Rewards and Fairies

Rewards and Fairies

Rudyard Kipling

Text illustrations by
Charles E. Brock, RI

Cover illustration by Nicola Bayley

A Piccolo book
Pan Books Ltd London and Sydney
in association with Macmillan & Co Ltd

First published 1910 by Macmillan and Co Ltd
This edition published 1975 by Pan Books Ltd
Cavaye Place, London sw10 9pg
in association with
Macmillan and Co Ltd
isbn 0 330 24260 1

Printed in Great Britain by
Richard Clay (The Chaucer Press) Ltd, Bungay, Suffolk

CONTENTS

ILLUSTRATIONS

A CHARM

Take of English earth as much
As either hand may rightly clutch.
In the taking of it breathe
Prayer for all who lie beneath —
Not the great nor well-bespoke,
But the mere uncounted folk
Of whose life and death is none
Report or lamentation.
      Lay that earth upon thy heart,
      And thy sickness shall depart!

It shall sweeten and make whole
Fevered breath and festered soul;
It shall mightily restrain
Over-busy hand and brain;
It shall ease thy mortal strife
'Gainst the immortal woe of life,
Till thyself restored shall prove
By what grace the Heavens do move.

Take of English flowers these —
Spring's full-facéd primroses,
Summer's wild wide-hearted rose,
Autumn's wall-flower of the close,
And, thy darkness to illume,
Winter's bee-thronged ivy-bloom.
Seek and serve them where they bide
From Candlemas to Christmas-tide,
      For these simples used aright
      Shall restore a failing sight.

These shall cleanse and purify
Webbed and inward-turning eye;
These shall show thee treasure hid,
Thy familiar fields amid,
At thy threshold, on thy hearth,
Or about thy daily path;
And reveal (which is thy need)
Every man a King indeed!

INTRODUCTION

Once upon a time, Dan and Una, brother and sister, living in the English country, had the good fortune to meet with Puck, *alias* Robin Goodfellow, *alias* Nick o' Lincoln, *alias* Lob-lie-by-the-Fire, the last survivor in England of those whom mortals call Fairies. Their proper name, of course, is 'The People of the Hills'. This Puck, by means of the magic of Oak, Ash, and Thorn, gave the children power

> To see what they should see and hear what they should hear,
> Though it should have happened three thousand year.

The result was that from time to time, and in different places on the farm and in the fields and the country about, they saw and talked to some rather interesting people. One of these, for instance, was a Knight of the Norman Conquest, another a young Centurion of a Roman Legion stationed in England, another a builder and decorator of King Henry VII's time; and so on and so forth; as I have tried to explain in a book called *Puck of Pook's Hill*.

A year or so later, the children met Puck once more, and though they were then older and wiser, and wore boots regularly instead of going barefooted when they got the chance, Puck was as kind to them as ever, and introduced them to more people of the old days.

He was careful, of course, to take away their memory of their walks and conversations afterwards, but otherwise he did not interfere; and Dan and Una would find the strangest sort of persons in their gardens or woods.

In the stories that follow I am trying to tell something about those people.

Cold Iron

Cold Iron

WHEN Dan and Una had arranged to go out before break-fast, they did not remember that it was Midsummer Morning. They only wanted to see the otter which, old Hobden said, had been fishing their brook for weeks; and early morning was the time to surprise him. As they tiptoed out of the house into the wonderful stillness, the church clock struck five. Dan took a few steps across the dew-blobbed lawn, and looked at his black footprints.

'I think we ought to be kind to our poor boots,' he said. 'They'll get horrid wet.'

It was their first summer in boots, and they hated them, so they took them off, and slung them round their necks, and paddled joyfully over the dripping turf where the shadows lay the wrong way, like evening in the East.

The sun was well up and warm, but by the brook the last of the night mist still fumed off the water. They picked up the chain of otter's footprints on the mud, and followed it from the bank, between the weeds and the drenched mow-ing, while the birds shouted with surprise. Then the track left the brook and became a smear, as though a log had been dragged along.

They traced it into Three Cows meadow, over the mill-sluice to the Forge, round Hobden's garden, and then up the slope till it ran out on the short turf and fern of Pook's Hill, and they heard the cock-pheasants crowing in the woods behind them.

'No use!' said Dan, questing like a puzzled hound. 'The dew's drying off, and old Hobden says otters'll travel for miles.'

'I'm sure we've travelled miles.' Una fanned herself with her hat. 'How still it is! It's going to be a regular roaster.' She looked down the valley, where no chimney yet smoked.

'Hobden's up!' Dan pointed to the open door of the Forge cottage. 'What d'you suppose he has for breakfast?'

'One of *them*. He says they eat good all times of the year.' Una jerked her head at some stately pheasants going down to the brook for a drink.

A few steps farther on a fox broke almost under their bare feet, yapped, and trotted off.

'Ah, Mus' Reynolds – Mus' Reynolds' – Dan was quoting from old Hobden, – 'if I knowed all you knowed, I'd know something.'[1]

'I say,' – Una lowered her voice – 'you know that funny feeling of things having happened before. I felt it when you said "Mus' Reynolds." '

'So did I,' Dan began. 'What is it?'

They faced each other, stammering with excitement.

'Wait a shake! I'll remember in a minute. Wasn't it something about a fox – last year? Oh, I nearly had it then!' Dan cried.

'Be quiet!' said Una, prancing excitedly. 'There was something happened before we met the fox last year. Hills! Broken Hills – the play at the theatre – see what you see—'

'I remember now,' Dan shouted. 'It's as plain as the nose on your face – Pook's Hill – Puck's Hill – Puck!'

'I remember, too,' said Una. 'And it's Midsummer Day again!'

The young fern on a knoll rustled, and Puck walked out, chewing a green-topped rush.

'Good Midsummer Morning to you! Here's a happy meeting,' said he. They shook hands all round, and asked questions.

'You've wintered well,' he said after a while, and looked them up and down. 'Nothing much wrong with you, seemingly.'

'They've put us into boots,' said Una. 'Look at my feet –

[1] See 'The Winged Hats' in *Puck of Pook's Hill*.

they're all pale white, and my toes are squdged together awfully.'

'Yes – boots make a difference.' Puck wriggled his brown, square, hairy foot, and cropped a dandelion flower between the big toe and the next.

'I could do that – last year,' Dan said dismally, as he tried and failed. 'And boots simply ruin one's climbing.'

'There must be some advantage to them, I suppose,' said Puck, 'or folk wouldn't wear them. Shall we come this way?'

They sauntered along side by side till they reached the gate at the far end of the hillside. Here they halted just like cattle, and let the sun warm their backs while they listened to the flies in the wood.

'Little Lindens is awake,' said Una, as she hung with her chin on the top rail. 'See the chimney smoke?'

'Today's Thursday, isn't it?' Puck turned to look at the old pink farmhouse across the little valley. 'Mrs Vincey's baking day. Bread should rise well this weather.' He yawned, and that set them both yawning.

The bracken about rustled and ticked and shook in every direction. They felt that little crowds were stealing past.

'Doesn't that sound like – er – the People of the Hills?' said Una.

'It's the birds and wild things drawing up to the woods before people get about,' said Puck, as though he were Ridley the keeper.

'Oh, we know that. I only said it sounded like.'

'As I remember 'em, the People of the Hills used to make more noise. They'd settle down for the day rather like small birds settling down for the night. But that was in the days when they carried the high hand. Oh, me! The deeds that I've had act and part in, you'd scarcely believe!'

'I like that!' said Dan. 'After all you told us last year, too!'

'Only, the minute you went away, you made us forget everything,' said Una.

Puck laughed and shook his head. 'I shall this year, too.

I've given you seizin of Old England, and I've taken away your Doubt and Fear, but your memory and remembrance between whiles I'll keep where old Billy Trott kept his night-lines – and that's where he could draw 'em up and hide 'em at need. Does that suit?' He twinkled mischievously.

'It's got to suit,' said Una, and laughed. 'We can't magic back at you.' She folded her arms and leaned against the gate. 'Suppose, now, you wanted to magic me into something – an otter? Could you?'

'Not with those boots round your neck.'

'I'll take them off.' She threw them on the turf. Dan's followed immediately. 'Now!' she said.

'Less than ever now you've trusted me. Where there's true faith, there's no call for magic.' Puck's slow smile broadened all over his face.

'But what have boots to do with it?' said Una, perching on the gate.

'There's Cold Iron in them,' said Puck, and settled beside her. 'Nails in the soles, I mean. It makes a difference.'

'How?'

'Can't you feel it does? You wouldn't like to go back to bare feet again, same as last year, would you? Not really?'

'No – o. I suppose I shouldn't – not for always. I'm growing up, you know,' said Una.

'But you told us last year, in the Long Slip – at the theatre – that you didn't mind Cold Iron,' said Dan.

'*I* don't; but folk in housen, as the People of the Hills call them, must be ruled by Cold Iron. Folk in housen are born on the near side of Cold Iron – there's iron in every man's house, isn't there? They handle Cold Iron every day of their lives, and their fortune's made or spoilt by Cold Iron in some shape or other. That's how it goes with Flesh and Blood, and one can't prevent it.'

'I don't quite see. How do you mean?' said Dan.

'It would take me some time to tell you.'

'Oh, it's ever so long to breakfast,' said Dan. 'We looked in the larder before we came out.' He unpocketed one big hunk of bread and Una another, which they shared with Puck.

'That's Little Lindens' baking,' he said, as his white teeth sunk in it. 'I know Mrs Vincey's hand.' He ate with a slow sideways thrust and grind, just like old Hobden, and, like Hobden, hardly dropped a crumb. The sun flashed on Little Lindens' windows, and the cloudless sky grew stiller and hotter in the valley.

'Ah – Cold Iron,' he said at last to the impatient children. 'Folk in housen, as the People of the Hills say, grow careless about Cold Iron. They'll nail the Horseshoe over the front door, and forget to put it over the back. Then, some time or other, the People of the Hills slip in, find the cradle-babe in the corner, and—'

'Oh, I know. Steal it and leave a changeling,' Una cried.

'No,' said Puck firmly. 'All that talk of changelings is people's excuse for their own neglect. Never believe 'em. I'd whip 'em at the cart-tail through three parishes if I had my way.'

'But they don't do it now,' said Una.

'Whip, or neglect children? Umm! Some folks and some fields never alter. But the People of the Hills didn't work any changeling tricks. They'd tiptoe in and whisper and weave round the cradle-babe in the chimney-corner – a fag-end of a charm here, or half a spell there – like kettles singing; but when the babe's mind came to bud out afterwards, it would act differently from other people in its station. That's no advantage to man or maid. So I wouldn't allow it with my folks' babies here. I told Sir Huon so once.'

'Who was Sir Huon?' Dan asked, and Puck turned on him in quiet astonishment.

'Sir Huon of Bordeaux – he succeeded King Oberon. He had been a bold knight once, but he was lost on the road to Babylon, a long while back. Have you ever heard "How many miles to Babylon?"?'

'Of course,' said Dan, flushing.

'Well, Sir Huon was young when that song was new. But

about tricks on mortal babies. I said to Sir Huon in the fern here, on just such a morning as this: "If you crave to act and influence on folk in housen, which I know is your desire, why don't you take some human cradle-babe by fair dealing, and bring him up among yourselves on the far side of Cold Iron – as Oberon did in time past? Then you could make him a splendid fortune, and send him out into the world."

' "Time past is past time," says Sir Huon. "I doubt if we could do it. For one thing, the babe would have to be taken without wronging man, woman, or child. For another, he'd have to be born on the far side of Cold Iron – in some house where no Cold Iron ever stood; and for yet the third, he'd have to be kept from Cold Iron all his days till we let him find his fortune. No, it's not easy," he said, and he rode off, thinking. You see, Sir Huon had been a man once.

'I happened to attend Lewes Market next Woden's Day even, and watched the slaves being sold there – same as pigs are sold at Robertsbridge Market nowadays. Only, the pigs have rings on their noses, and the slaves had rings round their necks.'

'What sort of rings?' said Dan.

'A ring of Cold Iron, four fingers wide, and a thumb thick, just like a quoit, but with a snap to it for to snap round the slave's neck. They used to do a big trade in slave-rings at the Forge here, and ship them to all parts of Old England, packed in oak sawdust. But, as I was saying, there was a farmer out of the Weald who had bought a woman with a babe in her arms, and he didn't want any encumbrances to her driving his beasts home for him.'

'Beast himself!' said Una, and kicked her bare heel on the gate.

'So he blamed the auctioneer. "It's none o' my baby," the wench puts in. "I took it off a woman in our gang who died on Terrible Down yesterday." "I'll take it off to the church then," says the farmer. "Mother Church'll make a monk of it, and we'll step along home."

'It was dusk then. He slipped down to St Pancras' Church,

and laid the babe at the cold chapel door. I breathed on the back of his stooping neck – and – I've *heard* he never could be warm at any fire afterwards. I should have been surprised if he could! Then I whipped up the babe, and came flying home here like a bat to his belfry.

'On the dewy break of morning of Thor's own day – just such a day as this – I laid the babe outside the Hill here, and the People flocked up and wondered at the sight.

' "You've brought him, then?" Sir Huon said, staring like any mortal man.

' "Yes, and he's brought his mouth with him too," I said. The babe was crying loud for his breakfast.

' "What is he?" says Sir Huon, when the womenfolk had drawn him under to feed him.

' "Full Moon and Morning Star may know," I says. "*I* don't. By what I could make out of him in the moonlight, he's without brand or blemish. I'll answer for it that he's born on the far side of Cold Iron, for he was born under a shaw on Terrible Down, and I've wronged neither man, woman, nor child in taking him, for he is the son of a dead slave-woman."

' "All to the good, Robin," Sir Huon said. "He'll be the less anxious to leave us. Oh, we'll give him a splendid fortune, and he shall act and influence on folk in housen as we have always craved." His Lady came up then, and drew him under to watch the babe's wonderful doings.'

'Who was his Lady?' said Dan.

'The Lady Esclairmonde. She had been a woman once, till she followed Sir Huon across the fern, as we say. Babies are no special treat to me – I've watched too many of them – so I stayed on the Hill. Presently I heard hammering down at the Forge there.' Puck pointed towards Hobden's cottage. 'It was too early for any workmen, but it passed through my mind that the breaking day was Thor's own day. A slow north-east wind blew up and set the oaks sawing and fretting in a way I remembered; so I slipped over to see what I could see.'

'And what did you see?'

'A smith forging something or other out of Cold Iron. When it was finished, he weighed it in his hand (his back was towards me), and tossed it from him a longish quoit-throw down the valley. I saw Cold Iron flash in the sun, but I couldn't quite make out where it fell. *That* didn't trouble me. I knew it would be found sooner or later by some one.'

'How did you know?' Dan went on.

'Because I knew the Smith that made it,' said Puck quietly.

'Wayland Smith?'[1] Una suggested.

'No. I should have passed the time o' day with Wayland Smith, of course. This other was different. So' – Puck made a queer crescent in the air with his finger – 'I counted the blades of grass under my nose till the wind dropped and he had gone – he and his Hammer.'

'Was it Thor then?' Una murmured under her breath.

'Who else? It was Thor's own day.' Puck repeated the sign. 'I didn't tell Sir Huon or his Lady what I'd seen. Borrow trouble for yourself if that's your nature, but don't lend it to your neighbours. Moreover, I might have been mistaken about the Smith's work. He might have been making things for mere amusement, though it wasn't like him, or he might have thrown away an old piece of made iron. One can never be sure. So I held my tongue and enjoyed the babe. He was a wonderful child – and the People of the Hills were so set on him, they wouldn't have believed me. He took to me wonderfully. As soon as he could walk he'd putter forth with me all about my Hill here. Fern makes soft falling! He knew when day broke on earth above, for he'd thump, thump, thump, like an old buck-rabbit in a bury, and I'd hear him say "Opy!" till some one who knew the Charm let him out, and then it would be "Robin! Robin!" all round Robin Hood's barn, as we say, till he'd found me.'

'The dear!' said Una. 'I'd like to have seen him!'

'Yes, he was a boy. And when it came to learning his

[1] See 'Weland's Sword' in *Puck of Pook's Hill*.

words – spells and such-like – he'd sit on the Hill in the long shadows, worrying out bits of charms to try on passers-by. And when the bird flew to him, or the tree bowed to him for pure love's sake (like everything else on my Hill), he'd shout, "Robin! Look – see! Look, see, Robin!" and sputter out some spell or other that they had taught him, *all* wrong end first, till I hadn't the heart to tell him it was his own dear self and not the words that worked the wonder. When he got more abreast of his words, and could cast spells for sure, as we say, he took more and more notice of things and people in the world. People, of course, always drew him, for he was mortal all through.

'Seeing that he was free to move among folk in housen, under or over Cold Iron, I used to take him along with me night-walking, where he could watch folk, and I could keep him from touching Cold Iron. That wasn't so difficult as it sounds, because there are plenty of things besides Cold Iron in housen to catch a boy's fancy. He *was* a handful, though! I shan't forget when I took him to Little Lindens – his first night under a roof. The smell of the rushlights and the bacon on the beams – they were stuffing a feather-bed too, and it was a drizzling warm night – got into his head. Before I could stop him – we were hiding in the bakehouse – he'd whipped up a storm of wildfire, with flashlights and voices, which sent the folk shrieking into the garden, and a girl overset a hive there, and – of course *he* didn't know till then such things could touch him – he got badly stung, and came home with his face looking like kidney potatoes!

'You can imagine how angry Sir Huon and Lady Esclair-monde were with poor Robin! They said the Boy was never to be trusted with me night-walking any more – and he took about as much notice of their order as he did of the bee-stings. Night after night, as soon as it was dark, I'd pick up his whistle in the wet fern, and off we'd flit together among folk in housen till break of day – he asking questions, and I answering according to my knowledge. Then we fell into mischief again!' Puck shook till the gate rattled.

'We came across a man up at Brightling who was beating his wife with a bat in the garden. I was just going to toss the man over his own woodlump when the Boy jumped the hedge and ran at him. Of course the woman took her husband's part, and while the man beat him, the woman scratted his face. It wasn't till I danced among the cabbages like Brightling Beacon all ablaze that they gave up and ran indoors. The Boy's fine green-and-gold clothes were torn all *to* pieces, and he had been welted in twenty places with the man's bat, and scratted by the woman's nails to pieces. He looked like a Robertsbridge hopper on a Monday morning.

' "Robin," said he, while I was trying to clean him down with a bunch of hay, "I don't quite understand folk in housen. I went to help that old woman, and she hit me, Robin!"

' "What else did you expect?" I said. "That was the one time when you might have worked one of your charms, instead of running into three times your weight."

' "I didn't think," he says. "But I caught the man one on the head that was as good as any charm. Did you see it work, Robin?"

' "Mind your nose," I said. "Bleed it on a dockleaf – not your sleeve, for pity's sake." I knew what the Lady Esclairmonde would say.

'*He* didn't care. He was as happy as a gipsy with a stolen pony, and the front part of his gold coat, all blood and grass stains, looked like ancient sacrifices.

'Of course the People of the Hills laid the blame on me. The Boy could do nothing wrong, in their eyes.

' "You are bringing him up to act and influence on folk in housen, when you're ready to let him go,". I said. "Now he's begun to do it, why do you cry shame on me? That's no shame. It's his nature drawing him to his kind."

' "But we don't want him to begin *that* way," the Lady Esclairmonde said. "We intend a splendid fortune for him – not your flitter-by-night, hedge-jumping, gipsy-work."

' "I don't blame you, Robin," says Sir Huon, "but I *do* think you might look after the Boy more closely."

' "I've kept him away from Cold Iron these sixteen years," I said. "You know as well as I do, the first time he touches Cold Iron he'll find his own fortune, in spite of everything you intend for him. You owe me something for that."

'Sir Huon, having been a man, was going to allow me the right of it, but the Lady Esclairmonde, being the Mother of all Mothers, over-persuaded him.

' "We're very grateful," Sir Huon said, "but we think that just for the present you are about too much with him on the Hill."

' "Though you have said it," I said, "I will give you a second chance." I did not like being called to account for my doings on my own Hill. I wouldn't have stood it even that far except I loved the Boy.

' "No! No!" says the Lady Esclairmonde. "He's never any trouble when he's left to me and himself. It's your fault."

' "You have said it," I answered. "Hear me! From now on till the Boy has found his fortune, whatever that may be, I vow to you all on my Hill, by Oak, and Ash, and Thorn, *and* by the Hammer of Asa Thor" ' – again Puck made that curious double-cut in the air – ' "that you may leave me out of all your counts and reckonings." Then I went out' – he snapped his fingers – 'like the puff of a candle, and though they called and cried, they made nothing by it. I didn't promise not to keep an eye on the Boy, though. I watched him close – close – close!

'When he found what his people had forced me to do, he gave them a piece of his mind, but they all kissed and cried round him, and being only a boy, he came over to their way of thinking (I don't blame him), and called himself unkind and ungrateful; and it all ended in fresh shows and plays, and magics to distract him from folk in housen. Dear heart alive! How he used to call and call on me, and I couldn't answer, or even let him know that I was near!'

'Not even once?' said Una. 'If he was very lonely?'

'No, he couldn't,' said Dan, who had been thinking. 'Didn't you swear by the Hammer of Thor that you wouldn't, Puck?'

'By that Hammer!' was the deep rumbled reply. Then he came back to his soft speaking voice. 'And the Boy *was* lonely, when he couldn't see me any more. He began to try to learn all learning (he had good teachers), but I saw him lift his eyes from the big black books towards folk in housen all the time. He studied song-making (good teachers he had too!), but he sang those songs with his back toward the Hill, and his face toward folk. *I* know! I have sat and grieved over him grieving within a rabbit's jump of him. Then he studied the High, Low, and Middle Magic. He had promised the Lady Esclairmonde he would never go near folk in housen; so he had to make shows and shadows for his mind to chew on.'

'What sort of shows?' said Dan.

'Just boy's Magic as we say. I'll show you some, some time. It pleased him for the while, and it didn't hurt any one in particular except a few men coming home late from the taverns. But I knew what it was a sign of, and I followed him like a weasel follows a rabbit. As good a boy as ever lived! I've seen him with Sir Huon and the Lady Esclairmonde stepping just as they stepped to avoid the track of Cold Iron in a furrow, or walking wide of some old ash-tot because a man had left his swop-hook or spade there; and all his heart aching to go straightforward among folk in housen all the time. Oh, a good boy! They always intended a fine fortune for him – but they could never find it in their heart to let him begin. I've heard that many warned them, but they wouldn't be warned. So it happened *as* it happened.

'One hot night I saw the Boy roving about here wrapped in his flaming discontents. There was flash on flash against the clouds, and rush on rush of shadows down the valley till the shaws were full of his hounds giving tongue, and the woodways were packed with his knights in armour riding down into the water-mists – all his own Magic, of course. Behind them you could see great castles lifting slow and splendid on arches of moonshine, with maidens waving their hands at the windows, which all turned into roaring rivers; and then would come the darkness of his own young heart wiping out the whole slateful. But boy's Magic doesn't trouble me – or Merlin's either for that matter. I followed the Boy by the flashes and the whirling wildfire of his discontent, and oh, but I grieved for him! Oh, but I grieved for him! He pounded back and forth like a bullock in a strange pasture – sometimes alone – sometimes waist-deep among his shadow-hounds – sometimes leading his shadow-knights on a hawk-winged horse to rescue his shadow-girls. I never guessed he had such Magic at his command; but it's often that way with boys.

'Just when the owl comes home for the second time, I saw Sir Huon and the Lady ride down my Hill, where there's not much Magic allowed except mine. They were very pleased at the Boy's Magic – the valley flared with it – and I heard them settling his splendid fortune when they should find it in their hearts to let him go to act and influence among folk in housen. Sir Huon was for making him a great King somewhere or other, and the Lady was for making him a marvellous wise man whom all should praise for his skill and kindness. She was very kind-hearted.

'Of a sudden we saw the flashes of his discontents turned back on the clouds, and his shadow-hounds stopped baying.

' "There's Magic fighting Magic over yonder," the Lady Esclairmonde cried, reining up. "Who is against him?"

'I could have told her, but I did not count it any of my business to speak of Asa Thor's comings and goings.'

'How did you know?' said Una.

'A slow North-East wind blew up, sawing and fretting through the oaks in a way I remembered. The wildfire roared up, one last time in one sheet, and snuffed out like a rushlight, and a bucketful of stinging hail fell. We heard the Boy walking in the Long Slip – where I first met you.

' "Here, oh, come here!" said the Lady Esclairmonde, and stretched out her arms in the dark.

'He was coming slowly, but he stumbled in the footpath, being, of course, mortal man.

' "Why, what's this?" he said to himself. We three heard him.

' "Hold, lad, hold! 'Ware Cold Iron!" said Sir Huon, and they two swept down like nightjars, crying as they rode.

'I ran at their stirrups, but it was too late. We felt that the Boy had touched Cold Iron somewhere in the dark, for the Horses of the Hill shied off, and whipped round, snorting.

'Then I judged it was time for me to show myself in my own shape; so I did.

' "Whatever it is," I said, "he has taken hold of it. Now we must find out whatever it *is* that he has taken hold of; for that will be his fortune."

' "Come here, Robin," the Boy shouted, as soon as he heard my voice. "I don't know what I've hold of."

' "It is in your hands," I called back. "Tell us if it is hard and cold, with jewels atop. For that will be a King's Sceptre."

' "Not by a furrow-long," he said, and stooped and tugged in the dark. We heard him.

' "Has it a handle and two cutting edges?" I called. "For that'll be a Knight's Sword."

' "No, it hasn't," he says. "It's neither ploughshare, whittle, hook, nor crook, nor aught I've yet seen men handle." By this time he was scratting in the dirt to prise it up.

' "Whatever it is, you know who put it there, Robin," said Sir Huon to me, "or you would not ask those questions. You should have told me as soon as you knew."

' "What could you or I have done against the Smith that made it and laid it for him to find?" I said, and I whispered Sir Huon what I had seen at the Forge on Thor's Day, when the babe was first brought to the Hill.

' "Oh, good-bye, our dreams!" said Sir Huon. "It's neither sceptre, sword, nor plough! Maybe yet it's a bookful of learning, bound with iron clasps. There's a chance for a splendid fortune in that sometimes."

'But we knew we were only speaking to comfort ourselves, and the Lady Esclairmonde, having been a woman, said so.

' "Thur aie! Thor help us!" the Boy called. "It is round, without end, Cold Iron, four fingers wide and a thumb thick, and there is writing on the breadth of it."

' "Read the writing if you have the learning," I called. The darkness had lifted by then, and the owl was out over the fern again.

'He called back, reading the runes on the iron:

> "Few can see
> Further forth
> Than when the child
> Meets the Cold Iron."

And there he stood, in clear starlight, with a new, heavy, shining slave-ring round his proud neck.

' "Is this how it goes?" he asked, while the Lady Esclairmonde cried.

' "That is how it goes," I said. He hadn't snapped the catch home yet, though.

' "What fortune does it mean for him?" said Sir Huon, while the Boy fingered the ring. "You who walk under Cold Iron, you must tell us and teach us."

' "Tell I can, but teach I cannot," I said. "The virtue of the Ring is only that he must go among folk in housen henceforward, doing what they want done, or what he knows they need, all Old England over. Never will he be his own master, nor yet ever any man's. He will get half he gives, and give twice what he gets, till his life's last breath; and if he lays aside his load before he draws that last breath, all his work will go for naught."

' "Oh, cruel, wicked Thor!" cried the Lady Esclairmonde. "Ah, look, see, all of you! The catch is still open! He hasn't locked it. He can still take it off. He can still come back. Come back!" She went as near as she dared, but she could not lay hands on Cold Iron. The Boy could have taken

'Come back!' She went as near as she dared

it off, yes. We waited to see if he would, but he put up his hand, and the snap locked home.

' "What else could I have done?" said he.

' "Surely, then, you will do," I said. "Morning's coming, and if you three have any farewells to make, make them now, for, after sunrise, Cold Iron must be your master."

'So the three sat down, cheek by wet cheek, telling over their farewells till morning light. As good a boy as ever lived, he was.'

'And what happened to him?' asked Dan.

'When morning came, Cold Iron was master of him and his fortune, and he went to work among folk in housen. Presently he came across a maid like-minded with himself, and they were wedded, and had bushels of children, as the saying is. Perhaps you'll meet some of his breed, this year.'

'Thank you,' said Una. 'But what did the poor Lady Esclairmonde do?'

'What *can* you do when Asa Thor lays the Cold Iron in a lad's path? She and Sir Huon were comforted to think they had given the Boy good store of learning to act and influence on folk in housen. For he *was* a good boy! Isn't it getting on for breakfast-time? I'll walk with you a piece.'

When they were well in the centre of the bone-dry fern, Dan nudged Una, who stopped and put on a boot as quickly as she could.

'Now,' she said, 'you can't get any Oak, Ash, and Thorn leaves from here, and' – she balanced wildly on one leg – 'I'm standing on Cold Iron. What'll you do if we don't go away?'

'E-eh? Of all mortal impudence!' said Puck, as Dan, also in one boot, grabbed his sister's hand to steady himself. He walked round them, shaking with delight. 'You think I can only work with a handful of dead leaves? This comes of taking away your Doubt and Fear! I'll show you!'

A minute later they charged into old Hobden at his simple breakfast of cold roast pheasant, shouting that there was a wasps' nest in the fern which they had nearly stepped on, and asking him to come and smoke it out.

'It's too early for wops-nestës, an' I don't go diggin' in the Hill, not for shillin's,' said the old man placidly. 'You've a thorn in your foot, Miss Una. Sit down, and put on your t'other boot. You're too old to be caperin' barefoot on an empty stomach. Stay it with this chicken o' mine.'

COLD IRON

'Gold is for the mistress — silver for the maid!
Copper for the craftsman cunning at his trade.'
'Good!' said the Baron, sitting in his hall,
'But Iron — Cold Iron — is master of them all!'

So he made rebellion 'gainst the King his liege,
Camped before his citadel and summoned it to siege —
'Nay!' said the cannoneer on the castle wall,
'But Iron — Cold Iron — shall be master of you all!'

Woe for the Baron and his knights so strong,
When the cruel cannon-balls laid 'em all along!
He was taken prisoner, he was cast in thrall,
And Iron — Cold Iron — was master of it all!

Yet his King spake kindly (Oh, how kind a Lord!)
'What if I release thee now and give thee back thy sword?'
'Nay!' said the Baron, 'mock not at my fall,
For Iron — Cold Iron — is master of men all.'

'Tears are for the craven, prayers are for the clown —
Halters for the silly neck that cannot keep a crown.'
'As my loss is grievous, so my hope is small,
For Iron — Cold Iron — must be master of men all!'

Yet his King made answer (few such Kings there be!)
'Here is Bread and here is Wine — sit and sup with me.
Eat and drink in Mary's Name, the whiles I do recall
How Iron — Cold Iron — can be master of men all!'

He took the Wine and blessed It; He blessed and brake the
    Bread.
With His own Hands He served Them, and presently He said:
'Look! These Hands they pierced with nails outside my city wall
Show Iron — Cold Iron — to be master of men all!

'Wounds are for the desperate, blows are for the strong,
Balm and oil for weary hearts all cut and bruised with wrong.
I forgive thy treason – I redeem thy fall –
For Iron – Cold Iron – must be master of men all!'

'Crowns are for the valiant – sceptres for the bold!
Thrones and powers for mighty men who dare to take and hold.'
'Nay!' said the Baron, kneeling in his hall,
'But Iron – Cold Iron – is master of men all!
        Iron, out of Calvary, is master of men all!'

Gloriana

THE TWO COUSINS

Valour and Innocence
Have latterly gone hence
To certain death by certain shame attended.
Envy – ah! even to tears! –
The fortune of their years
Which, though so few, yet so divinely ended.

Scarce had they lifted up
Life's full and fiery cup,
Than they had set it down untouched before them.
Before their day arose
They beckoned it to close –
Close in destruction and confusion o'er them.

They did not stay to ask
What prize should crown their task,
Well sure that prize was such as no man strives for;
But passed into eclipse,
Her kiss upon their lips –
Even Belphoebe's, whom they gave their lives for!

Gloriana

WILLOW SHAW, the little fenced wood where the hop-poles are stacked like Indian wigwams, had been given to Dan and Una for their very own kingdom when they were quite small. As they grew older, they contrived to keep it most particularly private. Even Phillips, the gardener, told them every time that he came in to take a hop-pole for his beans, and old Hobden would no more have thought of setting his rabbit-wires there without leave, given fresh each spring, than he would have torn down the calico and marking ink notice on the big willow which said: 'Grown-ups not allowed in the Kingdom unless brought.'

Now you can understand their indignation when, one blowy July afternoon, as they were going up for a potato-roast, they saw somebody moving among the trees. They hurled themselves over the gate, dropping half the potatoes, and while they were picking them up Puck came out of a wigwam.

'Oh, it's you, is it?' said Una. 'We thought it was people.'

'I saw you were angry – from your legs,' he answered with a grin.

'Well, it's our own Kingdom – not counting you, of course.'

'That's rather why I came. A lady here wants to see you.'

'What about?' said Dan cautiously.

'Oh, just Kingdoms and things. She knows about Kingdoms.'

There was a lady near the fence dressed in a long dark cloak that hid everything except her high red-heeled shoes. Her face was half covered by a black silk fringed mask, without goggles. And yet she did not look in the least as if she motored.

Puck led them up to her and bowed solemnly. Una made the best dancing-lesson curtsy she could remember. The lady answered with a long, deep, slow, billowy one.

'Since it seems that you are a Queen of this Kingdom,' she said, 'I can do no less than acknowledge your sovereignty.' She turned sharply on staring Dan. 'What's in your head, lad? Manners?'

'I was thinking how wonderfully you did that curtsy,' he answered.

She laughed a rather shrill laugh. 'You're a courtier already. Do you know anything of dances, wench – or Queen, must I say?'

'I've had some lessons, but I can't really dance a bit,' said Una.

'You should learn, then.' The lady moved forward as though she would teach her at once. 'It gives a woman alone among men or her enemies time to think how she shall win or – lose. A woman can only work in man's play-time. Heigho!' She sat down on the bank.

Old Middenboro, the lawn-mower pony, stumped across the paddock and hung his sorrowful head over the fence.

'A pleasant Kingdom,' said the lady, looking round. 'Well enclosed. And how does your Majesty govern it? Who is your Minister?'

Una did not quite understand. 'We don't play that,' she said.

'Play?' The lady threw up her hands and laughed.

'We have it for our own, together,' Dan explained.

'And d'you never quarrel, young Burleigh?'

'Sometimes, but then we don't tell.'

The lady nodded. 'I've no brats of my own, but I understand keeping a secret between Queens and their Ministers. *Ay de mi!* But with no disrespect to present majesty, methinks your realm is small, and therefore likely to be coveted by man and beast. For example' – she pointed to Middenboro – 'yonder old horse, with the face of a Spanish friar – does he never break in?'

'He can't. Old Hobden stops all our gaps for us,' said Una, 'and we let Hobden catch rabbits in the Shaw.'

The lady laughed like a man. 'I see! Hobden catches conies – rabbits – for himself, and guards your defences for you. Does he make a profit out of his coney-catching?'

'We never ask,' said Una. 'Hobden's a particular friend of ours.'

'Hoity-toity!' the lady began angrily. Then she laughed. 'But I forget. It is your Kingdom. I knew a maid once that had a larger one than this to defend, and so long as her men kept the fences stopped, she asked 'em no questions either.'

'Was she trying to grow flowers?' said Una.

'No, trees – perdurable trees. Her flowers all withered.' The lady leaned her head on her hand.

'They do if you don't look after them. We've got a few. Would you like to see? I'll fetch you some.' Una ran off to the rank grass in the shade behind the wigwam, and came back with a handful of red flowers. 'Aren't they pretty?' she said. 'They're Virginia stock.'

'Virginia?' said the lady, and lifted them to the fringe of her mask.

'Yes. They come from Virginia. Did your maid ever plant any?'

'Not herself – but her men adventured all over the earth to pluck or to plant flowers for her crown. They judged her worthy of them.'

'And was she?' said Dan cheerfully.

'*Quien sabe?* [who knows?] But at least, while her men toiled abroad she toiled in England, that they might find a safe home to come back to.'

'And what was she called?'

'Gloriana – Belphoebe – Elizabeth of England.' Her voice changed at each word.

'You mean Queen Bess?'

The lady bowed her head a little towards Dan. 'You name her lightly enough, young Burleigh. What might you know of her?' said she.

'Well, I – I've seen the little green shoes she left at Brick-wall House – down the road, you know. They're in a glass case – awfully tiny things.'

'Oh, Burleigh, Burleigh!' she laughed. 'You are a courtier too soon.'

'But they are,' Dan insisted. 'As little as dolls' shoes. Did you really know her well?'

'Well. She was a – woman. I've been at her Court all my life. Yes, I remember when she danced after the banquet at Brickwall. They say she danced Philip of Spain out of a brand-new kingdom that day. Worth the price of a pair of old shoes – hey?'

She thrust out one foot, and stooped forward to look at its broad flashing buckle.

'You've heard of Philip of Spain – long-suffering Philip,' she said, her eyes still on the shining stones. 'Faith, what some men will endure at some women's hands passes belief! If *I* had been a man, and a woman had played with me as Elizabeth played with Philip, I would have—' She nipped off one of the Virginia stocks and held it up between finger and thumb. 'But for all that' – she began to strip the leaves one by one – 'they say – and I am persuaded – that Philip loved her.' She tossed her head sideways.

'I don't quite understand,' said Una.

'The high heavens forbid that you should, wench!' She swept the flowers from her lap and stood up in the rush of shadows that the wind chased through the wood.

'I should like to know about the shoes,' said Dan.

'So ye shall, Burleigh. So ye shall, if ye watch me. 'Twill be as good as a play.'

'We've never been to a play,' said Una.

The lady looked at her and laughed. 'I'll make one for you. Watch! You are to imagine that she – Gloriana, Belphoebe, Elizabeth – has gone on a progress to Rye to comfort her sad heart (maids are often melancholic), and while she halts at Brickwall House, the village – what was its name?' She pushed Puck with her foot.

'Norgem,' he croaked, and squatted by the wigwam.

'Norgem village loyally entertains her with a masque or play, and a Latin oration spoken by the parson, for whose false quantities, if *I*'d made 'em in my girlhood, I should have been whipped.'

'You whipped?' said Dan.

'Soundly, sirrah, soundly! She stomachs the affront to her scholarship, makes her grateful, gracious thanks from the teeth outwards, thus' – (the lady yawned) – 'Oh, a Queen may love her subjects in her heart, and yet be dog-wearied of 'em in body and mind – and so sits down' – her skirts foamed about her as she sat – 'to a banquet beneath Brickwall Oak. Here for her sins she is waited upon by— What were the young cockerels' names that served Gloriana at table?'

'Frewens, Courthopes, Fullers, Husseys,' Puck began.

She held up her long jewelled hand. 'Spare the rest! They were the best blood of Sussex, and by so much the more clumsy in handling the dishes and plates. Wherefore' – she looked funnily over her shoulder – 'you are to think of Gloriana in a green and gold-laced habit, dreadfully expecting that the jostling youths behind her would, of pure jealousy or devotion, spatter it with sauces and wines. The gown was Philip's gift, too! At this happy juncture a Queen's messenger, mounted and mired, spurs up the Rye road and delivers her a letter' – she giggled – 'a letter from a good, simple, frantic Spanish gentleman called – Don Philip.'

'That wasn't Philip, King of Spain?' Dan asked.

'Truly, it was. 'Twixt you and me and the bedpost, young Burleigh, these kings and queens are very like men and women, and I've heard they write each other fond, foolish letters that none of their ministers should open.'

'Did her ministers ever open Queen Elizabeth's letters?' said Una.

'Faith, yes! But she'd have done as much for theirs, any day. You are to think of Gloriana, then (they say she had a pretty hand), excusing herself thus to the company – for the

Queen's time is never her own – and, while the music strikes up, reading Philip's letter, as I do.' She drew a real letter from her pocket, and held it out almost at arm's length, like the old post-mistress in the village when she reads telegrams.

'Hm! Hm! Hm! Philip writes as ever most lovingly. He says his Gloriana is cold, for which reason he burns for her through a fair written page.' She turned it with a snap. 'What's here? Philip complains that certain of her gentlemen have fought against his generals in the Low Countries. He prays her to hang 'em when they re-enter her realms. (Hm, that's as may be.) Here's a list of burnt shipping slipped between two vows of burning adoration. Oh, poor Philip! His admirals at sea – no less than three of 'em – have been boarded, sacked, and scuttled on their lawful voyages by certain English mariners (gentlemen, he will not call them), who are now at large and working more piracies in *his* American ocean, which the Pope gave him. (He and the Pope should guard it, then!) Philip hears, but his devout ears will not credit it, that Gloriana in some fashion countenances these villains' misdeeds, shares in their booty, and – oh, shame! – has even lent them ships royal for their sinful thefts. Therefore he requires (which is a word Gloriana loves not), *requires* that she shall hang 'em when they return to England, and afterwards shall account to him for all the goods and gold they have plundered. A most loving request! If Gloriana will not be Philip's bride, she shall be his broker and his butcher! Should she still be stiff-necked, he writes – see where the pen digged the innocent paper! – that he hath both the means and the intention to be revenged on her. Aha! Now we come to the Spaniard in his shirt!' (She waved the letter merrily.) 'Listen here! Philip will prepare for Gloriana a destruction from the West – a destruction from the West – far exceeding that which Pedro de Avila wrought upon the Huguenots. And he rests and remains, kissing her feet and her hands, her slave, her enemy, or her conqueror, as he shall find that she uses him.'

She thrust back the letter under her cloak, and went on acting, but in a softer voice. 'All this while – hark to it – the wind blows through Brickwall Oak, the music plays, and, with the company's eyes upon her, the Queen of England must think what this means. She cannot remember the name of Pedro de Avila, nor what he did to the Huguenots, nor when, nor where. She can only see darkly some dark motion moving in Philip's dark mind, for he hath never written before in this fashion. She must smile above the letter as though it were good news from her ministers – the smile that tires the mouth and the poor heart. What shall she do?' Again her voice changed.

'You are to fancy that the music of a sudden wavers away. Chris Hatton, Captain of her bodyguard, quits the table all red and ruffled, and Gloriana's virgin ear catches the clash of swords at work behind a wall. The mothers of Sussex look round to count their chicks – I mean those young game-cocks that waited on her. Two dainty youths have stepped aside into Brickwall garden with rapier and dagger on a private point of honour. They are haled out through the gate, disarmed and glaring – the lively image of a brace of young Cupids transformed into pale, panting Cains. Ahem! Gloriana beckons awfully – thus! They come up for judg-ment. Their lives and estates lie at her mercy whom they have doubly offended, both as Queen and woman. But la! what will not foolish young men do for a beautiful maid?'

'Why? What did she do? What had they done?' said Una.

'Hsh! You mar the play! Gloriana had guessed the cause of the trouble. They were handsome lads. So she frowns a while and tells 'em not to be bigger fools than their mothers had made 'em, and warns 'em, if they do not kiss and be friends on the instant, she'll have Chris Hatton horse and birch 'em in the style of the new school at Harrow. (Chris looks sour at that.) Lastly, because she needed time to think on Philip's letter burning in her pocket, she signifies her pleasure to dance with 'em and teach 'em better manners. Whereat the revived company call down Heaven's blessing on her gracious head; Chris and the others prepare Brickwall House for a dance; and she walks in the clipped garden between those two lovely young sinners who are both ready to sink for shame. They confess their fault. It appears that midway in the banquet the elder – they were cousins – conceived that the Queen looked upon him with special favour. The younger, taking the look to himself, after some words gives the elder the lie. Hence, as she guessed, the duel.'

'And which had she really looked at?' Dan asked.

'Neither – except to wish them farther off. She was afraid all the while they'd spill dishes on her gown. She tells 'em this, poor chicks – and it completes their abasement. When they had grilled long enough, she says: "And so you would have fleshed your maiden swords for me – for me?" Faith, they would have been at it again if she'd egged 'em on! but their swords – oh, prettily they said it! – had been drawn for her once or twice already.

' "And where?" says she. "On your hobby-horses before you were breeched?"

' "On my own ship," says the elder. "My cousin was vice-admiral of our venture in his pinnace. We would not have you think of us as brawling children."

' "No, no," says the younger, and flames like a very Tudor rose. "At least the Spaniards know us better."

' "Admiral Boy – Vice-Admiral Babe," says Gloriana, "I cry your pardon. The heat of these present times ripens childhood to age more quickly than I can follow. But we are at peace with Spain. Where did you break your Queen's peace?"

' "On the sea called the Spanish Main, though 'tis no more Spanish than my doublet," says the elder. Guess how that warmed Gloriana's already melting heart! She would never suffer any sea to be called Spanish in her private hearing.

' "And why was I not told? What booty got you, and

where have you hid it? Disclose," says she. "You stand in some danger of the gallows for pirates."

' "The axe, most gracious lady," says the elder, "for we are gentle born." He spoke truth, but no woman can brook contradiction. "Hoity-toity!" says she, and, but that she remembered that she was Queen, she'd have cuffed the pair of 'em. "It shall be gallows, hurdle, and dung-cart if I choose."

' "Had our Queen known of our going beforehand, Philip might have held her to blame for some small things we did on the seas," the younger lisps.

' "As for treasure," says the elder, "we brought back but our bare lives. We were wrecked on the Gascons' Graveyard, where our sole company for three months was the bleached bones of De Avila's men."

'Gloriana's mind jumped back to Philip's last letter.

' "De Avila that destroyed the Huguenots? What d'you know of him?" she says. The music called from the house here, and they three turned back between the yews.

' "Simply that De Avila broke in upon a plantation of Frenchmen on that coast, and very Spaniardly hung them all for heretics – eight hundred or so. The next year Dominique de Gorgues, a Gascon, broke in upon De Avila's men, and very justly hung 'em all for murderers – five hundred or so. No Christians inhabit there now," says the elder lad, "though 'tis a goodly land north of Florida."

' "How far is it from England?" asks prudent Gloriana.

' "With a fair wind, six weeks. They say that Philip will plant it again soon." This was the younger, and he looked at her out of the corner of his innocent eye.

'Chris Hatton, fuming, meets and leads her into Brickwall Hall, where she dances – thus. A woman can think while she dances – can think. I'll show you. Watch!'

She took off her cloak slowly, and stood forth in dove-coloured satin, worked over with pearls that trembled like running water in the running shadows of the trees. Still talking – more to herself than to the children – she swam into a majestical dance of the stateliest balancings, the haughtiest wheelings and turnings aside, the most dignified sinkings, the gravest risings, all joined together by the elaboratest interlacing steps and circles.

They leaned forward breathlessly to watch the splendid acting.

'Would a Spaniard,' she began, looking on the ground, 'speak of his revenge till his revenge were ripe? No. Yet a man who loved a woman might threaten her in the hope that his threats would make her love him. Such things have been.' She moved slowly across a bar of sunlight. 'A destruction from the West may signify that Philip means to descend on Ireland. But then my Irish spies would have had some warning. The Irish keep no secrets. No – it is not Ireland. Now why – why – why' – the red shoes clicked and paused – 'does Philip name Pedro Melendez de Avila, a general in his Americas, unless' – she turned more quickly – 'unless he intends to work his destruction from the Americas? Did he say De Avila only to put her off her guard, or for this once has his black pen betrayed his black heart? We' – she raised herself to her full height – 'England must forestall Master Philip. But not openly,' – she sank again – 'we cannot fight Spain openly – not yet – not yet.' She stepped three paces as though she were pegging down some snare with her twinkling shoe-buckles. 'The Queen's mad gentlemen may fight Philip's poor admirals where they find 'em, but England, Gloriana, Harry's daughter, must keep the peace. Perhaps, after all, Philip loves her – as many men and boys do. That may help England. Oh, *what* shall help England?'

She raised her head – the masked head that seemed to have nothing to do with the busy feet – and stared straight at the children.

'I think this is rather creepy,' said Una with a shiver. 'I wish she'd stop.'

The lady held out her jewelled hand as though she were taking some one else's hand in the Grand Chain.

'Can a ship go down into the Gascons' Graveyard and

wait there?' she asked into the air, and passed on rustling.

'She's pretending to ask one of the cousins, isn't she?' said Dan, and Puck nodded.

Back she came in the silent, swaying, ghostly dance. They saw she was smiling beneath the mask, and they could hear her breathing hard.

'I cannot lend you any of my ships for the venture; Philip would hear of it,' she whispered over her shoulder; 'but as much guns and powder as you ask, if you do not ask too—' Her voice shot up and she stamped her foot thrice. 'Louder! Louder, the music in the gallery! Oh, me, but I have burst out of my shoe!'

She gathered her skirts in each hand, and began a curtsy. 'You will go at your own charges,' she whispered straight before her. 'Oh, enviable and adorable age of youth!' Her eyes shone through the mask-holes. 'But I warn you you'll repent it. Put not your trust in princes – or Queens. Philip's ships'll blow you out of water. You'll not be frightened? Well, we'll talk on it again, when I return from Rye, dear lads.'

The wonderful curtsy ended. She stood up. Nothing stirred on her except the rush of the shadows.

'And so it was finished,' she said to the children. 'Why d'you not applaud?'

'What was finished?' said Una.

'The dance,' the lady replied offendedly. 'And a pair of green shoes.'

'I don't understand a bit,' said Una.

'Eh? What did *you* make of it, young Burleigh?'

'I'm not quite sure,' Dan began, 'but—'

'You never can be – with a woman. But—'

'But I thought Gloriana meant the cousins to go back to the Gascons' Graveyard, wherever that was.'

' 'Twas Virginia afterwards. Her plantation of Virginia.'

'Virginia afterwards, and stop Philip from taking it. Didn't she say she'd lend 'em guns?'

'Right so. But not ships – *then*.'

'And I thought you meant they must have told her they'd do it off their own bat, without getting her into a row with Philip. Was I right?'

'Near enough for a Minister of the Queen. But remember she gave the lads full time to change their minds. She was three long days at Rye Royal – knighting of fat Mayors. When she came back to Brickwall, they met her a mile down the road, and she could feel their eyes burn through her riding-mask. Chris Hatton, poor fool, was vexed at it.

' "You would not birch them when I gave you the chance," says she to Chris. "Now you must get me half an hour's private speech with 'em in Brickwall garden. Eve tempted Adam in a garden. Quick, man, or I may repent!" '

'She was a Queen. Why did she not send for them herself?' said Una.

The lady shook her head. 'That was never her way. I've seen her walk to her own mirror by bye-ends, and the woman that cannot walk straight *there* is past praying for. Yet I would have you pray for her! What else – what else in England's name could she have done?' She lifted her hand to her throat for a moment. 'Faith,' she cried, 'I'd forgotten the little green shoes! She left 'em at Brickwall – so she did. And I remember she gave the Norgem parson – John Withers, was he? – a text for his sermon – "Over Edom have I cast out my shoe." Neat, if he'd understood!'

'I don't understand,' said Una. 'What about the two cousins?'

'You are as cruel as a woman,' the lady answered. '*I* was not to blame. I told you I gave 'em time to change their minds. On my honour (*ay de mi!*), she asked no more of 'em at first than to wait a while off that coast – the Gascons' Graveyard – to hover a little if their ships chanced to pass that way – they had only one tall ship and a pinnace – only to watch and bring me word of Philip's doings. One must watch Philip always. What a murrain right had he to make any plantation there, a hundred leagues north of his Spanish

Main, and only six weeks from England? By my dread
father's soul, I tell you he had none – none!' She stamped
her red foot again, and the two children shrunk back for a
second.

'Nay, nay. You must not turn from me too! She laid it all
fairly before the lads in Brickwall garden between the yews.
I told 'em that if Philip sent a fleet (and to make a plantation
he could not well send less), their poor little cock-boats could
not sink it. They answered that, with submission, the fight
would be their own concern. She showed 'em again that
there could be only one end to it – quick death on the sea, or
slow death in Philip's prisons. They asked no more than to
embrace death for my sake. Many men have prayed to me
for life. I've refused 'em, and slept none the worse after; but
when my men, my tall, fantastical young men, beseech me
on their knees for leave to die for me, it shakes me – ah, it
shakes me to the marrow of my old bones.'

Her chest sounded like a board as she hit it.

'She showed 'em all. I told 'em that this was no time for
open war with Spain. If by miracle inconceivable they
prevailed against Philip's fleet, Philip would hold me
accountable. For England's sake, to save war, I should e'en
be forced (I told 'em so) to give him up their young lives. If
they failed, and again by some miracle escaped Philip's
hand, and crept back to England with their bare lives, they
must lie – oh, I told 'em all – under my sovereign dis-
pleasure. She could not know them, see them, nor hear their
names, nor stretch out a finger to save them from the gallows,
if Philip chose to ask it.

' "Be it the gallows, then," says the elder. (I could have
wept, but that my face was made for the day.)

' "Either way – any way – this venture is death, which I
know you fear not. But it is death with assured dishonour,"
I cried.

' "Yet our Queen will know in her heart what we have
done," says the younger.

' "Sweetheart," I said. "A queen has no heart."

'Nay, dear lads – but here!' I said

' "But she is a woman, and a woman would not forget,"
says the elder. "We will go!" They knelt at my feet.

' "Nay, dear lads – but here!" I said, and I opened my
arms to them and I kissed them.

' "Be ruled by me," I said. "We'll hire some ill-featured
old tarry-breeks of an admiral to watch the Graveyard, and
you shall come to Court."

' "Hire whom you please," says the elder; "we are ruled
by you, body and soul"; and the younger, who shook most
when I kissed 'em, says between his white lips, "I think you
have power to make a god of a man."

' "Come to Court and be sure of it," I said.

'They shook their heads and I knew – I knew, that go
they would. If I had not kissed them – perhaps I might have
prevailed.'

'Then why did you do it?' said Una. 'I don't think you
knew really what you wanted done.'

'May it please your Majesty' – the lady bowed her head
low – 'this Gloriana whom I have represented for your
pleasure was a woman and a Queen. Remember her when
you come to your Kingdom.'

'But did the cousins go to the Gascons' Graveyard?' said
Dan, as Una frowned.

'They went,' said the lady.

'Did they ever come back?' Una began; but – 'Did they
stop King Philip's fleet?' Dan interrupted.

The lady turned to him eagerly.

'D'you think they did right to go?' she asked.

'I don't see what else they could have done,' Dan replied,
after thinking it over.

'D'you think she did right to send 'em?' The lady's voice
rose a little.

'Well,' said Dan, 'I don't see what else she could have
done, either – do you? How did they stop King Philip from
getting Virginia?'

'There's the sad part of it. They sailed out that autumn
from Rye Royal, and there never came back so much as a

single rope-yarn to show what had befallen them. The winds blew, and they were not. Does that make you alter your mind, young Burleigh?'

'I expect they were drowned, then. Anyhow, Philip didn't score, did he?'

'Gloriana wiped out her score with Philip later. But if Philip had won, would you have blamed Gloriana for wasting those lads' lives?'

'Of course not. She was bound to try to stop him.'

The lady coughed. 'You have the root of the matter in you. Were I Queen, I'd make you Minister.'

'We don't play that game,' said Una, who felt that she disliked the lady as much as she disliked the noise the high wind made tearing through Willow Shaw.

'Play!' said the lady with a laugh, and threw up her hands affectedly. The sunshine caught the jewels on her many rings and made them flash till Una's eyes dazzled, and she had to rub them. Then she saw Dan on his knees picking up the potatoes they had spilled at the gate.

'There wasn't anybody in the Shaw, after all,' he said. 'Didn't you think you saw some one?'

'I'm most awfully glad there isn't,' said Una. Then they went on with the potato-roast.

THE LOOKING-GLASS

Queen Bess was Harry's daughter!

The Queen was in her chamber, and she was middling old,
Her petticoat was satin and her stomacher was gold.
Backwards and forwards and sideways did she pass,
Making up her mind to face the cruel looking-glass.
  The cruel looking-glass that will never show a lass
  As comely or as kindly or as young as once she was!

The Queen was in her chamber, a-combing of her hair,
There came Queen Mary's spirit and it stood behind her chair,
Singing, 'Backwards and forwards and sideways may you pass,
But I will stand behind you till you face the looking-glass.
  The cruel looking-glass that will never show a lass
  As lovely or unlucky or as lonely as I was!'

The Queen was in her chamber, a-weeping very sore,
There came Lord Leicester's spirit and it scratched upon the
    door,
Singing, 'Backwards and forwards and sideways may you pass,
But I will walk beside you till you face the looking-glass.
  The cruel looking-glass that will never show a lass
  As hard and unforgiving or as wicked as you was!'

The Queen was in her chamber; her sins were on her head;
She looked the spirits up and down and statelily she said:
'Backwards and forwards and sideways though I've been,
Yet I am Harry's daughter and I am England's Queen!'
  And she faced the looking-glass (and whatever else there was),
  And she saw her day was over and she saw her beauty pass
  In the cruel looking-glass that can always hurt a lass
  More hard than any ghost there is or any man there was!

The Wrong Thing

A TRUTHFUL SONG

I

THE BRICKLAYER:

I tell this tale, which is strictly true,
  Just by way of convincing you
How very little since things were made
  Things have altered in the building trade.

A year ago, come the middle o' March,
We was building flats near the Marble Arch,
When a thin young man with coal-black hair
Came up to watch us working there.

Now there wasn't a trick in brick or stone
That this young man hadn't seen or known;
Nor there wasn't a tool from trowel to maul
But this young man could use 'em all!

Then up and spoke the plumbyers bold,
Which was laying the pipes for the hot and cold:
'Since you with us have made so free,
Will you kindly say what your name might be?'

The young man kindly answered them:
'It might be Lot or Methusalem,
Or it might be Moses (a man I hate),
Whereas it is Pharaoh surnamed the Great.

'Your glazing is new and your plumbing's strange,
But otherwise I perceive no change,
And in less than a month, if you do as I bid,
I'd learn you to build me a Pyramid.'

II

THE SAILOR:

I tell this tale, which is stricter true,
  Just by way of convincing you
How very little since things was made
  Things have altered in the shipwright's trade.

In Blackwall Basin yesterday
A China barque re-fitting lay,
When a fat old man with snow-white hair
Came up to watch us working there.

Now there wasn't a knot which the riggers knew
But the old man made it – and better too;
Nor there wasn't a sheet, or a lift, or a brace,
But the old man knew its lead and place.

Then up and spake the caulkyers bold,
Which was packing the pump in the after-hold:
'Since you with us have made so free,
Will you kindly tell what your name might be?'

The old man kindly answered them:
'It might be Japhet, it might be Shem,
Or it might be Ham (though his skin was dark),
Whereas it is Noah, commanding the Ark.

'Your wheel is new and your pumps are strange,
But otherwise I perceive no change,
And in less than a week, if she did not ground,
I'd sail this hooker the wide world round!'

BOTH: *We tell these tales, which are strictest true, etc.*

The Wrong Thing

DAN had gone in for building model boats; but after he had filled the schoolroom with chips, which he expected Una to clear away, they turned him out of doors and he took all his tools up the hill to Mr Springett's yard, where he knew he could make as much mess as he chose. Old Mr Springett was a builder, contractor, and sanitary engineer, and his yard, which opened off the village street, was always full of interesting things. At one end of it was a long loft, reached by a ladder, where he kept his iron-bound scaffold-planks, tins of paints, pulleys, and odds and ends he had found in old houses. He would sit here by the hour watching his carts as they loaded or unloaded in the yard below, while Dan gouged and grunted at the carpenter's bench near the loft window. Mr Springett and Dan had always been particular friends, for Mr Springett was so old he could remember when railways were being made in the southern counties of England, and people were allowed to drive dogs in carts.

One hot, still afternoon – the tar-paper on the roof smelt like ships – Dan, in his shirt-sleeves, was smoothing down a new schooner's bow, and Mr Springett was talking of barns and houses he had built. He said he never forgot any stick or stone he had ever handled, or any man, woman, or child he had ever met. Just then he was very proud of the Village Hall at the entrance to the village, which he had finished a few weeks before.

'An' I don't mind tellin' you, Mus' Dan,' he said, 'that the Hall will be my last job top of this mortal earth. I didn't make ten pounds – no, nor yet five – out o' the whole contrac', but my name's lettered on the foundation stone – *Ralph Springett, Builder* – and the stone she's bedded on four foot good concrete. If she shifts any time these five hundred years, I'll sure-ly turn in my grave. I told the Lunnon architec' so when he come down to oversee my work.'

'What did he say?' Dan was sandpapering the schooner's port bow.

'Nothing. The Hall ain't more than one of his small jobs for *him*, but 'tain't small to me, an' my name is cut and lettered, frontin' the village street, I do hope an' pray, for time everlastin'. You'll want the little round file for that holler in her bow. Who's there?' Mr Springett turned stiffly in his chair.

A long pile of scaffold-planks ran down the centre of the loft. Dan looked, and saw Hal o' the Draft's touzled head beyond them.[1]

'Be you the builder of the Village Hall?' he asked of Mr Springett.

'I be,' was the answer. 'But if you want a job—'

Hal laughed. 'No, faith!' he said. 'Only the Hall is as good and honest a piece of work as I've ever run a rule over. So, being born hereabouts, and being reckoned a master among masons, and accepted as a master mason, I made bold to pay my brotherly respects to the builder.'

'Aa – um!' Mr Springett looked important. 'I be a bit rusty, but I'll try ye!'

He asked Hal several curious questions, and the answers must have pleased him, for he invited Hal to sit down. Hal moved up, always keeping behind the pile of planks so that only his head showed, and sat down on a trestle in the dark corner at the back of Mr Springett's desk. He took no notice of Dan, but talked at once to Mr Springett about bricks, and cement, and lead and glass, and after a while Dan went on with his work. He knew Mr Springett was pleased, because he tugged his white sandy beard, and smoked his pipe in short puffs. The two men seemed to agree about everything, but when grown-ups agree they interrupt each other almost as much as if they were quarrelling. Hal said something about workmen.

[1] See 'Hal o' the Draft' in *Puck of Pook's Hill*.

'Why, that's what *I* always say,' Mr Springett cried. 'A man who can only do one thing, he's but next-above-fool to the man that can't do nothin'. That's where the Unions make their mistake.'

'My thought to the very dot.' Dan heard Hal slap his tight-hosed leg. 'I've suffered in my time from these same Guilds – Unions, d'you call 'em? All their precious talk of the mysteries of their trades – why, what does it come to?'

'Nothin'! You've justabout hit it,' said Mr Springett, and rammed his hot tobacco with his thumb.

'Take the art of wood-carving,' Hal went on. He reached across the planks, grabbed a wooden mallet, and moved his other hand as though he wanted something. Mr Springett without a word passed him one of Dan's broad chisels. 'Ah! Wood-carving, for example. If you can cut wood and have a fair draft of what ye mean to do, a' Heaven's name take chisel and maul and let drive at it, say I! You'll soon find all the mystery, forsooth, of wood-carving under your proper hand!' Whack, came the mallet on the chisel, and a sliver of wood curled up in front of it. Mr Springett watched like an old raven.

'All art is one, man – one!' said Hal between whacks; 'and to wait on another man to finish out—'

'To finish out your work ain't no sense,' Mr Springett cut in. 'That's what I'm always sayin' to the boy here.' He nodded towards Dan. 'That's what I said when I put the new wheel into Brewster's Mill in Eighteen hundred Seventy-two. I reckoned I was millwright enough for the job 'thout bringin' a man from Lunnon. An' besides, dividin' work eats up profits, no bounds.'

Hal laughed his beautiful deep laugh, and Mr Springett joined in till Dan laughed too.

'You handle your tools, I can see,' said Mr Springett. 'I reckon, if you're any way like me, you've found yourself hindered by those – Guilds, did you call 'em? – Unions, we say.'

'You may say so!' Hal pointed to a white scar on his

cheek-bone. 'This is a remembrance from the Master watching-Foreman of Masons on Magdalen Tower, because, please you, I dared to carve stone without their leave. They said a stone had slipped from the cornice by accident.'

'I know them accidents. There's no way to disprove 'em. An' stones ain't the only things that slip,' Mr Springett grunted. Hal went on:

'I've seen a scaffold-plank keckle and shoot a too-clever workman thirty foot on to the cold chancel floor below. And a rope can break—'

'Yes, natural as nature; an' lime 'll fly up in a man's eyes without any breath o' wind sometimes,' said Mr Springett. 'But who's to show 'twasn't a accident?'

'Who do these things?' Dan asked, and straightened his back at the bench as he turned the schooner end-for-end in the vice to get at her counter.

'Them which don't wish other men to work no better nor quicker than they do,' growled Mr Springett. 'Don't pinch her so hard in the vice, Mus' Dan. Put a piece o' rag in the jaws, or you'll bruise her. More than that' – he turned towards Hal – 'if a man has his private spite laid up against you, the Unions give him his excuse for workin' it off.'

'Well I know it,' said Hal.

'They never let you go, them spiteful ones. I knowed a plasterer in Eighteen hundred Sixty-one – down to the wells. He was a Frenchy – a bad enemy he was.'

'I had mine too. He was an Italian, called Benedetto. I met him first at Oxford on Magdalen Tower when I was learning my trade – or trades, I should say. A bad enemy he was, as you say, but he came to be my singular good friend,' said Hal as he put down the mallet and settled himself comfortably.

'What might his trade have been – plasterin'?' Mr Springett asked.

'Plastering of a sort. He worked in stucco – fresco we call it. Made pictures on plaster. Not but what he had a fine sweep of the hand in drawing. He'd take the long sides of a cloister, trowel on his stuff, and roll out his great all-abroad pictures of saints and croppy-topped trees quick as a webster unrolling cloth almost. Oh, Benedetto could draw, but 'a was a little-minded man, professing to be full of secrets of colour or plaster – common tricks, all of 'em – and his one single talk was how Tom, Dick or Harry had stole this or t'other secret art from him.'

'I know that sort,' said Mr Springett. 'There's no keeping peace or making peace with such. An' they're mostly born an' bone idle.'

'True. Even his fellow-countrymen laughed at his jealousy. We two came to loggerheads early on Magdalen Tower. I was a youngster then. Maybe I spoke my mind about his work.'

'You shouldn't never do that.' Mr Springett shook his head. 'That sort lay it up against you.'

'True enough. This Benedetto did most specially. Body o' me, the man lived to hate me! But I always kept my eyes open on a plank or a scaffold. I was mighty glad to be shut of him when he quarrelled with his Guild foreman, and went off, nose in air, and paints under his arm. But' – Hal leaned forward – 'if you hate a man or a man hates you—'

'*I* know. You're everlastin' running acrost him,' Mr Springett interrupted. 'Excuse me, sir.' He leaned out of the window, and shouted to a carter who was loading a cart with bricks.

'Ain't you no more sense than to heap 'em up that way?' he said. 'Take an' throw a hundred of 'em off. It's more than the team can compass. Throw 'em off, I tell you, and make another trip for what's left over. Excuse me, sir. You was sayin'—'

'I was saying that before the end of the year I went to Bury to strengthen the lead-work in the great Abbey east window there.'

'Now that's just one of the things I've never done. But I mind there was a cheap excursion to Chichester in Eighteen hundred Seventy-nine, an' I went an' watched 'em leadin' a won'erful fine window in Chichester Cathedral. I stayed watchin' till 'twas time for us to go back. Dunno as I had two drinks p'raps, all that day.'

Hal smiled. 'At Bury, then, sure enough, I met my enemy Benedetto. He had painted a picture in plaster on the south wall of the Refectory – a noble place for a noble thing – a picture of Jonah.'

'Ah! Jonah an' his whale. I've never been as fur as Bury. You've worked about a lot,' said Mr Springett, with his eyes on the carter below.

'No. Not the whale. This was a picture of Jonah and the pompion that withered. But all that Benedetto had shown was a peevish grey-beard huggled up in angle-edged drapery beneath a pompion on a wooden trellis. This last, being a dead thing, he'd drawn it as 'twere to the life. But fierce old Jonah, bared in the sun, angry even to death that his cold prophecy was disproven – Jonah, ashamed, and already hearing the children of Nineveh running to mock him – ah, that was what Benedetto had *not* drawn!'

'He better ha' stuck to his whale, then,' said Mr Springett.

'He'd ha' done no better with that. He draws the damp cloth off the picture, an' shows it to me. I was a craftsman too, d'ye see?

' " 'Tis good," I said, "but it goes no deeper than the plaster."

' "What?" he said in a whisper.

' "Be thy own judge, Benedetto," I answered. "Does it go deeper than the plaster?"

'He reeled against a piece of dry wall. "No," he says, "and I know it. I could not hate thee more than I have done these five years, but if I live, I will try, Hal. I will try." Then he goes away. I pitied him, but I had spoken truth. His picture went no deeper than the plaster.'

'Ah!' said Mr Springett, who had turned quite red. 'You was talkin' so fast I didn't understand what you was drivin' at. I've seen men – good workmen they was – try to do more

than they could do, and – and they couldn't compass it.
They knowed it, and it nigh broke their hearts like. You was
in your right, o' course, sir, to say what you thought o' his
work; but if you'll excuse me, was you in your duty?'

'I was wrong to say it,' Hal replied. 'God forgive me – I
was young! He was workman enough himself to know where
he failed. But it all came evens in the long run. By the same
token, did ye ever hear o' one Torrigiano – Torrisany we
called him?'

'I can't say I ever did. Was he a Frenchy like?'

'No, a hectoring, hard-mouthed, long-sworded Italian
builder, as vain as a peacock and as strong as a bull, but,
mark you, a master workman. More than that – he could get
his best work out of the worst men.'

'Which it's a gift. I had a foreman-bricklayer like him
once,' said Mr Springett. 'He used to prod 'em in the back
like with a pointing-trowel, and they did wonders.'

'I've seen our Torrisany lay a 'prentice down with one
buffet and raise him with another – to make a mason of him.
I worked under him at building a chapel in London – a
chapel and a tomb for the King.'

'I never knew kings went to chapel much,' said Mr
Springett. 'But I always hold with a man – don't care who
he be – seein' about his own grave before he dies. 'Tidn't the
sort of thing to leave to your family after the will's read. I
reckon 'twas a fine vault?'

'None finer in England. This Torrigiano had the contract
for it, as you'd say. He picked master craftsmen from all
parts – England, France, Italy, the Low Countries – no odds
to him so long as they knew their work, and he drove them
like – like pigs at Brightling Fair. He called us English all
pigs. We suffered it because he was a master in his craft. If
he misliked any work that a man had done, with his own
great hands he'd rive it out, and tear it down before us all.
"Ah, you pig – you English pig!" he'd scream in the dumb
wretch's face. "You answer me? You look at me? You think
at me? Come out with me into the cloisters. I will teach you

carving myself. I will gild you all over!" But when his
passion had blown out, he'd slip his arm round the man's
neck, and impart knowledge worth gold. 'Twould have done
your heart good, Mus' Springett, to see the two hundred of
us – masons, jewellers, carvers, gilders, iron-workers and the
rest – all toiling like cock-angels, and this mad Italian hornet
fleeing one to next up and down the chapel. Done your
heart good, it would!'

'I believe you,' said Mr Springett. 'In Eighteen hundred
Fifty-four, I mind, the railway was bein' made into Hastin's.
There was two thousand navvies on it – all young – all
strong – an' I was one of 'em. Oh, dearie me! Excuse me,
sir, but was your enemy workin' with you?'

'Benedetto? Be sure he was. He followed me like a lover.
He painted pictures on the chapel ceiling – slung from a
chair. Torrigiano made us promise not to fight till the work
should be finished. We were both master craftsmen, do ye
see, and he needed us. None the less, I never went aloft to
carve 'thout testing all my ropes and knots each morning.
We were never far from each other. Benedetto 'ud sharpen
his knife on his sole while he waited for his plaster to dry –
wheet, wheet, wheet. I'd hear it where I hung chipping round
a pillar-head, and we'd nod to each other friendly-like. Oh,
he was a craftsman, was Benedetto, but his hate spoiled his
eye and his hand. I mind the night I had finished the models
for the bronze saints round the tomb; Torrigiano embraced
me before all the chapel, and bade me to supper. I met
Benedetto when I came out. He was slavering in the porch
like a mad dog.'

'Workin' himself up to it?' said Mr Springett. 'Did he
have it in at ye that night?'

'No, no. That time he kept his oath to Torrigiano. But I
pitied him. Eh, well! Now I come to my own follies. I had
never thought too little of myself; but after Torrisany had
put his arm round my neck, I – I' – Hal broke into a laugh –
'I lay there was not much odds 'twixt me and a cock-
sparrow in his pride.'

'I was pretty middlin' young once on a time,' said Mr Springett.

'Then ye know that a man can't drink and dice and dress fine, and keep company above his station, but his work suffers for it, Mus' Springett.'

'I never held much with dressin' up, but – you're right! The worst mistakes *I* ever made they was made of a Monday morning,' Mr Springett answered. 'We've all been one sort of fool or t'other. Mus' Dan, Mus' Dan, take the smallest gouge, or you'll be spluttin' her stern works clean out. Can't ye see the grain of the wood don't favour a chisel?'

'I'll spare you some of my follies. But there was a man called Brygandyne – Bob Brygandyne – Clerk of the King's Ships, a little, smooth, bustling atomy, as clever as a woman to get work done for nothin' – a won'erful smooth-tongued pleader. He made much o' me, and asked me to draft him out a drawing, a piece of carved and gilt scroll-work for the bows of one of the King's Ships – the *Sovereign* was her name.'

'Was she a man-of-war?' asked Dan.

'She was a warship, and a woman called Catherine of Castile desired the King to give her the ship for a pleasure-ship of her own. *I* did not know at the time, but she'd been at Bob to get this scroll-work done and fitted that the King might see it. I made him the picture, in an hour, all of a heat after supper – one great heaving play of dolphins and a Neptune or so reining in webby-footed sea-horses, and Arion with his harp high atop of them. It was twenty-three foot long, and maybe nine foot deep – painted and gilt.'

'It must ha' justabout looked fine,' said Mr Springett.

'That's the curiosity of it. 'Twas bad – rank bad. In my conceit I must needs show it to Torrigiano, in the chapel. He straddles his legs, hunches his knife behind him, and whistles like a storm-cock through a sleet-shower. Benedetto was behind him. We were never far apart, I've told you.

' "That is pig's work," says our Master. "Swine's work. You make any more such things, even after your fine Court suppers, and you shall be sent away." '

'Benedetto licks his lips like a cat. "Is it so bad then, Master?" he says. "What a pity!"

' "Yes," says Torrigiano. "Scarcely *you* could do things so bad. I will condescend to show."

'He talks to me then and there. No shouting, no swearing (it was too bad for that); but good, memorable counsel, bitten in slowly. Then he sets me to draft out a pair of iron gates, to take, as he said, the taste of my naughty dolphins out of my mouth. Iron's sweet stuff if you don't torture her, and hammered work is all pure, truthful line, with a reason and a support for every curve and bar of it. A week at that settled my stomach handsomely, and the Master let me put the work through the smithy, where I sweated out more of my foolish pride.'

'Good stuff is good iron,' said Mr Springett. 'I done a pair of lodge gates once in Eighteen hundred Sixty-three.'

'Oh, I forgot to say that Bob Brygandyne whipped away my draft of the ship's scroll-work, and would not give it back to me to re-draw. He said 'twould do well enough. Howsoever, my lawful work kept me too busied to remember him. Body o' me, but I worked that winter upon the gates and the bronzes for the tomb as I'd never worked before! I was leaner than a lath, but I lived – I lived then!' Hal looked at Mr Springett with his wise, crinkled-up eyes, and the old man smiled back.

'Ouch!' Dan cried. He had been hollowing out the schooner's after-deck, the little gouge had slipped and gashed the ball of his left thumb, – an ugly, triangular tear.

'That came of not steadying your wrist,' said Hal calmly. 'Don't bleed over the wood. *Do* your work with your heart's blood, but no need to let it show.' He rose and peered into a corner of the loft.

Mr Springett had risen too, and swept down a ball of cobwebs from a rafter.

'Clap that on,' was all he said, 'and put your handkerchief atop. 'Twill cake over in a minute. It don't hurt now, do it?'

'No,' said Dan indignantly. 'You know it has happened lots of times. I'll tie it up myself. Go on, sir.'

'And it'll happen hundreds of times more,' said Hal with a friendly nod as he sat down again. But he did not go on till Dan's hand was tied up properly. Then he said:

'One dark December day – too dark to judge colour – we was all sitting and talking round the fires in the chapel (you heard good talk there), when Bob Brygandyne bustles in and – "Hal, you're sent for," he squeals. I was at Torrigiano's feet on a pile of put-locks, as I might be here, toasting a herring on my knife's point. 'Twas the one English thing our Master liked – salt herring.

' "I'm busy, about my art," I calls.

' "Art?" says Bob. "What's Art compared to your scroll-work for the *Sovereign*? Come."

' "Be sure your sins will find you out," says Torrigiano. "Go with him and see." As I followed Bob out I was aware of Benedetto, like a black spot when the eyes are tired, sliddering up behind me.

'Bob hurries through the streets in the raw fog, slips into a doorway, up stairs, along passages, and at last thrusts me into a little cold room vilely hung with Flemish tapestries, and no furnishing except a table and my draft of the *Sovereign*'s scroll-work. Here he leaves me. Presently comes in a dark, long-nosed man in a fur cap.

' "Master Harry Dawe?" said he.

' "The same," I says. "Where a plague has Bob Brygandyne gone?"

'His thin eyebrows surged up a piece and come down again in a stiff bar. "He went to the King," he says.

' "All one. What's your pleasure with me?" I says, shivering, for it was mortal cold.

'He lays his hand flat on my draft. "Master Dawe," he says, "do you know the present price of gold leaf for all this wicked gilding of yours?"

'By that I guessed he was some cheese-paring clerk or other of the King's Ships, so I gave him the price. I forget it now, but it worked out to thirty pounds – carved, gilt, and fitted in place.

' "Thirty pounds!" he said, as though I had pulled a tooth of him. "You talk as though thirty pounds was to be had for the asking. None the less," he says, "your draft's a fine piece of work."

'I'd been looking at it ever since I came in, and 'twas viler even than I judged it at first. My eye and hand had been purified the past months, d'ye see, by my iron work.

' "I could do it better now," I said. The more I studied my squabby Neptunes the less I liked 'em; and Arion was a pure flaming shame atop of the unbalanced dolphins.

' "I doubt it will be fresh expense to draft it again," he says.

' "Bob never paid me for the first draft. I lay he'll never pay me for the second. 'Twill cost the King nothing if I re-draw it," I says.

' "There's a woman wishes it to be done quickly," he says. "We'll stick to your first drawing, Master Dawe. But thirty pounds is thirty pounds. You must make it less.'

'And all the while the faults in my draft fair leaped out and hit me between the eyes. At any cost, I thinks to myself, I must get it back and re-draft it. He grunts at me impatiently, and a splendid thought comes to me, which shall save me. By the same token, 'twas quite honest.'

'They ain't always,' says Mr Springett. 'How did you get out of it?'

'By the truth. I says to Master Fur Cap, as I might to you here, I says, "I'll tell you something, since you seem a knowledgeable man. Is the *Sovereign* to lie in Thames river all her days, or will she take the high seas?"

' "Oh," he says quickly, "the King keeps no cats that don't catch mice. She must sail the seas, Master Dawe. She'll be hired to merchants for the trade. She'll be out in all shapes o' weathers. Does that make any odds?"

' "Why, then," says I, "the first heavy sea she sticks her nose into'll claw off half that scroll-work, and the next will finish it. If she's meant for a pleasure-ship give me my draft again, and I'll porture you a pretty, light piece of scroll-work, good cheap. If she's meant for the open sea, pitch the draft into the fire. She can never carry that weight on her bows."

'He looks at me squintlings and plucks his under-lip.

' "Is this your honest, unswayed opinion?" he says.

' "Body o' me! Ask about!" I says. "Any seaman could tell you 'tis true. I'm advising you against my own profit, but why I do so is my own concern."

' "Not altogether," he says. "It's some of mine. You've saved me thirty pounds, Master Dawe, and you've given me good arguments to use against a wilful woman that wants my fine new ship for her own toy. We'll not have any scroll-work." His face shined with pure joy.

' "Then see that the thirty pounds you've saved on it are honestly paid the King," I says, "and keep clear o' women-folk." I gathered up my draft and crumpled it under my arm. "If that's all you need of me I'll be gone," I says. "I'm pressed."

'He turns him round and fumbles in a corner. "Too pressed to be made a knight, Sir Harry?" he says, and comes at me smiling, with three-quarters of a rusty sword.

'I pledge you my Mark I never guessed it was the King till that moment. I kneeled, and he tapped me on the shoulder.

' "Rise up, Sir Harry Dawe," he says, and, in the same breath, "I'm pressed, too," and slips through the tapestries, leaving me like a stuck calf.

'It come over me, in a bitter wave like, that here was I, a master craftsman, who had worked no bounds, soul or body, to make the King's tomb and chapel a triumph and a glory for all time; and here, d'ye see, I was made knight, not for anything I'd slaved over, or given my heart and guts to, but expressedly because I'd saved him thirty pounds and a tongue-lashing from Catherine of Castile – she that had asked for the ship. That thought shrivelled me withinsides

while I was folding away my draft. On the heels of it – maybe
you'll see why – I began to grin to myself. I thought of the
earnest simplicity of the man – the King, I should say –
because I'd saved him the money; his smile as though he'd
won half France! I thought of my own silly pride and foolish
expectations that some day he'd honour me as a master
craftsman. I thought of the broken-tipped sword he'd found
behind the hangings; the dirt of the cold room, and his cold
eye, wrapped up in his own concerns, scarcely resting on me.
Then I remembered the solemn chapel roof and the bronzes
about the stately tomb he'd lie in, and – d'ye see? – the
unreason of it all – the mad high humour of it all – took hold
on me till I sat me down on a dark stair-head in a passage,
and laughed till I could laugh no more. What else could I
have done?

'I never heard his feet behind me – he always walked like
a cat – but his arm slid round my neck, pulling me back
where I sat, till my head lay on his chest, and his left hand
held the knife plumb over my heart – Benedetto! Even so I
laughed – the fit was beyond my holding – laughed while he
ground his teeth in my ear. He was stark crazed for the time.

' "Laugh," he said. "Finish the laughter. I'll not cut ye
short. Tell me now" – he wrenched at my head – "why the
King chose to honour you, – you – you – you lickspittle
Englishman? I am full of patience now. I have waited so
long." Then he was off at score about his Jonah in Bury
Refectory, and what I'd said of it, and his pictures in the
chapel which all men praised and none looked at twice (as
if that was *my* fault!), and a whole parcel of words and looks
treasured up against me through years.

' "Ease off your arm a little," I said. "I cannot die by
choking, for I am just dubbed knight, Benedetto."

' "Tell me, and I'll confess ye, Sir Harry Dawe, Knight.
There's a long night before ye. Tell," says he.

'So I told him – his chin on my crown – told him all; told
it as well and with as many words as I have ever told a tale
at a supper with Torrigiano. I knew Benedetto would

'Laugh,' he said. 'Finish the laughter'

understand, for, mad or sad, he was a craftsman. I believed
it to be the last tale I'd ever tell top of mortal earth, and I
would not put out bad work before I left the Lodge. All art's
one art, as I said. I bore Benedetto no malice. My spirits,
d'ye see, were catched up in a high, solemn exaltation, and
I saw all earth's vanities foreshortened and little, laid out
below me like a town from a cathedral scaffolding. I told
him what befell, and what I thought of it. I gave him the
King's very voice at "Master Dawe, you've saved me thirty
pounds!"; his peevish grunt while he looked for the sword;
and how the badger-eyed figures of Glory and Victory leered
at me from the Flemish hangings. Body o' me, 'twas a fine,
noble tale, and, as I thought, my last work on earth.

   ' "That is how I was honoured by the King," I said.
"They'll hang ye for killing me, Benedetto. And, since you've
killed in the King's Palace, they'll draw and quarter you;
but you're too mad to care. Grant me, though, ye never
heard a better tale."

   'He said nothing, but I felt him shake. My head on his
chest shook; his right arm fell away, his left dropped the
knife, and he leaned with both hands on my shoulder –
shaking – shaking! I turned me round. No need to put my
foot on his knife. The man was speechless with laughter –
honest craftsman's mirth. The first time I'd ever seen him
laugh. You know the mirth that cuts off the very breath,
while ye stamp and snatch at the short ribs? That was
Benedetto's case.

   'When he began to roar and bay and whoop in the
passage, I haled him out into the street, and there we leaned
against the wall and had it all over again – waving our
hands and wagging our heads – till the watch came to know
if we were drunk.

   'Benedetto says to 'em, solemn as an owl: "You have
saved me thirty pound, Mus' Dawe," and off he pealed. In
some sort we were mad-drunk – I because dear life had been
given back to me, and he because, as he said afterwards,
because the old crust of hatred round his heart was broke up

and carried away by laughter. His very face had changed too.

' "Hal," he cries, "I forgive thee. Forgive me too, Hal. Oh, you English, you English! Did it gall thee, Hal, to see the rust on the dirty sword? Tell me again, Hal, how the King grunted with joy. Oh, let us tell the Master."

'So we reeled back to the chapel, arms round each other's necks, and when we could speak – he thought we'd been fighting – we told the Master. Yes, we told Torrigiano, and he laughed till he rolled on the new cold pavement. Then he knocked our heads together.

' "Ah, you English!" he cried. "You are more than pigs. You are English. Now you are well punished for your dirty fishes. Put the draft in the fire, and never do so any more. You are a fool, Hal, and you are a fool, Benedetto, but I need your works to please this beautiful English King—"

' "And I meant to kill Hal," says Benedetto. "Master, I meant to kill him because the English King had made him a knight."

' "Ah!" says the Master, shaking his finger. "Benedetto, if you had killed my Hal, I should have killed you – in the cloister. But you are a craftsman too, so I should have killed you like a craftsman, very, very slowly – in an hour, if I could spare the time!" That was Torrigiano – the Master!'

Mr Springett sat quite still for some time after Hal had finished. Then he turned dark red; then he rocked to and fro; then he coughed and wheezed till the tears ran down his face. Dan knew by this that he was laughing, but it surprised Hal at first.

'Excuse me, sir,' said Mr Springett, 'but I was thinkin' of some stables I built for a gentleman in Eighteen hundred Seventy-four. They was stables in blue brick – very particular work. Dunno as they weren't the best job which ever I'd done. But the gentleman's lady – she'd come from Lunnon, new married – she was all for buildin' what she called a haw-haw – what you an' me 'ud call a dik – right acrost his park. A middlin' big job which I'd have had the contract of, for she spoke to me in the library about it. But I told her there was a line o' springs just where she wanted to dig her ditch, an' she'd flood the park if she went on.'

'Were there any springs at all?' said Hal.

'Bound to be springs everywhere if you dig deep enough, ain't there? But what I said about the springs put her out o' conceit o' diggin' haw-haws, an' she took an' built a white tile dairy instead. But when I sent in my last bill for the stables, the gentleman he paid it 'thout even lookin' at it, and I hadn't forgotten nothin', I do assure you. More than that, he slips two five-pound notes into my hand in the library, an' "Ralph," he says – he allers called me by name – "Ralph," he says, "you've saved me a heap of expense an' trouble this autumn." I didn't say nothin', o' course. I knowed he didn't want any haw-haws digged acrost his park no more'n *I* did, but I never said nothin'. No more he didn't say nothin' about my blue-brick stables, which was really the best an' honestest piece o' work I'd done in quite a while. He give me ten pounds for savin' him a hem of a deal o' trouble at home. I reckon things are pretty much alike, all times, in all places.'

Hal and he laughed together. Dan couldn't quite understand what they thought so funny, and went on with his work for some time without speaking.

When he looked up, Mr Springett, alone, was wiping his eyes with his green-and-yellow pocket-handkerchief.

'Bless me, Mus' Dan, I've been asleep,' he said. 'An' I've dreamed a dream which has made me laugh – laugh as I ain't laughed in a long day. I can't remember what 'twas all about, but they do say that when old men take to laughin' in their sleep, they're middlin' ripe for the next world. Have you been workin' honest, Mus' Dan?'

'Ra-ather,' said Dan, unclamping the schooner from the vice. 'And look how I've cut myself with the small gouge.'

'Ye-es. You want a lump o' cobwebs to that,' said Mr Springett. 'Oh, I see you've put it on already. That's right, Mus' Dan.'

KING HENRY VII AND THE SHIPWRIGHTS

Harry our King in England from London town is gone,
And comen to Hamull on the Hoke in the countie of Suthampton.
For there lay the *Mary of the Tower*, his ship of war so strong,
And he would discover, certaynely, if his shipwrights did him
    wrong.

He told not none of his setting forth, nor yet where he would go
(But only my Lord of Arundel), and meanly did he show,
In an old jerkin and patched hose that no man might him mark;
With his frieze hood and cloak about, he looked like any clerk.

He was at Hamull on the Hoke about the hour of the tide,
And saw the *Mary* haled into dock, the winter to abide,
With all her tackle and habiliments which are the King his own;
But then ran on his false shipwrights and stripped her to the bone.

They heaved the main-mast overboard, that was of a trusty tree,
And they wrote down it was spent and lost by force of weather
    at sea.
But they sawen it into planks and strakes as far as it might go,
To maken beds for their own wives and little children also.

There was a knave called Slingawai, he crope beneath the deck,
Crying: 'Good felawes, come and see! The ship is nigh a wreck!
For the storm that took our tall main-mast, it blew so fierce and
    fell,
Alack! it hath taken the kettles and pans, and this brass pott as
    well!'

With that he set the pott on his head and hied him up the hatch,
While all the shipwrights ran below to find what they might
    snatch;
All except Bob Brygandyne and he was a yeoman good,
He caught Slingawai round the waist and threw him on to the
    mud.

'I have taken plank and rope and nail, without the King his leave,
After the custom of Portesmouth, but I will not suffer a thief.
Nay, never lift up thy hand at me! There's no clean hands in the trade.
Steal in measure,' quo' Brygandyne. 'There's measure in all things made!'

'Gramercy, yeoman!' said our King. 'Thy counsel liketh me.'
And he pulled a whistle out of his neck and whistled whistles three.
Then came my Lord of Arundel pricking across the down,
And behind him the Mayor and Burgesses of merry Suthampton town.

They drew the naughty shipwrights up, with the kettles in their hands,
And bound them round the forecastle to wait the King's commands.
But 'Since ye have made your beds,' said the King, 'ye needs must lie thereon.
For the sake of your wives and little ones – felawes, get you gone!'

When they had beaten Slingawai, out of his own lips,
Our King appointed Brygandyne to be Clerk of all his ships.
'Nay, never lift up thy hands to me – there's no clean hands in the trade.
But steal in measure,' said Harry our King. 'There's measure in all things made!'

God speed the 'Mary of the Tower,' the 'Sovereign' and 'Grace Dieu,'
The 'Sweepstakes' and the 'Mary Fortune,' and the 'Henry of Bristol' too!
All tall ships that sail on the sea, or in our harbours stand,
That they may keep measure with Harry our King and peace in England!

Marklake Witches

THE WAY THROUGH THE WOODS

They shut the road through the woods
  Seventy years ago.
Weather and rain have undone it again,
  And now you would never know
There was once a road through the woods
  Before they planted the trees.
It is underneath the coppice and heath,
  And the thin anemones.
  Only the keeper sees
That, where the ring-dove broods,
  And the badgers roll at ease,
There was once a road through the woods.

Yet, if you enter the woods
  Of a summer evening late,
When the night-air cools on the trout-ringed pools
  Where the otter whistles his mate
(They fear not men in the woods
  Because they see so few),
You will hear the beat of a horse's feet
  And the swish of a skirt in the dew,
  Steadily cantering through
The misty solitudes,
  As though they perfectly knew
The old lost road through the woods . . .
But there is no road through the woods!

Marklake Witches

WHEN Dan took up boat-building, Una coaxed Mrs Vincey, the farmer's wife at Little Lindens, to teach her to milk. Mrs Vincey milks in the pasture in summer, which is different from milking in the shed, because the cows are not tied up, and until they know you they will not stand still. After three weeks Una could milk Red Cow or Kitty Shorthorn quite dry, without her wrists aching, and then she allowed Dan to look. But milking did not amuse him, and it was pleasanter for Una to be alone in the quiet pastures with quiet-spoken Mrs Vincey. So, evening after evening, she slipped across to Little Lindens, took her stool from the fern-clump beside the fallen oak, and went to work, her pail between her knees, and her head pressed hard into the cow's flank. As often as not, Mrs Vincey would be milking cross Pansy at the other end of the pasture, and would not come near till it was time to strain and pour off.

Once, in the middle of a milking, Kitty Shorthorn boxed Una's ear with her tail.

'You old pig!' said Una, nearly crying, for a cow's tail can hurt.

'Why didn't you tie it down, child?' said a voice behind her.

'I meant to, but the flies are so bad I let her off – and this is what she's done!' Una looked round, expecting Puck, and saw a curly-haired girl, not much taller than herself, but older, dressed in a curious high-waisted, lavender-coloured riding-habit, with a high hunched collar and a deep cape and a belt fastened with a steel clasp. She wore a yellow velvet cap and tan gauntlets, and carried a real hunting-crop. Her cheeks were pale except for two pretty pink patches in the middle, and she talked with little gasps at the end of her sentences, as though she had been running.

'You don't milk so badly, child,' she said, and when she smiled her teeth showed small and even and pearly.

'Can you milk?' Una asked, and then flushed, for she heard Puck's chuckle.

He stepped out of the fern and sat down, holding Kitty Shorthorn's tail. 'There isn't much,' he said, 'that Miss Philadelphia doesn't know about milk – or, for that matter, butter and eggs. She's a great housewife.'

'Oh,' said Una. 'I'm sorry I can't shake hands. Mine are all milky; but Mrs Vincey is going to teach me butter-making this summer.'

'Ah! *I'm* going to London this summer,' the girl said, 'to my aunt in Bloomsbury.' She coughed as she began to hum, ' "Oh, what a town! What a wonderful metropolis!" '

'You've got a cold,' said Una.

'No. Only my stupid cough. But it's vastly better than it was last winter. It will disappear in London air. Every one says so. D'you like doctors, child?'

'I don't know any,' Una replied. 'But I'm sure I shouldn't.'

'Think yourself lucky, child. I beg your pardon,' the girl laughed, for Una frowned.

'I'm not a child, and my name's Una,' she said.

'Mine's Philadelphia. But everybody except René calls me Phil. I'm Squire Bucksteed's daughter – over at Mark-lake yonder.' She jerked her little round chin towards the south behind Dallington. 'Sure-ly you know Marklake?'

'We went a picnic to Marklake Green once,' said Una. 'It's awfully pretty. I like all those funny little roads that don't lead anywhere.'

'They lead over our land,' said Philadelphia stiffly, 'and the coach road is only four miles away. One can go anywhere from the Green. I went to the Assize Ball at Lewes last year.' She spun round and took a few dancing steps, but stopped with her hand to her side.

'It gives me a stitch,' she explained. 'No odds. 'Twill go

away in London air. That's the latest French step, child. René taught it me. D'you hate the French, chi – Una?'

'Well, I hate French, of course, but I don't mind Ma'm'selle. She's rather decent. Is René your French governess?'

Philadelphia laughed till she caught her breath again.

'Oh no! René's a French prisoner – on parole. That means he's promised not to escape till he has been properly exchanged for an Englishman. He's only a doctor, so I hope they won't think him worth exchanging. My uncle captured him last year in the *Ferdinand* privateer, off Belle Isle, and he cured my uncle of a r-r-raging toothache. Of course, after *that* we couldn't let him lie among the common French prisoners at Rye, and so he stays with us. He's of very old family – a Breton, which is nearly next door to being a true Briton, my father says – and he wears his hair clubbed – not powdered. *Much* more becoming, don't you think?'

'I don't know what you're—' Una began, but Puck, the other side of the pail, winked, and she went on with her milking.

'He's going to be a great French physician when the war is over. He makes me bobbins for my lace-pillow now – he's very clever with his hands; but he'd doctor our people on the Green if they would let him. Only our Doctor – Doctor Break – says he's an emp— or imp something – worse than impostor. But my Nurse says—'

'Nurse! You're ever so old. What have you got a nurse for?' Una finished milking, and turned round on her stool as Kitty Shorthorn grazed off.

'Because I can't get rid of her. Old Cissie nursed my mother, and she says she'll nurse me till she dies. The idea! She never lets me alone. She thinks I'm delicate. She has grown infirm in her understanding, you know. Mad – quite mad, poor Cissie!'

'Really mad?' said Una. 'Or just silly?'

'Crazy, I should say – from the things she does. Her devotion to me is terribly embarrassing. You know I have all the keys of the Hall except the brewery and the tenants' kitchen. I give out all stores and the linen and plate.'

'How jolly! I love store-rooms and giving out things.'

'Ah, it's a great responsibility, you'll find, when you come to my age. Last year Dad said I was fatiguing myself with my duties, and he actually wanted me to give up the keys to old Amoore, our housekeeper. I wouldn't. I hate her. I said, "No, sir. I am Mistress of Marklake Hall just as long as I live, because I'm never going to be married, and I shall give out stores and linen till I die!"'

'And what did your father say?'

'Oh, I threatened to pin a dishclout to his coat-tail. He ran away. Every one's afraid of Dad, except me.' Philadelphia stamped her foot. 'The idea! If I can't make my own father happy in his own house, I'd like to meet the woman that can, and – and – I'd have the living hide off her!'

She cut with her long-thonged whip. It cracked like a pistol-shot across the still pasture. Kitty Shorthorn threw up her head and trotted away.

'I beg your pardon,' Philadelphia said; 'but it makes me furious. Don't you hate those ridiculous old quizzes with their feathers and fronts, who come to dinner and call you "child" in your own chair at your own table?'

'I don't always come to dinner,' said Una, 'but I hate being called "child." Please tell me about store-rooms and giving out things.'

'Ah, it's a great responsibility – particularly with that old cat Amoore looking at the lists over your shoulder. And such a shocking thing happened last summer! Poor crazy Cissie, my Nurse that I was telling you of, she took three solid silver tablespoons.'

'Took! But isn't that stealing?' Una cried.

'Hsh!' said Philadelphia, looking round at Puck. 'All I say is she took them without my leave. I made it right afterwards. So, as Dad says – and he's a magistrate –, it wasn't a legal offence; it was only compounding a felony.'

'It sounds awful,' said Una.

'It was. My dear, I was furious! I had had the keys for ten months, and I'd never lost anything before. I said nothing at first, because a big house offers so many chances of things being mislaid, and coming to hand later. "Fetching up in the lee-scuppers," my uncle calls it. But next week I spoke to old Cissie about it when she was doing my hair at night, and she said I wasn't to worry my heart for trifles!'

'Isn't it like 'em?' Una burst out. 'They see you're worried over something that really matters, and they say, "Don't worry"; as if *that* did any good!'

'I quite agree with you, my dear; quite agree with you! I told Ciss the spoons were solid silver, and worth forty shillings, so if the thief were found, he'd be tried for his life.'

'Hanged, do you mean?' Una said.

'They ought to be; but Dad says no jury will hang a man nowadays for a forty-shilling theft. They transport 'em into penal servitude at the uttermost ends of the earth beyond the seas, for the term of their natural life. I told Cissie that, and I saw her tremble in my mirror. Then she cried, and caught hold of my knees, and I couldn't for my life understand what it was all about, – she cried so. *Can* you guess, my dear, what that poor crazy thing had done? It was midnight before I pieced it together. She had given the spoons to Jerry Gamm, the Witchmaster on the Green, so that he might put a charm on me! Me!'

'Put a charm on you? Why?'

'That's what *I* asked; and then I saw how mad poor Cissie was! You know this stupid little cough of mine? It will disappear as soon as I go to London. She was troubled about *that*, and about my being so thin, and she told me Jerry had promised her, if she would bring him three silver spoons, that he'd charm my cough away and make me plump – "flesh up," she said. I couldn't help laughing; but it was a terrible night! I had to put Cissie into my own bed, and stroke her hand till she cried herself to sleep. What else could I have done? When she woke, and I coughed – I suppose I *can* cough in my own room if I please – she said that she'd killed me, and asked me to have her hanged at Lewes sooner than send her to the uttermost ends of the earth away from me.'

'How awful! What did you do, Phil?'

'Do? I rode off at five in the morning to talk to Master Jerry, with a new lash on my whip. Oh, I was *furious*! Witchmaster or no Witchmaster, I meant to—'

'Ah! what's a Witchmaster?'

'A master of witches, of course. *I* don't believe there are witches; but people say every village has a few, and Jerry was the master of all ours at Marklake. He has been a smuggler, and a man-of-war's man, and now he pretends to be a carpenter and joiner – he can make almost anything – but he really is a white wizard. He cures people by herbs and charms. He can cure them after Doctor Break has given them up, and that's why Doctor Break hates him so. He used to make me toy carts, and charm off my warts when I was a child.' Philadelphia spread out her hands with the delicate shiny little nails. 'It isn't counted lucky to cross him. He has his ways of getting even with you, they say. But *I* wasn't afraid of Jerry! I saw him working in his garden, and I leaned out of my saddle and double-thonged him between the shoulders, over the hedge. Well, my dear, for the first time since Dad gave him to me, my Troubadour (I wish you could see the sweet creature!) shied across the road, and I spilled out into the hedge-top. *Most* undignified! Jerry pulled me through to his side and brushed the leaves off me. I was horribly pricked, but I didn't care. "Now, Jerry," I said, "I'm going to take the hide off you first, and send you to Lewes afterwards. You well know why." "Oh!" he said, and he sat down among his bee-hives. "Then I reckon you've come about old Cissie's business, my dear." "I reckon I justabout have," I said. "Stand away from these hives. I can't get at you there." "That's why I be where I be," he said. "If you'll excuse me, Miss Phil, I don't hold with bein' flogged before breakfast, at my time o' life." He's

But *I* wasn't afraid of Jerry

a huge big man, but he looked so comical squatting among the hives that – I know I oughtn't to – I laughed, and he laughed. I always laugh at the wrong time. But I soon recovered my dignity, and I said, "Then give me back what you made poor Cissie steal!"

' "Your pore Cissie," he said. "She's a hatful o' trouble. But you shall have 'em, Miss Phil. They're all ready put by for you." And, would you believe it, the old sinner pulled my three silver spoons out of his dirty pocket, and polished them on his cuff! "Here they be," he says, and he gave them to me, just as cool as though I'd come to have my warts charmed. That's the worst of people having known you when you were young. But I preserved my composure. "Jerry," I said, "what in the world are we to do? If you'd been caught with these things on you, you'd have been hanged."

' "I know it," he said. "But they're yours now."

' "But you made my Cissie steal them," I said.

' "That I didn't," he said. "Your Cissie, she was pickin' at me an' tarrifyin' me all the long day an' every day for weeks, to put a charm on you, Miss Phil, an' take away your little spitty cough."

' "Yes. I knew that, Jerry, and to make me flesh-up!" I said. "I'm much obliged to you, but I'm not one of your pigs!"

' "Ah! I reckon she've been talking to you, then," he said. "Yes, she give me no peace, and bein' tarrified – for I don't hold with old women – I laid a task on her which I thought 'ud silence her. *I* never reckoned the old scrattle 'ud risk her neckbone at Lewes Assizes for your sake, Miss Phil. But she did. She up an' stole, I tell ye, as cheerful as a tinker. You might ha' knocked me down with any one of them liddle spoons when she brung 'em in her apron."

' "Do you mean to say, then, that you did it to try my poor Cissie?" I screamed at him.

' "What else for, dearie?" he said. "*I* don't stand in need of hedge-stealings. I'm a freeholder, with money in the bank; and now I won't trust women no more! Silly old besom! I do beleft she'd ha' stole the Squire's big fob-watch, if I'd required her."

'"Then you're a wicked, wicked old man," I said, and I was so angry that I couldn't help crying, and of course that made me cough.

'Jerry was in a fearful taking. He picked me up and carried me into his cottage – it's full of foreign curiosities – and he got me something to eat and drink, and he said he'd be hanged by the neck any day if it pleased me. He said he'd even tell old Cissie he was sorry. That's a great comedown for a Witchmaster, you know.

'I was ashamed of myself for being so silly, and I dabbed my eyes and said, "The least you can do now is to give poor Ciss some sort of a charm for me."

'"Yes, that's only fair dealings," he said. "You know the names of the Twelve Apostles, dearie? You say them names, one by one, before your open window, rain or storm, wet or shine, five times a day fasting. But mind you, 'twixt every name you draw in your breath through your nose, right down to your pretty liddle toes, as long and as deep as you can, and let it out slow through your pretty liddle mouth. There's virtue for your cough in those names spoke that way. And I'll give you something you can see, moreover. Here's a stick of maple, which is the warmest tree in the wood." '

'That's true,' Una interrupted. 'You can feel it almost as warm as yourself when you touch it.'

'"It's cut one inch long for your every year," Jerry said. "That's sixteen inches. You set it in your window so that it holds up the sash, and thus you keep it, rain or shine, or wet or fine, day and night. I've said words over it which will have virtue on your complaints."

'"I haven't any complaints, Jerry," I said. "It's only to please Cissie."

'"I know that as well as you do, dearie," he said. And – and that was all that came of my going to give him a flogging. I wonder whether he made poor Troubadour shy when I lashed at him? Jerry has his ways of getting even with people.'

'I wonder,' said Una. 'Well, did you try the charm? Did it work?'

'What nonsense! I told René about it, of course, because he's a doctor. He's going to be a most famous doctor. That's why our doctor hates him. René said, "Oho! Your Master Gamm, he is worth knowing," and he put up his eyebrows – like this. He made joke of it all. He can see my window from the carpenter's shed, where he works, and if ever the maple stick fell down, he pretended to be in a fearful taking till I propped the window up again. He used to ask me whether I had said my Apostles properly, and how I took my deep breaths. Oh yes, and the next day, though he had been there ever so many times before, he put on his new hat and paid Jerry Gamm a visit of state – as a fellow-physician. Jerry never guessed René was making fun of him, and so he told René about the sick people in the village, and how he cured them with herbs after Doctor Break had given them up. Jerry could talk smugglers' French, of course, and I had taught René plenty of English, if only he wasn't so shy. They called each other Monsieur Gamm and Mosheur Lanark, just like gentlemen. I suppose it amused poor René. He hasn't much to do, except to fiddle about in the carpenter's shop. He's like all the French prisoners – always making knick-knacks; and Jerry had a little lathe at his cottage, and so – and so – René took to being with Jerry much more than I approved of. The Hall is so big and empty when Dad's away, and I will *not* sit with old Amoore – she talks so horridly about every one – specially about René.

'I was rude to René, I'm afraid; but I was properly served out for it. One always is. You see, Dad went down to Hastings to pay his respects to the General who commanded the brigade there, and to bring him to the Hall afterwards. Dad told me he was a very brave soldier from India – he was Colonel of Dad's Regiment, the Thirty-third Foot, after Dad left the Army, and then he changed his name from Wesley to Wellesley, or else the other way about; and Dad said I was to get out all the silver for him, and I knew that meant a big dinner. So I sent down to the sea for early mackerel, and had *such* a morning in the kitchen and the store-rooms. Old Amoore nearly cried.

'However, my dear, I made all my preparations in ample time, but the fish didn't arrive – it never does – and I wanted René to ride to Pevensey and bring it himself. He had gone over to Jerry, of course, as he always used, unless I requested his presence beforehand. *I* can't send for René every time I want him. He should be there. Now, don't you ever do what I did, child, because it's in the highest degree unladylike; but – but one of our woods runs up to Jerry's garden, and if you climb – it's ungenteel, but I can climb like a kitten – there's an old hollow oak just above the pigsty where you can hear and see everything below. Truthfully, I only went to tell René about the mackerel, but I saw him and Jerry sitting on the seat playing with wooden toy trumpets. So I slipped into the hollow, and choked down my cough, and listened. René had never shown *me* any of these trumpets.'

'Trumpets? Aren't you too old for trumpets?' said Una.

'They weren't real trumpets, because Jerry opened his shirt-collar, and René put one end of his trumpet against Jerry's chest, and put his ear to the other. Then Jerry put his trumpet against René's chest, and listened while René breathed and coughed. I was afraid *I* would cough too.

' "This hollywood one is the best," said Jerry. " 'Tis won'erful like hearin' a man's soul whisperin' in his innards; but unless I've a buzzin' in my ears, Mosheur Lanark, you make much about the same kind o' noises as old Gaffer Macklin – but not quite so loud as young Copper. It sounds like breakers on a reef – a long way off. Comprenny?"

' "Perfectly," said René. "I drive on the breakers. But before I strike, I shall save hundreds, thousands, millions perhaps, by my little trumpets. Now tell me what sounds the old Gaffer Macklin have made in his chest, and what the young Copper also."

'Jerry talked for nearly a quarter of an hour about sick people in the village, while René asked questions. Then he sighed, and said, "You explain very well, Monsieur Gamm, but if only I had your opportunities to listen for myself! Do you think these poor people would let me listen to them through my trumpet – for a little money? No?" – René's as poor as a church mouse.

' "They'd kill you, Mosheur. It's all I can do to coax 'em to abide it, and I'm Jerry Gamm," said Jerry. He's very proud of his attainments.

' "Then these poor people are alarmed – No?" said René.

' "They've had it in at me for some time back because o' my tryin' your trumpets on their sick; and I reckon by the talk at the alehouse they won't stand much more. Tom Dunch an' some of his kidney was drinkin' themselves riot-ripe when I passed along after noon. Charms an' mutterin's an' bits o' red wool an' black hens is in the way o' nature to these fools, Mosheur; but anything likely to do 'em real service is devil's work by their estimation. If I was you, I'd go home before they come." Jerry spoke quite quietly, and René shrugged his shoulders.

' "I am prisoner on parole, Monsieur Gamm," he said. "I have no home."

'Now that was unkind of René. He's often told me that he looked on England as his home. I suppose it's French politeness.

' "Then we'll talk o' something that matters," said Jerry. "Not to name no names, Mosheur Lanark, what might be your own opinion o' some one who ain't old Gaffer Macklin nor young Copper? Is that person better or worse?"

' "Better – for time that is," said René. He meant for the time being, but I never could teach him some phrases.

' "I thought so too," said Jerry. "But how about time to come?"

'René shook his head, and then he blew his nose. You

don't know how odd a man looks blowing his nose when you are sitting directly above him.

' "I've thought that too," said Jerry. He rumbled so deep I could scarcely catch. "It don't make much odds to me, because I'm old. But you're young, Mosheur – you're young," and he put his hand on René's knee, and René covered it with his hand. I didn't know they were such friends.

' "Thank you, *mon ami*," said René. "I am much oblige. Let us return to our trumpet-making. But I forget" – he stood up – "it appears that you receive this afternoon!"

'You can't see into Gamm's Lane from the oak, but the gate opened, and fat little Doctor Break stumped in, mopping his head, and half-a-dozen of our people following him, very drunk.

'You ought to have seen René bow; he does it beautifully.

' "A word with you, Laennec," said Doctor Break. "Jerry has been practising some devilry or other on these poor wretches, and they've asked me to be arbiter."

' "Whatever that means, I reckon it's safer than asking you to be doctor," said Jerry, and Tom Dunch, one of our carters, laughed.

' "That ain't right feeling of you, Tom," Jerry said, "seeing how clever Doctor Break put away your thorn in the flesh last winter." Tom's wife had died at Christmas, though Doctor Break bled her twice a week. Doctor Break danced with rage.

' "This is all beside the mark," he said. "These good people are willing to testify that you've been impudently prying into God's secrets by means of some papistical contrivance which this person" – he pointed to poor René – "has furnished you with. Why, here are the things themselves!" René was holding a trumpet in his hand.

'Then all the men talked at once. They said old Gaffer Macklin was dying from stitches in his side where Jerry had put the trumpet – they called it the devil's ear-piece; and they said it left round red witch-marks on people's skins, and dried up their lights, and made 'em spit blood, and threw 'em into sweats. Terrible things they said. You never heard such a noise. I took advantage of it to cough.

'René and Jerry were standing with their backs to the pigsty. Jerry fumbled in his big flap pockets and fished up a pair of pistols. You ought to have seen the men give back when he cocked his. He passed one to René.

' "Wait! Wait!" said René. "I will explain to the doctor if he permits." He waved a trumpet at him, and the men at the gate shouted, "Don't touch it, Doctor! Don't lay a hand to the thing."

' "Come, come!" said René. "You are not so big fool as you pretend. No?"

'Doctor Break backed toward the gate, watching Jerry's pistol, and René followed him with his trumpet, like a nurse trying to amuse a child, and put the ridiculous thing to his ear to show how it was used, and talked of *la Gloire*, and *l'Humanité*, and *la Science*, while Doctor Break watched Jerry's pistol and swore. I nearly laughed aloud.

' "Now listen! Now listen!" said René. "This will be moneys in your pockets, my dear *confrère*. You will become rich."

'Then Doctor Break said something about adventurers who could not earn an honest living in their own country creeping into decent houses and taking advantage of gentlemen's confidence to enrich themselves by base intrigues.

'René dropped his absurd trumpet and made one of his best bows. I knew he was angry from the way he rolled his "r's."

' "Ver-r-ry good," said he. "For that I shall have much pleasure to kill you now and here. Monsieur Gamm," – another bow to Jerry – "you will please lend him your pistol, or he shall have mine. I give you my word I know not which is best; and if he will choose a second from his friends over there" – another bow to our drunken yokels at the gate – "we will commence."

' "That's fair enough," said Jerry. "Tom Dunch, you owe it to the Doctor to be his second. Place your man."

' "No," said Tom. "No mixin' in gentry's quarrels for me." And he shook his head and went out, and the others followed him.

' "Hold on," said Jerry. "You've forgot what you set out to do up at the alehouse just now. You was goin' to search me for witch-marks; you was goin' to duck me in the pond; you was goin' to drag all my bits o' sticks out o' my little cottage here. What's the matter with you? Wouldn't you like to be with your old woman tonight, Tom?"

'But they didn't even look back, much less come. They ran to the village alehouse like hares.

' "No matter for these *canaille*," said René, buttoning up his coat so as not to show any linen. All gentlemen do that before a duel, Dad says – and he's been out five times. "You shall be his second, Monsieur Gamm. Give him the pistol."

'Doctor Break took it as if it was red-hot, but he said that if René resigned his pretensions in certain quarters he would pass over the matter. René bowed deeper than ever.

' "As for that," he said, "if you were not the ignorant which you are, you would have known long ago that the subject of your remarks is not for any living man."

'I don't know what the subject of his remarks might have been, but he spoke in a simply dreadful voice, my dear, and Doctor Break turned quite white, and said René was a liar; and then René caught him by the throat, and choked him black.

'Well, my dear, as if this wasn't deliciously exciting enough, just exactly at that minute I heard a strange voice on the other side of the hedge say, "What's this? What's this, Bucksteed?" and there was my father and Sir Arthur Wesley on horseback in the lane; and there was René kneeling on Doctor Break, and there was I up in the oak, listening with all my ears.

'I must have leaned forward too much, and the voice gave me such a start that I slipped. I had only time to make one jump on to the pigsty roof – another, before the tiles broke, on to the pigsty wall – and then I bounced down into the garden, just behind Jerry, with my hair full of bark. Imagine the situation!'

'Oh, I can!' Una laughed till she nearly fell off the stool.

'Dad said, "Phil – a – del – phia!" and Sir Arthur Wesley said, "Good Ged" and Jerry put his foot on the pistol René had dropped. But René was splendid. He never even looked at me. He began to untwist Doctor Break's neckcloth as fast as he'd twisted it, and asked him if he felt better.

' "What's happened? What's happened?" said Dad.

' "A fit!" said René. "I fear my *confrère* has had a fit. Do not be alarmed. He recovers himself. Shall I bleed you a little, my dear Doctor?" Doctor Break was very good too. He said, "I am vastly obliged, Monsieur Laennec, but I am restored now." And as he went out of the gate he told Dad it was a syncope – I think. Then Sir Arthur said, "Quite right, Bucksteed. Not another word! They are both gentlemen." And he took off his cocked hat to Doctor Break and René.

'But poor Dad wouldn't let well alone. He kept saying, "Philadelphia, what does all this mean?"

' "Well, sir," I said, "I've only just come down. As far as I could see, it looked as though Doctor Break had had a sudden seizure." That was quite true – if you'd seen René seize him. Sir Arthur laughed. "Not much change there, Bucksteed," he said. "She's a lady – a thorough lady."

' "Heaven knows she doesn't look like one," said poor Dad. "Go home, Philadelphia."

'So I went home, my dear – don't laugh so! – right under Sir Arthur's nose – a most enormous nose – feeling as though I were twelve years old, going to be whipped. Oh, I *beg* your pardon, child!'

'It's all right,' said Una. 'I'm getting on for thirteen. I've never been whipped, but I know how you felt. All the same, it must have been funny!'

'Funny! If you'd heard Sir Arthur jerking out, "Good Ged, Bucksteed!" every minute as they rode behind me; and poor Dad saying, " 'Pon my honour, Arthur, I can't account for it!" Oh, how my cheeks tingled when I reached my room! But Cissie had laid out my very best evening dress, the white satin one, vandyked at the bottom with spots of morone foil, and the pearl knots, you know, catching up the drapery from the left shoulder. I had poor mother's lace tucker and her coronet comb.'

'Oh, you lucky!' Una murmured. '*And* gloves?'

'French kid, my dear' – Philadelphia patted her shoulder – 'and morone satin shoes and a morone and gold crape fan. That restored my calm. Nice things always do. I wore my hair banded on my forehead with a little curl over the left ear. And when I descended the stairs, *en grande tenue*, old Amoore curtsied to me without my having to stop and look at her, which, alas! is too often the case. Sir Arthur highly approved of the dinner, my dear: the mackerel *did* come in time. We had all the Marklake silver out, and he toasted my health, and he asked me where my little bird's-nesting sister was. I *know* he did it to quiz me, so I looked him straight in the face, my dear, and I said, "I always send her to the nursery, Sir Arthur, when I receive guests at Marklake Hall." '

'Oh, how chee – clever of you. What did he say?' Una cried.

'He said, "Not much change there, Bucksteed. Ged, I deserved it," and he toasted me again. They talked about the French and what a shame it was that Sir Arthur only commanded a brigade at Hastings, and he told Dad of a battle in India at a place called Assaye. Dad said it was a terrible fight, but Sir Arthur described it as though it had been a whist-party – I suppose because a lady was present.'

'Of course you were the lady. I wish I'd seen you,' said Una.

'I wish you had, child. I had *such* a triumph after dinner. René and Doctor Break came in. They had quite made up their quarrel, and they told me they had the highest esteem for each other, and I laughed and said, "I heard every word of it up in the tree." You never saw two men so frightened in your life, and when I said, "What *was* 'the subject of your remarks,' René?" neither of them knew where to look. Oh, I quizzed them unmercifully. They'd seen me jump off the pigsty roof, remember.'

'But what *was* the subject of their remarks?' said Una.

'Oh, Doctor Break said it was a professional matter, so the laugh was turned on me. I was horribly afraid it might have been something unladylike and indelicate. But *that* wasn't my triumph. Dad asked me to play on the harp. Between just you and me, child, I had been practising a new song from London – I don't always live in trees – for weeks; and I gave it them for a surprise.'

'What was it?' said Una. 'Sing it.'

' "I have given my heart to a flower." Not very difficult fingering, but r-r-ravishing sentiment.'

Philadelphia coughed and cleared her throat.

'I've a deep voice for my age and size,' she explained. 'Contralto, you know, but it ought to be stronger,' and she began, her face all dark against the last of the soft pink sunset:

> 'I have given my heart to a flower,
>   Though I know it is fading away,
>   Though I know it will live but an hour
> And leave me to mourn its decay!

'Isn't that touchingly sweet? Then the last verse – I wish I had my harp, dear – goes as low as my register will reach.' She drew in her chin, and took a deep breath:

> 'Ye desolate whirlwinds that rave,
>   I charge you be good to my dear!
>   She is all – she is all that I have,
> And the time of our parting is near!'

'Beautiful!' said Una. 'And did they like it?'

'Like it? They were overwhelmed – *accablés*, as René says. My dear, if I hadn't seen it, I shouldn't have believed that I could have drawn tears, genuine tears, to the eyes of four grown men. But I did! René simply couldn't endure it! He's all French sensibility. He hid his face and said, "*Assez, Mademoiselle! C'est plus fort que moi! Assez!*" And Sir Arthur blew his nose and said, "Good Ged! This is worse than Assaye!" While Dad sat with the tears simply running down his cheeks.'

'And what did Doctor Break do?'

'He got up and pretended to look out of the window, but I saw his little fat shoulders jerk as if he had the hiccoughs. That *was* a triumph. I never suspected him of sensibility.'

'Oh, I wish I'd seen! I wish I'd been you,' said Una, clasping her hands. Puck rustled and rose from the fern, just as a big blundering cock-chafer flew smack against Una's cheek.

When she had finished rubbing the place, Mrs Vincey called to her that Pansy had been fractious, or she would have come long before to help her strain and pour off.

'It didn't matter,' said Una; 'I just waited. Is that old Pansy barging about the lower pasture now?'

'No,' said Mrs Vincey, listening. 'It sounds more like a horse being galloped middlin' quick through the woods; but there's no road there. I reckon it's one of Gleason's colts loose. Shall I see you up to the house, Miss Una?'

'Gracious, no! thank you. What's going to hurt me?' said Una, and she put her stool away behind the oak, and strolled home through the gaps that old Hobden kept open for her.

BROOKLAND ROAD

I was very well pleased with what I knowed,
    I reckoned myself no fool –
Till I met with a maid on the Brookland Road
    That turned me back to school.

    Low down – low down!
    Where the liddle green lanterns shine –
    Oh! maids, I've done with 'ee all but one,
    And she can never be mine!

'Twas right in the middest of a hot June night,
    With thunder duntin' round,
And I seed her face by the fairy light
    That beats from off the ground.

She only smiled and she never spoke,
    She smiled and went away;
But when she'd gone my heart was broke,
    And my wits was clean astray.

Oh! Stop your ringing and let me be –
    Let be, O Brookland bells!
You'll ring Old Goodman[1] out of the sea,
    Before I wed one else!

Old Goodman's farm is rank sea sand,
    And was this thousand year;
But it shall turn to rich plough land
    Before I change my dear!

Oh! Fairfield Church is water-bound
    From Autumn to the Spring;
But it shall turn to high hill ground
    Before my bells do ring!

    [1] Earl Godwin of the Goodwin Sands (?)

Oh! leave me walk on the Brookland Road,
  In the thunder and warm rain –
Oh! leave me look where my love goed
  And p'raps I'll see her again!

  Low down – low down!
  Where the liddle green lanterns shine –
  Oh! maids, I've done with 'ee all but one,
  And she can never be mine!

The Knife and the Naked Chalk

THE RUN OF THE DOWNS

The Weald is good, the Downs are best –
I'll give you the run of 'em, East to West.
Beachy Head and Winddoor Hill,
They were once and they are still.
Firle, Mount Caburn and Mount Harry
Go back as far as sums 'll carry.
Ditchling Beacon and Chanctonbury Ring,
They have looked on many a thing;
And what those two have missed between 'em
I reckon Truleigh Hill has seen 'em.
Highden, Bignor and Duncton Down
Knew Old England before the Crown.
Linch Down, Treyford and Sunwood
Knew Old England before the Flood.
And when you end on the Hampshire side –
Butser's old as Time and Tide.
   The Downs are sheep, the Weald is corn,
   You be glad you are Sussex born!

The Knife and the Naked Chalk

THE children went to the seaside for a month, and lived in a flint village on the bare windy chalk Downs, quite thirty miles away from home. They made friends with an old shepherd, called Mr Dudeney, who had known their Father when their Father was little. He did not talk like their own people in the Weald of Sussex, and he used different names for farm things, but he understood how they felt, and let them go with him. He had a tiny cottage about half a mile from the village, where his wife made mead from thyme honey, and nursed sick lambs in front of a coal fire, while Old Jim, who was Mr Dudeney's sheep-dog's father, lay at the door. They brought up beef-bones for Old Jim (you must never give a sheep-dog mutton bones), and if Mr Dudeney happened to be far in the Downs, Mrs Dudeney would tell the dog to take them to him, and he did.

One August afternoon when the village water-cart had made the street smell specially townified, they went to look for their shepherd as usual, and, as usual, Old Jim crawled over the door-step and took them in charge. The sun was hot, the dry grass was very slippery, and the distances were very distant.

'It's just like the sea,' said Una, when Old Jim halted in the shade of a lonely flint-barn on a bare rise. 'You see where you're going, and – you go there, and there's nothing between.'

Dan slipped off his shoes. 'When we get home I shall sit in the woods all day,' he said.

'Whuff!' said Old Jim, to show he was ready, and struck across a long rolling stretch of turf. Presently he asked for his beef bone.

'Not yet,' said Dan. 'Where's Mr Dudeney? Where's Master?'

Old Jim looked as if he thought they were mad, and asked again.

'Don't you give it him,' Una cried. 'I'm not going to be left howling in a desert.'

'Show, boy! Show!' said Dan, for the Downs seemed as bare as the palm of your hand.

Old Jim sighed, and trotted forward. Soon they spied the blob of Mr Dudeney's hat against the sky a long way off.

'Right! All right!' said Dan. Old Jim wheeled round, took his bone carefully between his blunted teeth, and returned to the shadow of the old barn, looking just like a wolf. The children went on. Two kestrels hung bivvering and squealing above them. A gull flapped lazily along the white edge of the cliffs. The curves of the Downs shook a little in the heat, and so did Mr Dudeney's distant head.

They walked toward it very slowly and found themselves staring into a horseshoe-shaped hollow a hundred feet deep, whose steep sides were laced with tangled sheep-tracks. The flock grazed on the flat at the bottom, under charge of Young Jim. Mr Dudeney sat comfortably knitting on the edge of the slope, his crook between his knees. They told him what Old Jim had done.

'Ah, he thought you could see my head as soon as he did. The closeter you be to the turf the more you see things. You look warm-like,' said Mr Dudeney.

'We be,' said Una, flopping down. '*And* tired.'

'Set beside o' me here. The shadow'll begin to stretch out in a little while, and a heat-shake o' wind will come up with it that'll overlay your eyes like so much wool.'

'We don't want to sleep,' said Una indignantly; but she settled herself as she spoke, in the first strip of early afternoon shade.

'O' course not. You come to talk with me same as your father used. *He* didn't need no dog to guide him to Norton Pit.'

'Well, he belonged here,' said Dan, and laid himself down at length on the turf.

'He did. And what beats me is why he went off to live among them messy trees in the Weald, when he might ha' stayed here and looked all about him. There's no profit to trees. They draw the lightning, and sheep shelter under 'em, and *so*, like as not, you'll lose a half-score ewes struck dead in one storm. Tck! Your father knew that.'

'Trees aren't messy.' Una rose on her elbow. 'And what about firewood? I don't like coal.'

'Eh? You lie a piece more uphill and you'll lie more natural,' said Mr Dudeney, with his provoking deaf smile. 'Now press your face down and smell to the turf. That's Southdown thyme which makes our Southdown mutton beyond compare, and, my mother told me, 'twill cure anything except broken necks, or hearts. I forget which.'

They sniffed, and somehow forgot to lift their cheeks from the soft thymy cushions.

'You don't get nothing like that in the Weald. Water-cress, maybe?' said Mr Dudeney.

'But we've water – brooks full of it – where you paddle in hot weather,' Una replied, watching a yellow-and-violet-banded snail-shell close to her eye.

'Brooks flood. Then you must shift your sheep – let alone foot-rot afterward. I put more dependence on a dew-pond any day.'

'How's a dew-pond made?' said Dan, and tilted his hat over his eyes. Mr Dudeney explained.

The air trembled a little as though it could not make up its mind whether to slide into the Pit or move across the open. But it seemed easiest to go downhill, and the children felt one soft puff after another slip and sidle down the slope in fragrant breaths that baffed on their eyelids. The little whisper of the sea by the cliffs joined with the whisper of the wind over the grass, the hum of insects in the thyme, the ruffle and rustle of the flock below, and a thickish mutter deep in the very chalk beneath them. Mr Dudeney stopped explaining, and went on with his knitting.

They were roused by voices. The shadow had crept half-way down the steep side of Norton Pit, and on the edge of it, his back to them, Puck sat beside a half-naked man who seemed busy at some work. The wind had dropped, and in that funnel of ground every least noise and movement reached them like whispers up a water-pipe.

'That is clever,' said Puck, leaning over. 'How truly you shape it!'

'Yes, but what does The Beast care for a brittle flint tip? Bah!' The man flicked something contemptuously over his shoulder. It fell between Dan and Una – a beautiful dark-blue flint arrow-head still hot from the maker's hand.

The man reached for another stone, and worked away like a thrush with a snail-shell.

'Flint work is fool's work,' he said at last. 'One does it because one always did it; but when it comes to dealing with The Beast – no good!' He shook his shaggy head.

'The Beast was dealt with long ago. He has gone,' said Puck.

'He'll be back at lambing-time. *I* know him.' He chipped very carefully, and the flints squeaked.

'Not he. Children can lie out on the Chalk now all day through and go home safe.'

'Can they? Well, call The Beast by his True Name, and I'll believe it,' the man replied.

'Surely!' Puck leaped to his feet, curved his hands round his mouth and shouted: 'Wolf! Wolf!'

Norton Pit threw back the echo from its dry sides – 'Wuff! Wuff!' like Young Jim's bark.

'You see? You hear?' said Puck. 'Nobody answers. Grey Shepherd is gone. Feet-in-the-Night has run off. There are no more wolves.'

'Wonderful!' The man wiped his forehead as though he were hot. 'Who drove him away? You?'

'Many men through many years, each working in his own country. Were you one of them?' Puck answered.

The man slid his sheepskin cloak to his waist, and without a word pointed to his side, which was all seamed and blotched with scars. His arms, too, were dimpled from shoulder to elbow with horrible white dimples.

'I see,' said Puck. 'It is The Beast's mark. What did you use against him?'

'Hand, hammer, and spear, as our fathers did before us.'

'So? Then how' – Puck twitched aside the man's dark-brown cloak – 'how did a Flint-worker come by *that*? Show, man, show!' He held out his little hand.

The man slipped a long dark iron knife, almost a short sword, from his belt, and after breathing on it, handed it hilt-first to Puck, who took it with his head on one side, as you should when you look at the works of a watch, squinted down the dark blade, and very delicately rubbed his forefinger from the point to the hilt.

'Good!' said he, in a surprised tone.

'It should be. The Children of the Night made it,' the man answered.

'So I see by the iron. What might it have cost you?'

'This!' The man raised his hand to his cheek. Puck whistled like a Weald starling.

'By the Great Rings of the Chalk!' he cried. 'Was *that* your price? Turn sunward that I may see better, and shut your eye.'

He slipped his hand beneath the man's chin and swung him till he faced the children up the slope. They saw that his right eye was gone, and the eyelid lay shrunk. Quickly Puck turned him round again, and the two sat down.

'It was for the sheep. The sheep are the people,' said the man, in an ashamed voice. 'What else could I have done? *You* know, Old One.'

Puck sighed a little fluttering sigh. 'Take the knife. I listen.'

The man bowed his head, drove the knife into the turf,

and while it still quivered said: 'This is witness between us that I speak the thing that has been. Before my Knife and the Naked Chalk I speak. Touch!'

Puck laid a hand on the hilt. It stopped shaking. The children wriggled a little nearer.

'I am of the People of the Worked Flint. I am the one son of the Priestess who sells the Winds to the Men of the Sea. I am the Buyer of the Knife – the Keeper of the People,' the man began, in a sort of singing shout. 'These are my names in this country of the Naked Chalk, between the Trees and the Sea.'

'Yours was a great country. Your names are great too,' said Puck.

'One cannot feed some things on names and songs.' The man hit himself on the chest. 'It is better – always better – to count one's children safe round the fire, their Mother among them.'

'Ahai!' said Puck. 'I think this will be a very old tale.'

'I warm myself and eat at any fire that I choose, but there is no *one* to light me a fire or cook my meat. I sold all that when I bought the Magic Knife for my people. It was not right that The Beast should master man. What else could I have done?'

'I hear. I know. I listen,' said Puck.

'When I was old enough to take my place in the Sheep-guard, The Beast gnawed all our country like a bone between his teeth. He came in behind the flocks at watering-time, and watched them round the Dew-ponds; he leaped into the folds between our knees at the shearing; he walked out alongside the grazing flocks, and chose his meat on the hoof while our boys threw flints at him; he crept by night into the huts, and licked the babe from between the mother's hands; he called his companions and pulled down men in broad daylight on the Naked Chalk. No – not always did he do so! *This* was his cunning! He would go away for a while to let us forget him. A year – two years perhaps – we neither smelt, nor heard, nor saw him. When our flocks had in-

'I am the Buyer of the Knife – the Keeper of the People'

creased; when our men did not always look behind them; when children strayed from the fenced places; when our women walked alone to draw water – back, back, back came the Curse of the Chalk, Grey Shepherd, Feet-in-the-Night – The Beast, The Beast, The Beast!

'He laughed at our little brittle arrows and our poor blunt spears. He learned to run in under the stroke of the hammer. I think he knew when there was a flaw in the flint. Often it does not show till you bring it down on his snout. Then – *Pouf!* – the false flint falls all to flinders, and you are left with the hammer-handle in your fist, and his teeth in your flank! I have felt them. At evening, too, in the dew, or when it has misted and rained, your spear-head lashings slack off, though you have kept them beneath your cloak all day. You are alone – but so close to the home ponds that you stop to tighten the sinews with hands, teeth, and a piece of drift-wood. You bend over and pull – so! That is the minute for which he has followed you since the stars went out. "Aarh!" he says. "Wurr-aarh!" he says.' (Norton Pit gave back the growl like a pack of real wolves.) 'Then he is on your right shoulder feeling for the vein in your neck, and – perhaps your sheep run on without you. To fight The Beast is nothing, but to be despised by The Beast when he fights you – that is like his teeth in the heart! Old One, why is it that men desire so greatly, and can do so little?'

'I do not know. Did you desire so much?' said Puck.

'I desired to master The Beast. It is not right that The Beast should master man. But my people were afraid. Even my Mother, the Priestess, was afraid when I told her what I desired. We were accustomed to be afraid of The Beast. When I was made a man, and a maiden – she was a Priestess – waited for me at the Dew-ponds, The Beast flitted from off the Chalk. Perhaps it was a sickness; perhaps he had gone to his Gods to learn how to do us new harm. But he went, and we breathed more freely. The women sang again; the children were not so much guarded; our flocks grazed far out. I took mine yonder' – he pointed inland to the hazy line of the Weald – 'where the new grass was best. They grazed north. I followed till we were close to the Trees' – he lowered his voice – 'close *there* where the Children of the Night live.' He pointed north again.

'Ah, now I remember a thing,' said Puck. 'Tell me, why did your people fear the Trees so extremely?'

'Because the Gods hate the Trees and strike them with lightning. We can see them burning for days all along the Chalk's edge. Besides, all the Chalk knows that the Children of the Night, though they worship our Gods, are magicians. When a man goes into their country, they change his spirit; they put words into his mouth; they make him like talking water. But a voice in my heart told me to go toward the north. While I watched my sheep there I saw three Beasts chasing a man, who ran toward the Trees. By this I knew he was a Child of the Night. We Flint-workers fear the Trees more than we fear The Beast. He had no hammer. He carried a knife like this one. A Beast leaped at him. He stretched out his knife. The Beast fell dead. The other Beasts ran away howling, which they would never have done from a Flint-worker. The man went in among the Trees. I looked for the dead Beast. He had been killed in a new way – by a single deep, clean cut, without bruise or tear, which had split his bad heart. Wonderful! So I saw that the man's knife was magic, and I thought how to get it, – thought strongly how to get it.

'When I brought the flocks to the shearing, my Mother the Priestess asked me, "What is the new thing which you have seen and I see in your face?" I said, "It is a sorrow to me"; and she answered, "All new things are sorrow. Sit in my place, and eat sorrow." I sat down in her place by the fire, where she talks to the ghosts in winter, and two voices spoke in my heart. One voice said, "Ask the Children of the Night for the Magic Knife. It is not fit that The Beast should master man." I listened to that voice.

'One voice said, "If you go among the Trees, the Children of the Night will change your spirit. Eat and sleep here."

The other voice said, "Ask for the Knife." I listened to that voice.

'I said to my Mother in the morning, "I go away to find a thing for the people, but I do not know whether I shall return in my own shape." She answered, "Whether you live or die, or are made different, I am your Mother." '

'True,' said Puck. 'The Old Ones themselves cannot change men's mothers even if they would.'

'Let us thank the Old Ones! I spoke to my Maiden, the Priestess who waited for me at the Dew-ponds. She promised fine things too.' The man laughed. 'I went away to that place where I had seen the magician with the knife. I lay out two days on the short grass before I ventured among the Trees. I felt my way before me with a stick. I was afraid of the terrible talking Trees. I was afraid of the ghosts in the branches; of the soft ground underfoot; of the red and black waters. I was afraid, above all, of the Change. It came!'

They saw him wipe his forehead once again, and his strong back-muscles quivered till he laid his hand on the knife-hilt.

'A fire without a flame burned in my head; an evil taste grew in my mouth; my eyelids shut hot over my eyes; my breath was hot between my teeth, and my hands were like the hands of a stranger. I was made to sing songs and to mock the Trees, though I was afraid of them. At the same time I saw myself laughing, and I was very sad for this fine young man, who was myself. Ah! The Children of the Night know magic.'

'I think that is done by the Spirits of the Mist. They change a man if he sleeps among them,' said Puck. 'Had you slept in any mists?'

'Yes – but *I* know it was the Children of the Night. After three days I saw a red light behind the Trees, and I heard a heavy noise. I saw the Children of the Night dig red stones from a hole, and lay them in fires. The stones melted like tallow, and the men beat the soft stuff with hammers. I wished to speak to these men, but the words were changed in my mouth, and all I could say was, "Do not make that noise. It hurts my head." By this I knew that I was bewitched, and I clung to the Trees, and prayed the Children of the Night to take off their spells. They were cruel. They asked me many questions which they would never allow me to answer. They changed my words between my teeth till I wept. Then they led me into a hut and covered the floor with hot stones and dashed water on the stones, and sang charms till the sweat poured off me like water. I slept. When I waked, my own spirit – not the strange, shouting thing – was back in my body, and I was like a cool bright stone on the shingle between the sea and the sunshine. The magicians came to hear me – women and men – each wearing a Magic Knife. Their Priestess was their Ears and their Mouth.

'I spoke. I spoke many words that went smoothly along like sheep in order when their shepherd, standing on a mound, can count those coming, and those far off getting ready to come. I asked for Magic Knives for my people. I said that my people would bring meat, and milk, and wool, and lay them in the short grass outside the Trees, if the Children of the Night would leave Magic Knives for our people to take away. They were pleased. Their Priestess said, "For whose sake have you come?" I answered, "The sheep are the people. If The Beast kills our sheep, our people die. So I come for a Magic Knife to kill The Beast."

'She said, "We do not know if our God will let us trade with the people of the Naked Chalk. Wait till we have asked."

'When they came back from the Question-place (their Gods are our Gods), their Priestess said, "The God needs a proof that your words are true." I said, "What is the proof?" She said, "The God says that if you have come for the sake of your people you will give him your right eye to be put out; but if you have come for any other reason you will not give it. This proof is between you and the God. We ourselves are sorry."

'I said, "This is a hard proof. Is there no other road?"

'She said, "Yes. You can go back to your people with

your two eyes in your head if you choose. But then you will not get any Magic Knives for your people."

'I said, "It would be easier if I knew that I were to be killed."

'She said, "Perhaps the God knew this too. See! I have made my knife hot."

'I said, "Be quick, then!" With her knife heated in the flame she put out my right eye. She herself did it. I am the son of a Priestess. She was a Priestess. It was not work for any common man.'

'True! Most true,' said Puck. 'No common man's work' that. And, afterwards?'

'Afterwards I did not see out of that eye any more. I found also that a one eye does not tell you truly where things are. Try it!'

At this Dan put his hand over one eye, and reached for the flint arrow-head on the grass. He missed it by inches. 'It's true,' he whispered to Una. 'You can't judge distances a bit with only one eye.'

Puck was evidently making the same experiment, for the man laughed at him.

'I know it is so,' said he. 'Even now I am not always sure of my blow. I stayed with the Children of the Night till my eye healed. They said I was the son of Tyr, the God who put his right hand in a Beast's mouth. They showed me how they melted their red stone and made the Magic Knives of it. They told me the charms they sang over the fires and at the beatings. I can sing many charms.' Then he began to laugh like a boy.

'I was thinking of my journey home,' he said, 'and of the surprised Beast. He had come back to the Chalk. I saw him – I smelt his lairs as soon as ever I left the Trees. He did not know I had the Magic Knife – I hid it under my cloak – the Knife that the Priestess gave me. Ho! Ho! That happy day was too short! See! A Beast would wind me. "Wow!" he would say. "Here is my Flint-worker!" He would come leaping, tail in air; he would roll; he would lay his head between his paws out of merriness of heart at his warm, waiting meal. He would leap – and, oh, his eye in mid-leap when he saw – when he saw the knife held ready for him! It pierced his hide as a rush pierces curdled milk. Often he had no time to howl. I did not trouble to flay any beasts I killed. Sometimes I missed my blow. Then I took my little flint hammer and beat out his brains as he cowered. He made no fight. He knew the Knife! But The Beast is very cunning. Before evening all The Beasts had smelt the blood on my knife, and were running from me like hares. *They* knew! Then I walked as a man should – the Master of The Beast!

'So came I back to my Mother's house. There was a lamb to be killed. I cut it in two halves with my knife, and I told her all my tale. She said, "This is the work of a God." I kissed her and laughed. I went to my Maiden who waited for me at the Dew-ponds. There was a lamb to be killed. I cut it in two halves with my knife, and told her all my tale. She said, "It is the work of a God." I laughed, but she pushed me away, and being on my blind side, ran off before I could kiss her. I went to the Men of the Sheepguard at watering-time. There was a sheep to be killed for their meat. I cut it in two halves with my knife, and told them all my tale. They said, "It is the work of a God." I said, "We talk too much about Gods. Let us eat and be happy, and tomorrow I will take you to the Children of the Night, and each man will find a Magic Knife."

'I was glad to smell our sheep again; to see the broad sky from edge to edge, and to hear the sea. I slept beneath the stars in my cloak. The men talked among themselves.

'I led them, the next day, to the Trees, taking with me meat, wool, and curdled milk, as I had promised. We found the Magic Knives laid out on the grass, as the Children of the Night had promised. They watched us from among the Trees. Their Priestess called to me and said, "How is it with your people?" I said, "Their hearts are changed. I cannot see their hearts as I used to." She said, "That is because you have only one eye. Come to me and I will be both your eyes." But I said, "I must show my people how to use their knives against The Beast, as you showed me how to use my knife." I said this because the Magic Knife does not balance like the flint. She said, "What you have done, you have done for the sake of a woman, and not for the sake of your people." I asked of her, "Then why did the God accept my right eye, and why are you so angry?" She answered, "Because any man can lie to a God, but no man can lie to a woman. And I am not angry with you. I am only very sorrowful for you. Wait a little, and you will see out of your one eye why I am sorry." So she hid herself.

'I went back with my people, each one carrying his Knife, and making it sing in the air – *tssee-sssse*. The Flint never sings. It mutters – *ump-ump*. The Beast heard. The Beast saw. *He* knew! Everywhere he ran away from us. We all laughed. As we walked over the grass my Mother's brother – the Chief on the Men's Side – he took off his Chief's necklace of yellow sea-stones.'

'How? Eh? Oh, I remember! Amber,' said Puck.

'And would have put them on my neck. I said, "No, I am content. What does my one eye matter if my other eye sees fat sheep and fat children running about safely?" My Mother's brother said to them, "I told you he would never take such things." Then they began to sing a song in the Old Tongue – *The Song of Tyr*. I sang with them, but my Mother's brother said, "This is *your* song, O Buyer of the Knife. Let *us* sing it, Tyr."

'Even then I did not understand, till I saw that – that no man stepped on my shadow; and I knew that they thought me to be a God, like the God Tyr, who gave his right hand to conquer a Great Beast.'

'By the Fire in the Belly of the Flint was that so?' Puck rapped out.

'By my Knife and the Naked Chalk, so it was! They made way for my shadow as though it had been a Priestess walking to the Barrows of the Dead. I was afraid. I said to myself, "My Mother and my Maiden will know I am not Tyr."

But *still* I was afraid, with the fear of a man who falls into a steep flint-pit while he runs, and feels that it will be hard to climb out.

'When we came to the Dew-ponds all our people were there. The men showed their knives and told their tale. The sheepguards also had seen The Beast flying from us. The Beast went west across the river in packs – howling! He knew the Knife had come to the Naked Chalk at last – at last! *He* knew! So my work was done. I looked for my Maiden among the Priestesses. She looked at me, but she did not smile. She made the sign to me that our Priestesses must make when they sacrifice to the Old Dead in the Barrows. I would have spoken, but my Mother's brother made himself my Mouth, as though I had been one of the Old Dead in the Barrows for whom our Priests speak to the people on Midsummer Mornings.'

'I remember. Well I remember those Midsummer Mornings!' said Puck.

'Then I went away angrily to my Mother's house. She would have knelt before me. Then I was more angry, but she said, "Only a God would have spoken to me thus, a Priestess. A man would have feared the punishment of the Gods." I looked at her and I laughed. I could not stop my unhappy laughing. They called me from the door by the name of Tyr himself. A young man with whom I had watched my first flocks, and chipped my first arrow, and fought my first Beast, called me by that name in the Old Tongue. He asked my leave to take my Maiden. His eyes were lowered, his hands were on his forehead. He was full of the fear of a God, but of *me*, a man, he had no fear when he asked. I did not kill him. I said, "Call the maiden." She came also without fear – this very one that had waited for me, that had talked with me, by our Dew-ponds. Being a Priestess, she lifted her eyes to me. As I look on a hill or a cloud, so she looked at me. She spoke in the Old Tongue which Priestesses use when they make prayers to the Old Dead in the Barrows. She asked leave that she might light the fire in my companion's house – and that I should bless their children. I did not kill her. I heard my own voice, little and cold, say, "Let it be as you desire," and they went away hand in hand. My heart grew little and cold; a wind shouted in my ears; my eye darkened. I said to my Mother, "Can a God die?" I heard her say, "What is it? What is it, my son?" and I fell into darkness full of hammer-noises. I was not.'

'Oh, poor – poor God!' said Puck. 'And your wise Mother?'

'*She* knew. As soon as I dropped she knew. When my spirit came back I heard her whisper in my ear, "Whether you live or die, or are made different, I am your Mother." That was good – better even than the water she gave me and the going away of the sickness. Though I was ashamed to have fallen down, yet I was very glad. She was glad too. Neither of us wished to lose the other. There is only the one Mother for the one son. I heaped the fire for her, and barred the doors, and sat at her feet as before I went away, and she combed my hair, and sang.

'I said at last, "What is to be done to the people who say that I am Tyr?"

'She said, "He who has done a God-like thing must bear himself like a God. I see no way out of it. The people are now your sheep till you die. You cannot drive them off."

'I said, "This is a heavier sheep than I can lift." She said, "In time it will grow easy. In time perhaps you will not lay it down for any maiden anywhere. Be wise – be very wise, my son, for nothing is left you except the words, and the songs, and the worship of a God."'

'Oh, poor God!' said Puck. 'But those are not altogether bad things.'

'I know they are not; but I would sell them all – all – all for one small child of my own, smearing himself with the ashes of our own house-fire.'

He wrenched his knife from the turf, thrust it into his belt and stood up.

Merriness of heart at his warm, waiting meal

'And yet, what else could I have done?' he said. 'The sheep are the people.'

'It is a very old tale,' Puck answered. 'I have heard the like of it not only on the Naked Chalk, but also among the Trees – under Oak, and Ash, and Thorn.'

The afternoon shadows filled all the quiet emptiness of Norton Pit. The children heard the sheep-bells and Young Jim's busy bark above them, and they scrambled up the slope to the level.

'We let you have your sleep out,' said Mr Dudeney, as the flock scattered before them. 'It's making for tea-time now.'

'Look what I've found,' said Dan, and held up a little blue flint arrow-head as fresh as though it had been chipped that very day.

'Oh,' said Mr Dudeney, 'the closeter you be to the turf the more you're apt to see things. I've found 'em often. Some says the fairies made 'em, but I says they was made by folks like ourselves – only a goodish time back. They're lucky to keep. Now, you couldn't ever have slept – not to any profit – among your father's trees same as you've laid out on Naked Chalk – could you?'

'One doesn't want to sleep in the woods,' said Una.

'Then what's the good of 'em?' said Mr Dudeney. 'Might as well set in the barn all day. Fetch 'em 'long, Jim boy!'

The Downs, that looked so bare and hot when they came, were full of delicious little shadow-dimples; the smell of the thyme and the salt mixed together on the south-west drift from the still sea; their eyes dazzled with the low sun, and the long grass under it looked golden. The sheep knew where their fold was, so Young Jim came back to his master, and they all four strolled home, the scabious-heads swishing about their ankles, and their shadows streaking behind them like the shadows of giants.

SONG OF THE MEN'S SIDE

ONCE we feared The Beast – when he followed us we ran,
  Ran very fast though we knew
It was not right that The Beast should master Man;
  But what could we Flint-workers do?
The Beast only grinned at our spears round his ears –
  Grinned at the hammers that we made;
But now we will hunt him for the life with the Knife –
  And this is the Buyer of the Blade!

  Room for his shadow on the grass – let it pass!
    To left and right – stand clear!
  This is the Buyer of the Blade – be afraid!
    This is the great God Tyr!

Tyr thought hard till he hammered out a plan,
  For he knew it was not right
(And it *is* not right) that The Beast should master Man;
  So he went to the Children of the Night.
He begged a Magic Knife of their make for our sake.
  When he begged for the Knife they said:
'The price of the Knife you would buy is an eye!'
  And that was the price he paid.

  Tell it to the Barrows of the Dead – run ahead!
    Shout it so the Women's Side can hear!
  This is the Buyer of the Blade – be afraid!
    This is the great God Tyr!

Our women and our little ones may walk on the Chalk,
  As far as we can see them and beyond.
We shall not be anxious for our sheep when we keep
  Tally at the shearing-pond.

We can eat with both our elbows on our knees, if we please,
  We can sleep after meals in the sun;
For Shepherd-of-the-Twilight is dismayed at the Blade,
  Feet-in-the-Night have run!
Dog-without-a-Master goes away (Hai, Tyr aie!),
  Devil-in-the-Dusk has run!

Then:
  Room for his shadow on the grass — let it pass!
    To left and right — stand clear!
  This is the Buyer of the Blade — be afraid!
    This is the great God Tyr!

Brother Square-Toes

PHILADELPHIA

IF you're off to Philadelphia in the morning,
   You mustn't take my stories for a guide.
There's little left indeed of the city you will read of,
   And all the folk I write about have died.
Now few will understand if you mention Talleyrand,
   Or remember what his cunning and his skill did.
And the cabmen at the wharf do not know Count Zinnendorf,
   Nor the Church in Philadelphia he builded.

     It is gone, gone, gone with lost Atlantis
     (Never say I didn't give you warning).
     In Seventeen Ninety-three 'twas there for all to see,
     But it's not in Philadelphia this morning.

If you're off to Philadelphia in the morning,
   You mustn't go by everything I've said.
Bob Bicknell's Southern Stages have been laid aside for ages,
   But the Limited will take you there instead.
Toby Hirte can't be seen at One Hundred and Eighteen,
   North Second Street – no matter when you call;
And I fear you'll search in vain for the wash-house down the lane
   Where Pharaoh played the fiddle at the ball.

     It is gone, gone, gone with Thebes the Golden
     (Never say I didn't give you warning).
     In Seventeen Ninety-four 'twas a famous dancing-floor –
     But it's not in Philadelphia this morning.

If you're off to Philadelphia in the morning,
   You must telegraph for rooms at some Hotel.
You needn't try your luck at Epply's or the 'Buck,'
   Though the Father of his Country liked them well.

It is not the slightest use to inquire for Adam Goos,
    Or to ask where Pastor Meder has removed – so
You must treat as out-of-date the story I relate
    Of the Church in Philadelphia he loved so.

        He is gone, gone, gone with Martin Luther
        (Never say I didn't give you warning).
        In Seventeen Ninety-five he was (rest his soul!) alive,
        But he's not in Philadelphia this morning.

If you're off to Philadelphia this morning,
    And wish to prove the truth of what I say,
I pledge my word you'll find the pleasant land behind
    Unaltered since Red Jacket rode that way.
Still the pine-woods scent the noon; still the cat-bird sings his
        tune;
    Still Autumn sets the maple-forest blazing.
Still the grape-vine through the dusk flings her soul-compelling
        musk;
    Still the fire-flies in the corn make night amazing.

        They are there, there, there with Earth immortal
        (Citizens, I give you friendly warning).
        The things that truly last when men and times have passed,
        They are all in Pennsylvania this morning!

Brother Square-Toes

It was almost the end of their visit to the seaside. They had turned themselves out of doors while their trunks were being packed, and strolled over the Downs towards the dull evening sea. The tide was dead low under the chalk cliffs, and the little wrinkled waves grieved along the sands up the coast to Newhaven and down the coast to long, grey Brighton, whose smoke trailed out across the Channel.

They walked to The Gap, where the cliff is only a few feet high. A windlass for hoisting shingle from the beach below stands at the edge of it. The Coastguard cottages are a little farther on, and an old ship's figurehead of a Turk in a turban stared at them over the wall.

'This time tomorrow we shall be at home, thank goodness,' said Una. 'I hate the sea!'

'I believe it's all right in the middle,' said Dan. 'The edges are the sorrowful parts.'

Cordery, the coastguard, came out of the cottage, levelled his telescope at some fishing-boats, shut it with a click and walked away. He grew smaller and smaller along the edge of the cliff, where neat piles of white chalk every few yards show the path even on the darkest night.

'Where's Cordery going?' said Una.

'Half-way to Newhaven,' said Dan. 'Then he'll meet the Newhaven coastguard and turn back. He says if coastguards were done away with, smuggling would start up at once.'

A voice on the beach under the cliff began to sing:

> 'The moon she shined on Telscombe Tye –
>   On Telscombe Tye at night it was –
>   She saw the smugglers riding by,
>   A very pretty sight it was!'

Feet scrabbled on the flinty path. A dark, thin-faced man in very neat brown clothes and broad-toed shoes came up, followed by Puck.

'Three Dunkirk boats was standin' in!'

the man went on.

'Hssh!' said Puck. 'You'll shock these nice young people.'

'Oh! Shall I? *Mille pardons!*' He shrugged his shoulders almost up to his ears – spread his hands abroad, and jabbered in French. 'No comprenny?' he said. 'I'll give it you in Low German.' And he went off in another language, changing his voice and manner so completely that they hardly knew him for the same person. But his dark beady-brown eyes still twinkled merrily in his lean face, and the children felt that they did not suit the straight, plain, snuffy-brown coat, brown knee-breeches, and broad-brimmed hat. His hair was tied in a short pigtail which danced wickedly when he turned his head.

'Ha' done!' said Puck, laughing. 'Be one thing or t'other, Pharaoh – French or English or German – no great odds which.'

'Oh, but it is, though,' said Una quickly. 'We haven't begun German yet, and – and we're going back to our French next week.'

'Aren't you English?' said Dan. 'We heard you singing just now.'

'Aha! That was the Sussex side o' me. Dad he married a French girl out o' Boulogne, and French she stayed till her dyin' day. She was an Aurette, of course. We Lees mostly marry Aurettes. Haven't you ever come across the saying:

'Aurettes and Lees,
Like as two peas.
What they can't smuggle,
They'll run over seas'?

'Then, are you a smuggler?' Una cried; and, 'Have you smuggled much?' said Dan.

Mr Lee nodded solemnly.

'Mind you,' said he, 'I don't uphold smuggling for the generality o' mankind – mostly they can't make a do of it – but I was brought up to the trade, d'ye see, in a lawful line o' descent on' – he waved across the Channel – 'on both sides the water. 'Twas all in the families, same as fiddling. The Aurettes used mostly to run the stuff across from Boulogne, and we Lees landed it here and ran it up to London Town, by the safest road.'

'Then where did you live?' said Una.

'You mustn't ever live too close to your business in *our* trade. We kept our little fishing smack at Shoreham, but otherwise we Lees was all honest cottager folk – at Warminghurst under Washington – Bramber way – on the old Penn estate.'

'Ah!' said Puck, squatted by the windlass. 'I remember a piece about the Lees at Warminghurst, I do:

> 'There was never a Lee to Warminghurst
> That wasn't a gipsy last and first.

I reckon that's truth, Pharaoh.'

Pharaoh laughed. 'Admettin' that's true,' he said, 'my gipsy blood must be wore pretty thin, for I've made and kept a worldly fortune.'

'By smuggling?' Dan asked.

'No, in the tobacco trade.'

'You don't mean to say you gave up smuggling just to go and be a tobacconist!' Dan looked so disappointed they all had to laugh.

'I'm sorry; but there's all sorts of tobacconists,' Pharaoh replied. 'How far out, now, would you call that smack with the patch on her foresail?' He pointed to the fishing-boats.

'A scant mile,' said Puck after a quick look.

'Just about. It's seven fathom under her – clean sand. That was where Uncle Aurette used to sink his brandy kegs from Boulogne, and we fished 'em up and rowed 'em into The Gap here for the ponies to run inland. One thickish night in January of 'Ninety-three, Dad and Uncle Lot and me came over from Shoreham in the smack, and we found Uncle Aurette and the L'Estranges, my cousins, waiting for us in their lugger with New Year's presents from Mother's folk in Boulogne. I remember Aunt Cécile she'd sent me a fine new red knitted cap, which I put on then and there, for the French was having their Revolution in those days, and red caps was all the fashion. Uncle Aurette tells us that they had cut off their King Louis' head, and, moreover, the Brest forts had fired on an English man-o'-war. The news wasn't a week old.

' "That means war again, when we was only just getting used to the peace," says Dad. "Why can't King George's men and King Louis' men do on their uniforms and fight it out over our heads?"

' "Me too, I wish that," says Uncle Aurette. "But they'll be pressing better men than themselves to fight for 'em. The press-gangs are out already on our side. You look out for yours."

' "I'll have to bide ashore and grow cabbages for a while, after I've run this cargo; but I do wish" – Dad says, going over the lugger's side with our New Year presents under his arm and young L'Estrange holding the lantern – "I just *do* wish that those folk which make war so easy had to run one cargo a month all this winter. It 'ud show 'em what honest work means."

' "Well, I've warned ye," says Uncle Aurette. "I'll be slipping off now before your Revenue cutter comes. Give my love to Sister and take care o' the kegs. It's thicking to southward."

'I remember him waving to us and young Stephen L'Estrange blowing out the lantern. By the time we'd fished up the kegs the fog came down so thick Dad judged it risky for me to row 'em ashore, even though we could hear the ponies stamping on the beach. So he and Uncle Lot took the dinghy and left me in the smack playing on my fiddle to guide 'em back.

'Presently I heard guns. Two of 'em sounded mighty like

Uncle Aurette's three-pounders. *He* didn't go naked about the seas after dark. Then come more, which I reckoned was Captain Giddens in the Revenue cutter. He was open-handed with his compliments, but he *would* lay his guns himself. I stopped fiddling to listen, and I heard a whole skyful o' French up in the fog – and a high bow come down on top o' the smack. I hadn't time to call or think. I remember the smack heeling over, and me standing on the gunwale pushing against the ship's side as if I hoped to bear her off. Then the square of an open port, with a lantern in it, slid by in front of my nose. I kicked back on our gunwale as it went under and slipped through that port into the French ship – me and my fiddle.'

'Gracious!' said Una. 'What an adventure!'

'Didn't anybody see you come in?' said Dan.

'There wasn't any one there. I'd made use of an orlop-deck port – that's the next deck below the gun-deck, which by rights should not have been open at all. The crew was standing by their guns up above. I rolled on to a pile of dunnage in the dark and I went to sleep. When I woke, men was talking all round me, telling each other their names and sorrows just like Dad told me pressed men used to talk in the last war. Pretty soon I made out they'd all been hove aboard together by the press-gangs, and left to sort 'emselves. The ship she was the *Embuscade*, a thirty-six-gun Republican frigate, Captain Jean Baptiste Bompard, two days out of Le Havre, going to the United States with a Republican French Ambassador of the name of Genêt. They had been up all night clearing for action on account of hearing guns in the fog. Uncle Aurette and Captain Giddens must have been passing the time o' day with each other off Newhaven, and the frigate had drifted past 'em. She never knew she'd run down our smack. Seeing so many aboard was total strangers to each other, I thought one more mightn't be noticed; so I put Aunt Cécile's red cap on the back of my head, and my hands in my pockets like the rest, and, as we French say, I circulated till I found the galley.

' "What! Here's one of 'em that isn't sick!" says a cook. "Take his breakfast to Citizen Bompard."

'I carried the tray to the cabin, but I didn't call this Bompard "Citizen." Oh no! "Mon Capitaine" was my little word, same as Uncle Aurette used to answer in King Louis' Navy. Bompard, he liked it. He took me on for cabin servant, and after that no one asked questions; and thus I got good victuals and light work all the way across to America. He talked a heap of politics, and so did his officers, and when this Ambassador Genêt got rid of his land-stomach and laid down the law after dinner, a rooks' parliament was nothing compared to their cabin. I learned to know most of the men which had worked the French Revolution, through waiting at table and hearing talk about 'em. One of our forecas'le six-pounders was called Danton and t'other Marat. I used to play the fiddle between 'em, sitting on the capstan. Day in and day out Bompard and Monsieur Genêt talked o' what France had done, and how the United States was going to join her to finish off the English in this war. Monsieur Genêt said he'd justabout make the United States fight for France. He was a rude common man. But I liked listening. I always helped drink any healths that was proposed – specially Citizen Danton's who'd cut off King Louis' head. An all-Englishman might have been shocked – but that's where my French blood saved me.

'It didn't save me from getting a dose of ship's fever though, the week before we put Monsieur Genêt ashore at Charleston; and what was left of me after bleeding and pills took the dumb horrors from living 'tween decks. The surgeon, Karaguen his name was, kept me down there to help him with his plasters – I was too weak to wait on Bompard. I don't remember much of any account for the next few weeks, till I smelled lilacs, and I looked out of the port, and we was moored to a wharf-edge and there was a town o' fine gardens and red-brick houses and all the green leaves o' God's world waiting for me outside.

' "What's this?" I said to the sick-bay man – old Pierre Tiphaigne he was. "Philadelphia," says Pierre. "You've missed it all. We're sailing next week."

'I just turned round and cried for longing to be amongst the laylocks.

' "If that's your trouble," says old Pierre, "you go straight ashore. None 'll hinder you. They're all gone mad on these coasts – French and American together. 'Tisn't *my* notion o' war." Pierre was an old King Louis man.

'My legs was pretty tottly, but I made shift to go on deck, which it was like a fair. The frigate was crowded with fine gentlemen and ladies pouring in and out. They sung and they waved French flags, while Captain Bompard and his officers – yes, and some of the men – speechified to all and sundry about war with England. They shouted, "Down with England!" – "Down with Washington!" – "Hurrah for France and the Republic!" *I* couldn't make sense of it. I wanted to get out from that crunch of swords and petticoats and sit in a field. One of the gentlemen said to me, "Is that a genuine cap o' Liberty you're wearing?" 'Twas Aunt Cécile's red one, and pretty near wore out. "Oh yes!" I says, "straight from France." "I'll give you a shilling for it," he says, and with that money in my hand and my fiddle under my arm I squeezed past the entry-port and went ashore. It was like a dream – meadows, trees, flowers, birds, houses, and people *all* different! I sat me down in a meadow and fiddled a bit, and then I went in and out the streets, looking and smelling and touching, like a little dog at a fair. Fine folk was setting on the white stone doorsteps of their houses, and a girl threw me a handful of laylock sprays, and when I said "Merci" without thinking, she said she loved the French. They all was the fashion in the city. I saw more tricolour flags in Philadelphia than ever I'd seen in Boulogne, and every one was shouting for war with England. A crowd o' folk was cheering after our French Ambassador – that same Monsieur Genêt which we'd left at Charleston. He was a-horseback behaving as if the place belonged to him –

and commanding all and sundry to fight the British. But
I'd heard that before. I got into a long straight street as
wide as the Broyle, where gentlemen was racing horses. I'm
fond o' horses. Nobody hindered 'em, and a man told me it
was called Race Street o' purpose for that. Then I followed
some black niggers, which I'd never seen close before; but I
left them to run after a great, proud, copper-faced man with
feathers in his hair and a red blanket trailing behind him. A
man told me he was a real Red Indian called Red Jacket,
and I followed him into an alley-way off Race Street by
Second Street, where there was a fiddle playing. I'm fond o'
fiddling. The Indian stopped at a baker's shop – Conrad
Gerhard's it was – and bought some sugary cakes. Hearing
what the price was I was going to have some too, but the
Indian asked me in English if I was hungry. "Oh yes!" I
says. I must have looked a sore scrattel. He opens a door on
to a staircase and leads the way up. We walked into a dirty
little room full of flutes and fiddles and a fat man fiddling
by the window, in a smell of cheese and medicines fit to
knock you down. I *was* knocked down too, for the fat man
jumped up and hit me a smack in the face. I fell against an
old spinet covered with pill-boxes and the pills rolled about
the floor. The Indian never moved an eyelid.

'"Pick up the pills! Pick up the pills!" the fat man
screeches.

'I started picking 'em up – hundreds of 'em – meaning to
run out under the Indian's arm, but I came on giddy all
over and I sat down. The fat man went back to his fiddling.

'"Toby!" says the Indian after quite a while. "I brought
the boy to be fed, not hit."

'"What?" says Toby, "I thought it was Gert Schwankfelder." He put down his fiddle and took a good look at me.
"Himmel!" he says. "I have hit the wrong boy. It is not the
new boy. Why are you not the new boy? Why are you not
Gert Schwankfelder?"

'"I don't know," I said. "The gentleman in the pink
blanket brought me."

'Himmel!' he says. 'I have hit the wrong boy'

'Says the Indian, "He is hungry, Toby. Christians always feed the hungry. So I bring him."

' "You should have said that first," said Toby. He pushed plates at me and the Indian put bread and pork on them, and a glass of Madeira wine. I told him I was off the French ship, which I had joined on account of my mother being French. That was true enough when you think of it, and besides I saw that the French was all the fashion in Philadelphia. Toby and the Indian whispered and I went on picking up the pills.

' "You like pills – eh?" says Toby.

' "No," I says. "I've seen our ship's doctor roll too many of 'em."

' "Ho!" he says, and he shoves two bottles at me. "What's those?"

' "Calomel," I says. "And t'other's senna."

' "Right," he says. "One week have I tried to teach Gert Schwankfelder the difference between them, yet he cannot tell. You like to fiddle?" he says. He'd just seen my kit on the floor.

' "Oh yes!" says I.

' "Oho!" he says. "What note is this?" drawing his bow acrost.

'He meant it for A, so I told him it was.

' "My brother," he says to the Indian. "I think this is the hand of Providence! I warned that Gert if he went to play upon the wharves any more he would hear from me. Now look at this boy and say what you think."

'The Indian looked me over whole minutes – there was a musical clock on the wall and dolls came out and hopped while the hour struck. He looked me over all the while they did it.

' "Good," he says at last. "This boy is good."

' "Good, then," says Toby. "Now I shall play my fiddle and you shall sing your hymn, brother. Boy, go down to the bakery and tell them you are young Gert Schwankfelder that was. The horses are in Davy Jones's locker. If you ask any questions you shall hear from me."

'I left 'em singing hymns and I went down to old Conrad Gerhard. He wasn't at all surprised when I told him I was young Gert Schwankfelder that was. He knew Toby. His wife she walked me into the back-yard without a word, and she washed me and she cut my hair to the edge of a basin, and she put me to bed, and oh! how I slept – how I slept in that little room behind the oven looking on the flower garden! I didn't know Toby went to the *Embuscade* that night and bought me off Dr Karaguen for twelve dollars and a dozen bottles of Seneca Oil. Karaguen wanted a new lace to his coat, and he reckoned I hadn't long to live; so he put me down as "discharged sick."'

'I like Toby,' said Una.

'Who was he?' said Puck.

'Apothecary Tobias Hirte,' Pharaoh replied. 'One Hundred and Eighteen, Second Street – the famous Seneca Oil man, that lived half of every year among the Indians. But let me tell my tale my own way, same as his brown mare used to go to Lebanon.'

'Then why did he keep her in Davy Jones's locker?' Dan asked.

'That was his joke. He kept her under David Jones's hat shop in the "Buck" tavern yard, and his Indian friends kept their ponies there when they visited him. I looked after the horses when I wasn't rolling pills on top of the old spinet, while he played his fiddle and Red Jacket sang hymns. I liked it. I had good victuals, light work, a suit o' clean clothes, a plenty music, and quiet, smiling German folk all around that let me sit in their gardens. My first Sunday, Toby took me to his church in Moravian Alley; and that was in a garden too. The women wore long-eared caps and handkerchiefs. They came in at one door and the men at another, and there was a brass chandeller you could see your face in, and a nigger-boy to blow the organ bellows. I carried

Toby's fiddle, and he played pretty much as he chose all against the organ and the singing. He was the only one they let do it, for they was a simple-minded folk. They used to wash each other's feet up in the attic to keep 'emselves humble: which Lord knows they didn't need.'

'How very queer!' said Una.

Pharaoh's eyes twinkled. 'I've met many and seen much,' he said; 'but I haven't yet found any better or quieter or forbearinger people than the Brethren and Sistern of the Moravian Church in Philadelphia. Nor will I ever forget my first Sunday – the service was in English that week – with the smell of the flowers coming in from Pastor Meder's garden where the big peach tree is, and me looking at all the clean strangeness and thinking of 'tween decks on the *Embuscade* only six days ago. Being a boy, it seemed to me it had lasted for ever, and was going on for ever. But I didn't know Toby then. As soon as the dancing clock struck midnight that Sunday – I was lying under the spinet – I heard Toby's fiddle. He'd just done his supper, which he always took late and heavy. "Gert," says he, "get the horses. Liberty and Independence for Ever! The flowers appear upon the earth, and the time of the singing of birds is come. We are going to my country seat in Lebanon."

'I rubbed my eyes, and fetched 'em out of the "Buck" stables. Red Jacket was there saddling his, and when I'd packed the saddle-bags we three rode up Race Street to the Ferry by starlight. So we went travelling. It's a kindly, softly country there, back of Philadelphia among the German towns, Lancaster way. Little houses and bursting big barns, fat cattle, fat women, and all as peaceful as Heaven might be if they farmed there. Toby sold medicines out of his saddle-bags, and gave the French war-news to folk along the roads. Him and his long-hilted umberell was as well known as the stage-coaches. He took orders for that famous Seneca Oil which he had the secret of from Red Jacket's Indians, and he slept in friends' farmhouses, but he *would* shut all the windows; so Red Jacket and me slept outside. There's nothing to hurt except snakes – and they slip away quick enough if you thrash in the bushes.'

'I'd have liked that!' said Dan.

'I'd no fault to find with those days. In the cool o' the morning the cat-bird sings. He's something to listen to. And there's a smell of wild grape-vine growing in damp hollows which you drop into, after long rides in the heat, which is beyond compare for sweetness. So's the puffs out of the pine woods of afternoons. Come sundown, the frogs strike up, and later on the fireflies dance in the corn. Oh me, the fireflies in the corn! We were a week or ten days on the road, tacking from one place to another – such as Lancaster, Bethlehem-Ephrata – "thou Bethlehem-Ephrata." No odds – I loved the going about. And so we jogged into dozy little Lebanon by the Blue Mountains, where Toby had a cottage and a garden of all fruits. He come north every year for this wonderful Seneca Oil the Seneca Indians made for him. They'd never sell to any one else, and he doctored 'em with von Swieten pills, which they valued more than their own oil. He could do what he chose with them, and, of course, he tried to make them Moravians. The Senecas are a seemly, quiet people, and they'd had trouble enough from white men – American and English – during the wars, to keep 'em in that walk. They lived on a Reservation by themselves away off by their lake. Toby took me up there, and they treated me as if I was their own blood brother. Red Jacket said the mark of my bare feet in the dust was just like an Indian's and my style of walking was similar. I know I took to their ways all over.'

'Maybe the gipsy drop in your blood helped you?' said Puck.

'Sometimes I think it did,' Pharaoh went on. 'Anyhow, Red Jacket and Cornplanter, the other Seneca chief, they let me be adopted into the tribe. It's only a compliment, of course, but Toby was angry when I showed up with my face painted. They gave me a side-name which means "Two Tongues," because, d'ye see, I talked French and English.

'They had their own opinions (*I*'ve heard 'em) about the French and the English, *and* the Americans. They'd suffered from all of 'em during the wars, and they only wished to be left alone. But they thought a heap of the President of the United States. Cornplanter had had dealings with him in some French wars out West when General Washington was only a lad. His being President afterwards made no odds to 'em. They always called him Big Hand, for he was a large-fisted man, and he was all of their notion of a white chief. Cornplanter 'ud sweep his blanket round him, and after I'd filled his pipe he'd begin – " In the old days, long ago, when braves were many and blankets were few, Big Hand said—" If Red Jacket agreed to the say-so he'd trickle a little smoke out of the corners of his mouth. If he didn't, he'd blow through his nostrils. Then Cornplanter 'ud stop and Red Jacket 'ud take on. Red Jacket was the better talker of the two. I've laid and listened to 'em for hours. Oh! they knew General Washington well. Cornplanter used to meet him at Epply's – the great dancing-place in the city before District Marshal William Nichols bought it. They told me he was always glad to see 'em, and he'd hear 'em out to the end if they had anything on their minds. They had a good deal in those days. I came at it by degrees, after I was adopted into the tribe. The talk up in Lebanon and everywhere else that summer was about the French war with England and whether the United States 'ud join in with France or make a peace treaty with England. Toby wanted peace so as he could go about the Reservation buying his oils. But most of the white men wished for war, and they was angry because the President wouldn't give the sign for it. The newspaper said men was burning Guy Fawkes images of General Washington and yelling after him in the streets of Phila-delphia. You'd have been astonished what those two fine old chiefs knew of the ins and outs of such matters. The little I've learned of politics I picked up from Cornplanter and Red Jacket on the Reservation. Toby used to read the *Aurora* newspaper. He was what they call a "Democrat,"

though our Church is against the Brethren concerning themselves with politics.'

'I hate politics, too,' said Una, and Pharaoh laughed.

'I might ha' guessed it,' he said. 'But here's something
that isn't politics. One hot evening late in August, Toby was
reading the newspaper on the stoop and Red Jacket was
smoking under a peach tree and I was fiddling. Of a sudden
Toby drops his *Aurora*.

' "I am an oldish man, too fond of my own comforts," he
says. "I will go to the Church which is in Philadelphia. My
brother, lend me a spare pony. I must be there tomorrow
night."

' "Good!" says Red Jacket, looking at the sun. "My
brother shall be there. I will ride with him and bring back
the ponies."

'I went to pack the saddle-bags. Toby had cured me of
asking questions. He stopped my fiddling if I did. Besides,
Indians don't ask questions much and I wanted to be like
'em.

'When the horses were ready I jumped up.

' "Get off," says Toby. "Stay and mind the cottage till I
come back. The Lord has laid this on me, not on you. I wish
He hadn't."

'He powders off down the Lancaster road, and I sat on
the doorstep wondering after him. When I picked up the
paper to wrap his fiddle-strings in, I spelled out a piece about
the yellow fever being in Philadelphia so dreadful every one
was running away. I was scared, for I was fond of Toby. We
never said much to each other, but we fiddled together, and
music's as good as talking to them that understand.'

'Did Toby die of yellow fever?' Una asked.

'Not him! There's justice left in the world still. He went
down to the City and bled 'em well again in heaps. He sent
back word by Red Jacket that, if there was war or he died,
I was to bring the oils along to the City, but till then I was
to go on working in the garden and Red Jacket was to see
me do it. Down at heart all Indians reckon digging a

squaw's business, and neither him nor Cornplanter, when he
relieved watch, was a hard task-master. We hired a nigger-
boy to do our work, and a lazy grinning runagate he was.
When I found Toby didn't die the minute he reached town,
why, boylike, I took him off my mind and went with my
Indians again. Oh! those days up north at Canasedago,
running races and gambling with the Senecas, or bee-
hunting in the woods, or fishing in the lake.' Pharaoh sighed
and looked across the water. 'But it's best,' he went on
suddenly, 'after the first frostës. You roll out o' your blanket
and find every leaf left green over night turned red and
yellow, not by trees at a time, but hundreds and hundreds
of miles of 'em, like sunsets splattered upside down. On one
of such days – the maples was flaming scarlet and gold, and
the sumach bushes were redder – Cornplanter and Red
Jacket came out in full war-dress, making the very leaves
look silly: feathered war-bonnets, yellow doeskin leggings,
fringed and tasselled, red horse-blankets, and their bridles
feathered and shelled and beaded no bounds. I thought it
was war against the British till I saw their faces weren't
painted, and they only carried wrist-whips. Then I hummed
"Yankee Doodle" at 'em. They told me they was going to
visit Big Hand and find out for sure whether he meant to
join the French in fighting the English or make a peace
treaty with England. I reckon those two would ha' gone out
on the war-path at a nod from Big Hand, but they knew well,
if there was war 'twixt England and the United States, their
tribe 'ud catch it from both parties same as in all the other
wars. They asked me to come along and hold the ponies.
That puzzled me, because they always put their ponies up at
the "Buck" or Epply's when they went to see General
Washington in the city, and horse-holding is a nigger's job.
Besides, I wasn't exactly dressed for it.'

'D'you mean you were dressed like an Indian?' Dan
demanded.

Pharaoh looked a little abashed. 'This didn't happen at
Lebanon,' he said, 'but a bit farther north, on the Reser-

vation; and at that particular moment of time, so far as
blanket, hair-band, moccasins, and sunburn went, there
wasn't much odds 'twix' me and a young Seneca buck. You
may laugh' – he smoothed down his long-skirted brown
coat – 'but I told you I took to their ways all over. I said
nothing, though I was bursting to let out the war-whoop
like the young men had taught me.'

'No, and you don't let out one here, either,' said Puck
before Dan could ask. 'Go on, Brother Square-toes.'

'We went on.' Pharaoh's narrow dark eyes gleamed and
danced. 'We went on – forty, fifty miles a day, for days on
end – we three braves. And how a great tall Indian a-horseback can carry his war-bonnet at a canter through thick
timber without brushing a feather beats *me*! My silly head
was banged often enough by low branches, but they slipped
through like running elk. We had evening hymn-singing
every night after they'd blown their pipe-smoke to the
quarters of heaven. Where did we go? I'll tell you, but don't
blame me if you're no wiser. We took the old war-trail from
the end of the Lake along the East Susquehanna through the
Nantego country, right down to Fort Shamokin on the
Senachse river. We crossed the Juniata by Fort Granville,
got into Shippensberg over the hills by the Ochwick trail,
and then to Williams Ferry (it's a bad one). From Williams
Ferry, across the Shanedore, over the Blue Mountains,
through Ashby's Gap, and so south-east by south from there,
till we found the President at the back of his own plantations.
I'd hate to be trailed by Indians in earnest. They caught him
like a partridge on a stump. After we'd left our ponies, we
scouted forward through a woody piece, and, creeping
slower and slower, at last if my moccasins even slipped Red
Jacket 'ud turn and frown. I heard voices – Monsieur
Genêt's for choice – long before I saw anything, and we
pulled up at the edge of a clearing where some niggers in
grey-and-red liveries were holding horses, and half-a-dozen
gentlemen – but one was Genêt – were talking among felled
timber. I fancy they'd come to see Genêt a piece on his road,

for his portmantle was with him. I hid in between two logs as near to the company as I be to that old windlass there. I didn't need anybody to show me Big Hand. He stood up, very still, his legs a little apart, listening to Genêt, that French Ambassador, which never had more manners than a Bosham tinker. Genêt was as good as ordering him to declare war on England at once. I had heard that clack before on the *Embuscade*. He said he'd stir up the whole United States to have war with England, whether Big Hand liked it or not.

'Big Hand heard him out to the last end. I looked behind me, and my two chiefs had vanished like smoke. Says Big Hand, "That is very forcibly put, Monsieur Genêt—" "Citizen – citizen!" the fellow spits in. "*I*, at least, am a Republican!" "Citizen Genêt," he says, "you may be sure it will receive my fullest consideration." This seemed to take Citizen Genêt back a piece. He rode off grumbling, and never gave his nigger a penny. No gentleman!

'The others all assembled round Big Hand then, and, in their way, they said pretty much what Genêt had said. They put it to him, here was France and England at war, in a manner of speaking, right across the United States' stomach, and paying no regards to any one. The French was searching American ships on pretence they was helping England, but really for to steal the goods. The English was doing the same, only t'other way round, and besides searching, they was pressing American citizens into their Navy to help them fight France, on pretence that those Americans was lawful British subjects. His gentlemen put this very clear to Big Hand. It didn't look to *them*, they said, as though the United States trying to keep out of the fight was any advantage to *her*, because she only catched it from both French and English. They said that nine out of ten good Americans was crazy to fight the English then and there. They wouldn't say whether that was right or wrong; they only wanted Big Hand to turn it over in his mind. He did – for a while. I saw Red Jacket and Cornplanter watching him from the far side of the clearing, and how they had slipped round there was another mystery. Then Big Hand drew himself up, and he let his gentlemen have it.'

'Hit 'em?' Dan asked.

'No, nor yet was it what you might call swearing. He – he blasted 'em with his natural speech. He asked them half-a-dozen times over whether the United States had enough armed ships for any shape or sort of war with any one. He asked 'em, if they thought she *had* those ships, to *give* him those ships, and they looked on the ground, as if they expected to find 'em *there*. He put it to 'em whether, setting ships aside, their country – I reckon he gave 'em good reasons – whether the United States was ready or able to face a new big war; she having but so few years back wound up one against England, and being all holds full of her own troubles. As I said, the strong way he laid it all before 'em blasted 'em, and when he'd done it was like a still in the woods after a storm. A little man – but they all looked little – pipes up like a young rook in a blowed-down nest, "Nevertheless, General, it seems you will be compelled to fight England." Quick Big Hand wheels on him, "And is there anything in my past which makes you think I am averse to fighting Great Britain?"

'Everybody laughed except him. "Oh, General, you mistake us entirely!" they says. "I trust so," he says. "But I know my duty. We *must* have peace with England."

' "At any price?" says the man with the rook's voice.

' "At any price," says he, word by word. "Our ships will be searched – our citizens will be pressed, but—"

' "Then what about the Declaration of Independence?" says one.

' "Deal with facts, not fancies," says Big Hand. "The United States are in no position to fight England."

' "But think of public opinion," another one starts up. "The feeling in Philadelphia alone is at fever heat."

'He held up one of his big hands. "Gentlemen," he says – slow he spoke, but his voice carried far – "I have to think of our country. Let me assure you that the treaty with Great

Britain will be made though every city in the Union burn me in effigy."

' "At any price?" the actor-like chap keeps on croaking.

' "The treaty must be made on Great Britain's own terms. What else can I do?"

'He turns his back on 'em and they looked at each other and slinked off to the horses, leaving him alone: and then I saw he was an old man. Then Red Jacket and Cornplanter rode down the clearing from the far end as though they had just chanced along. Back went Big Hand's shoulders, up went his head, and he stepped forward one single pace with a great deep Hough! so pleased he was. That was a statelified meeting to behold – three big men, and two of 'em looking like jewelled images among the spattle of gay-coloured leaves. I saw my chiefs' war-bonnets sinking together, down and down. Then they made the sign which no Indian makes outside of the Medicine Lodges – a sweep of the right hand just clear of the dust and an inbend of the left knee at the same time, and those proud eagle feathers almost touched his boot-top.'

'What did it mean?' said Dan.

'Mean!' Pharaoh cried. 'Why it's what you – what we – it's the Sachems' way of sprinkling the sacred corn-meal in front of – oh! it's a piece of Indian compliment really, and it signifies that you are a very big chief.

'Big Hand looked down on 'em. First he says quite softly, "My brothers know it is not easy to be a chief." Then his voice grew. "My children," says he, "what is in your minds?"

'Says Cornplanter, "We came to ask whether there will be war with King George's men, but we have heard what our Father has said to his chiefs. We will carry away that talk in our hearts to tell to our people."

' "No," says Big Hand. "Leave all that talk behind – it was between white men only – but take this message from *me* to your people – 'There will be no war.' "

'His gentlemen were waiting, so they didn't delay him;

only Cornplanter says, using his old side-name, "Big Hand, did you see us among the timber just now?"

' "Surely," says he. "*You* taught me to look behind trees when we were both young." And with that he cantered off.

'Neither of my chiefs spoke till we were back on our ponies again and a half-hour along the home-trail. Then Cornplanter says to Red Jacket, "We will have the Corn-dance this year. There will be no war." And that was all there was to it.'

Pharaoh stood up as though he had finished.

'Yes,' said Puck, rising too. 'And what came out of it in the long run?'

'Let me get at my story my own way,' was the answer. 'Look! it's later than I thought. That Shoreham smack's thinking of her supper.'

The children looked across the darkening Channel. A smack had hoisted a lantern and slowly moved west where Brighton pier lights ran out in a twinkling line. When they turned round The Gap was empty behind them.

'I expect they've packed our trunks by now,' said Dan. 'This time tomorrow we'll be home.'

IF—

IF you can keep your head when all about you
   Are losing theirs and blaming it on you;
If you can trust yourself when all men doubt you,
   But make allowance for their doubting too;
If you can wait and not be tired by waiting,
   Or being lied about, don't deal in lies,
Or being hated, don't give way to hating,
   And yet don't look too good, nor talk too wise;

If you can dream – and not make dreams your master;
   If you can think – and not make thoughts your aim,
If you can meet with Triumph and Disaster
   And treat those two impostors just the same;
If you can bear to hear the truth you've spoken
   Twisted by knaves to make a trap for fools,
Or watch the things you gave your life to, broken,
   And stoop and build 'em up with worn-out tools;

If you can make one heap of all your winnings
   And risk it on one turn of pitch-and-toss,
And lose, and start again at your beginnings
   And never breathe a word about your loss;
If you can force your heart and nerve and sinew
   To serve your turn long after they are gone,
And so hold on when there is nothing in you
   Except the Will which says to them: 'Hold on!'

If you can talk with crowds and keep your virtue,
   Or walk with Kings – nor lose the common touch,
If neither foes nor loving friends can hurt you,
   If all men count with you, but none too much;
If you can fill the unforgiving minute
   With sixty seconds' worth of distance run,
Yours is the Earth and everything that's in it,
   And – which is more – you'll be a Man, my son!

'A Priest in Spite of Himself'

A ST HELENA LULLABY

How far is St Helena from a little child at play?
  What makes you want to wander there with all the world
    between?
Oh, Mother, call your son again or else he'll run away.
  (*No one thinks of winter when the grass is green!*)

How far is St Helena from a fight in Paris street?
  I haven't time to answer now – the men are falling fast.
The guns begin to thunder, and the drums begin to beat.
  (*If you take the first step you will take the last!*)

How far is St Helena from the field at Austerlitz?
  You couldn't hear me if I told – so loud the cannons roar.
But not so far for people who are living by their wits.
  ('*Gay go up*' means '*gay go down*' *the wide world o'er!*)

How far is St Helena from an Emperor of France?
  I cannot see – I cannot tell – the crowns they dazzle so.
The Kings sit down to dinner, and the Queens stand up to dance.
  (*After open weather you may look for snow!*)

How far is St Helena from the Capes of Trafalgar?
  A longish way – a longish way – with ten year more to run.
It's South across the water underneath a setting star.
  (*What you cannot finish you must leave undone!*)

How far is St Helena from the Beresina ice?
  An ill way – a chill way – the ice begins to crack.
But not so far for gentlemen who never took advice.
  (*When you can't go forward you must e'en come back!*)

How far is St Helena from the field of Waterloo?
  A near way – a clear way – the ship will take you soon.
A pleasant place for gentlemen with little left to do.
  (*Morning never tries you till the afternoon!*)

How far from St Helena to the Gate of Heaven's Grace?
 That no one knows – that no one knows – and no one ever will.
But fold your hands across your heart and cover up your face,
 And after all your trapesings, child, lie still!

'A Priest in Spite of Himself'

THE day after they came home from the sea-side they set out on a tour of inspection to make sure everything was as they had left it. Soon they discovered that old Hobden had blocked their best hedge-gaps with stakes and thorn-bundles, and had trimmed up the hedges where the black-berries were setting.

'It can't be time for the gipsies to come along,' said Una. 'Why, it was summer only the other day!'

'There's smoke in Low Shaw!' said Dan, sniffing. 'Let's make sure!'

They crossed the fields towards the thin line of blue smoke that leaned above the hollow of Low Shaw which lies beside the King's Hill road. It used to be an old quarry till some-body planted it, and you can look straight down into it from the edge of Banky Meadow.

'I thought so,' Dan whispered, as they came up to the fence at the edge of the larches. A gipsy-van – not the show-man's sort, but the old black kind, with little windows high up and a baby-gate across the door – was getting ready to leave. A man was harnessing the horses; an old woman crouched over the ashes of a fire made out of broken fence-rails; and a girl sat on the van-steps singing to a baby on her lap. A wise-looking, thin dog snuffed at a patch of fur on the ground till the old woman put it carefully in the middle of the fire. The girl reached back inside the van and tossed her a paper parcel. This was laid on the fire too, and they smelt singed feathers.

'Chicken feathers!' said Dan. 'I wonder if they are old Hobden's.'

Una sneezed. The dog growled and crawled to the girl's feet, the old woman fanned the fire with her hat, while the man led the horses up to the shafts. They all moved as quickly and quietly as snakes over moss.

'Ah!' said the girl. 'I'll teach you!' She beat the dog, who seemed to expect it.

'Don't do that,' Una called down. 'It wasn't his fault.'

'How do you know what I'm beating him for?' she answered.

'For not seeing us,' said Dan. 'He was standing right in the smoke, and the wind was wrong for his nose, anyhow.'

The girl stopped beating the dog, and the old woman fanned faster than ever.

'You've fanned some of your feathers out of the fire,' said Una. 'There's a tail-feather by that chestnut-tot.'

'What of it?' said the old woman, as she grabbed it.

'Oh, nothing!' said Dan. 'Only I've heard say that tail-feathers are as bad as the whole bird, sometimes.'

That was a saying of Hobden's about pheasants. Old Hobden always burned all feather and fur before he sat down to eat.

'Come on, mother,' the man whispered. The old woman climbed into the van, and the horses drew it out of the deep-rutted shaw on to the hard road.

The girl waved her hands and shouted something they could not catch.

'That was gipsy for "Thank you kindly, Brother and Sister,"' said Pharaoh Lee.

He was standing behind them, his fiddle under his arm.

'Gracious, you startled me!' said Una.

'*You* startled old Priscilla Savile,' Puck called from below them. 'Come and sit by their fire. She ought to have put it out before they left.'

They dropped down the ferny side of the shaw. Una raked the ashes together, Dan found a dead wormy oak branch that burns without flame, and they watched the smoke while Pharaoh played a curious wavery air.

'That's what the girl was humming to the baby,' said Una.

'I know it,' he nodded, and went on:

> Ai Lumai, Lumai, Lumai! Luludia!
> Ai Luludia!'

He passed from one odd tune to another, and quite forgot the children. At last Puck asked him to go on with his adventures in Philadelphia and among the Seneca Indians.

'I'm telling it,' he said, staring straight in front of him as he played. 'Can't you hear?'

'Maybe, but *they* can't. Tell it aloud,' said Puck.

Pharaoh shook himself, laid his fiddle beside him, and began:

'I'd left Red Jacket and Cornplanter riding home with me after Big Hand had said that there wouldn't be any war. That's all there was to it. We believed Big Hand and we went home again – we three braves. When we reached Lebanon we found Toby at the cottage with his waistcoat a foot too big for him – so hard he had worked amongst the yellow-fever people. He beat me for running off with the Indians, but 'twas worth it – I was glad to see him, – and when we went back to Philadelphia for the winter, and I was told how he'd sacrificed himself over sick people in the yellow fever, I thought the world and all of him. No, I didn't neither. I'd thought that all along. That yellow fever must have been something dreadful. Even in December people had no more than begun to trinkle back to town. Whole houses stood empty and the niggers was robbing them out. But I can't call to mind that any of the Moravian Brethren had died. It seemed like they had just kept on with their own concerns, and the good Lord He'd just looked after 'em. That was the winter – yes, winter of 'Ninety-three – the Brethren bought a stove for the church. Toby spoke in favour of it because the cold spoiled his fiddle hand, but many thought stove-heat not in the Bible, and there was yet a third party which always brought hickory coal foot-warmers to service and wouldn't speak either way. They ended by casting the Lot

for it, which is like pitch-and-toss. After my summer with the
Senecas, church-stoves didn't highly interest me, so I took
to haunting round among the French *émigrés* which Philadelphia was full of. My French and my fiddling helped me
there, d'ye see. They come over in shiploads from France,
where, by what I made out, every one was killing every one
else by any means, and they spread 'emselves about the city –
mostly in Drinker's Alley and Elfrith's Alley – and they did
odd jobs till times should mend. But whatever they stooped
to, they were gentry and kept a cheerful countenance, and
after an evening's fiddling at one of their poor little proud
parties, the Brethren seemed old-fashioned. Pastor Meder
and Brother Adam Goos didn't like my fiddling for hire, but
Toby said it was lawful in me to earn my living by exercising
my talents. He never let me be put upon.

'In February of 'Ninety-four – No, March it must have
been, because a new Ambassador called Fauchet had come
from France, with no more manners than Genêt the old one –
in March, Red Jacket came in from the Reservation bringing
news of all kind friends there. I showed him round the city,
and we saw General Washington riding through a crowd of
folk that shouted for war with England. They gave him quite
rough music, but he looked 'twixt his horse's ears and made
out not to notice. His stirrup brished Red Jacket's elbow, and
Red Jacket whispered up, "My brother knows it is not easy
to be a chief?" Big Hand shot just one look at him and
nodded. Then there was a scuffle behind us over some one
who wasn't hooting at Washington loud enough to please
the people. We went away to be out of the fight. Indians
won't risk being hit.'

'What do they do if they are?' Dan asked.

'Kill, of course. That's why they have such proper
manners. Well, then, coming home by Drinker's Alley to
get a new shirt which a French Vicomte's lady was washing
to take the stiff out of (I'm always choice in my body-linen)
a lame Frenchman pushes a paper of buttons at us. He hadn't
long landed in the United States, and please would we buy.

He sure-ly was a pitiful scrattel – his coat half torn off, his face cut, but his hands steady; so I knew it wasn't drink. He said his name was Peringuey, and he'd been knocked about in the crowd round the Stadt – Independence Hall. One thing leading to another we took him up to Toby's rooms, same as Red Jacket had taken me the year before. The compliments he paid to Toby's Madeira wine fairly conquered the old man, for he opened a second bottle and he told this Monsieur Peringuey all about our great stove dispute in the church. I remember Pastor Meder and Brother Adam Goos dropped in, and although they and Toby were direct opposite sides regarding stoves, yet this Monsieur Peringuey he made 'em feel as if he thought each one was in the right of it. He said he had been a clergyman before he had to leave France. He admired at Toby's fiddling, and he asked if Red Jacket, sitting by the spinet, was a simple Huron. Senecas aren't Hurons, they're Iroquois, of course, and Toby told him so. Well, then, in due time he arose and left in a style which made us feel he'd been favouring us, instead of us feeding him. I've never seen that so strong before – in a man. We all talked him over but couldn't make head or tail of him, and Red Jacket come out to walk with me to the French quarter where I was due to fiddle at a party. Passing Drinker's Alley again we saw a naked window with a light in it, and there sat our button-selling Monsieur Peringuey throwing dice all alone, right hand against left.

'Says Red Jacket, keeping back in the dark, "Look at his face!"

'I was looking. I protest to you I wasn't frightened like I was when Big Hand talked to his gentlemen. I – I only looked, and I only wondered that even those dead dumb dice 'ud dare to fall different from what that face wished. It – it *was* a face!

' "He is bad," says Red Jacket. "But he is a great chief. The French have sent away a great chief. I thought so when he told us his lies. Now I know."

'I had to go on to the party, so I asked him to call round

for me afterwards and we'd have hymn-singing at Toby's as usual.

' "No," he says. "Tell Toby I am not Christian tonight. All Indian." He had those fits sometimes. I wanted to know more about Monsieur Peringuey, and the *émigré* party was the very place to find out. It's neither here nor there, of course, but those French *émigré* parties they almost make you cry. The men that you bought fruit of in Market Street, the hairdressers and fencing-masters and French teachers, they turn back again by candlelight to what they used to be at home, and you catch their real names. There wasn't much room in the washhouse, so I sat on top of the copper and played 'em the tunes they called for – "*Si le Roi m'avait donné*," and such nursery stuff. They cried sometimes. It hurt me to take their money afterwards, indeed it did. And there I found out about Monsieur Peringuey. He was a proper rogue too! None of 'em had a good word for him except the Marquise that kept the French boarding-house on Fourth Street. I made out that his real name was the Count Talleyrand de Périgord – a priest right enough, but sorely come down in the world. He'd been King Louis' Ambassador to England a year or two back, before the French had cut off King Louis' head; and, by what I heard, that head wasn't hardly more than hanging loose before he'd run back to Paris and prevailed on Danton, the very man which did the murder, to send him back to England again as Ambassador of the French Republic! That was too much for the English, so they kicked him out by Act of Parliament, and he'd fled to the Americas without money or friends or prospects. I'm telling you the talk in the washhouse. Some of 'em was laughing over it. Says the French Marquise, "My friends, you laugh too soon. That man will be on the winning side before any of us."

' "I did not know you were so fond of priests, Marquise," says the Vicomte. His lady did my washing, as I've told you.

' "I have my reasons," says the Marquise. "He sent my uncle and my two brothers to Heaven by the little door," –

that was one of the *émigré* names for the guillotine. "He will be on the winning side if it costs him the blood of every friend he has in the world."

' "Then what does he want here?" says one of 'em. "We have all lost our game."

' "My faith!" says the Marquise. "He will find out, if any one can, whether this *canaille* of a Washington means to help us to fight England. Genêt (that was my Ambassador in the *Embuscade*) has failed and gone off disgraced; Fauchet (he was the new man) hasn't done any better, but our Abbé will find out, and he will make his profit out of the news. Such a man does not fail."

' "He begins unluckily," says the Vicomte. "He was set upon today in the street for not hooting your Washington." They all laughed again, and one remarks, "How does the poor devil keep himself?"

'He must have slipped in through the washhouse door, for he flits past me and joins 'em, cold as ice.

' "One does what one can," he says. "I sell buttons. And you, Marquise?"

' "I?" – she waves her poor white hands all burned – "I am a cook – a very bad one – at your service, Abbé. We were just talking about you."

'They didn't treat him like they talked of him. They backed off and stood still.

' "I have missed something, then," he says. "But I spent this last hour playing – only for buttons, Marquise – against a noble savage, the veritable Huron himself."

' "You had your usual luck, I hope?" she says.

' "Certainly," he says. "I cannot afford to lose even buttons in these days."

' "Then I suppose the child of nature does not know that your dice are usually loaded, Father Tout-à-tous," she continues. I don't know whether she meant to accuse him of cheating. He only bows.

' "Not yet, Mademoiselle Cunégonde," he says, and goes on to make himself agreeable to the rest of the company.

And that was how I found out our Monsieur Peringuey was
Count Charles Maurice Talleyrand de Périgord.'

Pharaoh stopped, but the children said nothing.

'You've heard of him?' said Pharaoh.

Una shook her head.

'Was Red Jacket the Indian he played dice with?' Dan
asked.

'He was. Red Jacket told me the next time we met. I
asked if the lame man had cheated. Red Jacket said no – he
had played quite fair and was a master player. I allow Red
Jacket knew. I've seen him, on the Reservation, play himself
out of everything he had and in again. Then I told Red
Jacket all I'd heard at the party concerning Talleyrand.

' "I was right," he says. "I saw the man's war-face when
he thought he was alone. That is why I played him. I
played him face to face. He is a great chief. Do they say why
he comes here?"

' "They say he comes to find out if Big Hand makes war
against the English," I said.

'Red Jacket grunted. "Yes," he says. "He asked me that
too. If he had been a small chief I should have lied. But he
is a great chief. He knew I was a chief, so I told him the
truth. I told him what Big Hand said to Cornplanter and
me in the clearing – 'There will be no war.' I could not see
what he thought. I could not see behind his face. But he is a
great chief. He will believe."

' "Will he believe that Big Hand can keep his people
back from war?" I said, thinking of the crowds that hooted
Big Hand whenever he rode out.

' "He is as bad as Big Hand is good, but he is not as
strong as Big Hand," says Red Jacket. "When he talks with
Big Hand he will feel this in his heart. The French have
sent away a great chief. Presently he will go back and make
them afraid."

'Now wasn't that comical? The French woman that
knew him and owed all her losses to him; the Indian that
picked him up, cut and muddy on the street, and played

dice with him; they neither of 'em doubted that Talleyrand was something by himself – appearances notwithstanding.'

'And was he something by himself?' asked Una.

Pharaoh began to laugh, but stopped. 'The way *I* look at it,' he said, 'Talleyrand was one of just three men in this world who are quite by themselves. Big Hand I put first, because I've seen him.'

'Ay,' said Puck. 'I'm sorry we lost him out of Old England. Who d'you put second?'

'Talleyrand: maybe because I've seen him too,' said Pharaoh.

'Who's third?' said Puck.

'Boney – even though I've seen him.'

'Whew!' said Puck. 'Every man has his own weights and measures, but that's queer reckoning.'

'Boney?' said Una. 'You don't mean you've ever met Napoleon Bonaparte?'

'There, I knew you wouldn't have patience with the rest of my tale after hearing that! But wait a minute. Talleyrand he come round to Hundred and Eighteen in a day or two to thank Toby for his kindness. I didn't mention the dice-playing, but I could see that Red Jacket's doings had made Talleyrand highly curious about Indians – though he *would* call him the Huron. Toby, as you may believe, was all holds full of knowledge concerning their manners and habits. He only needed a listener. The Brethren don't study Indians much till they join the Church, but Toby knew 'em wild. So evening after evening Talleyrand crossed his sound leg over his game one and Toby poured forth. Having been adopted into the Senecas I, naturally, kept still, but Toby 'ud call on me to back up some of his remarks, and by that means, and a habit he had of drawing you on in talk, Talleyrand saw I knew something of his noble savages too. Then he tried a trick. Coming back from an *émigré* party he turns into his little shop and puts it to me, laughing like, that I'd gone with the two chiefs on their visit to Big Hand. *I* hadn't told. Red Jacket hadn't told, and Toby, of course,

didn't know. 'Twas just Talleyrand's guess. "Now," he
says, "my English and Red Jacket's French was so bad that
I am not sure I got the rights of what the President really
said to the unsophisticated Huron. Do me the favour of
telling it again." I told him every word Red Jacket had told
him and not one word more. I had my suspicions, having
just come from an *émigré* party where the Marquise was
hating and praising him as usual.

' "Much obliged," he said. "But I couldn't gather from
Red Jacket exactly what the President said to Monsieur
Genêt, or to his American gentlemen after Monsieur Genêt
had ridden away."

'I saw Talleyrand was guessing again, for Red Jacket
hadn't told him a word about the white men's pow-wow.'

'Why hadn't he?' Puck asked.

'Because Red Jacket was a chief. He told Talleyrand
what the President had said to him and Cornplanter; but he
didn't repeat the talk, between the white men, that Big
Hand ordered him to leave behind.

'Oh!' said Puck. 'I see. What did *you* do?'

'First I was going to make some sort of tale round it, but
Talleyrand was a chief too. So I said, "As soon as I get Red
Jacket's permission to tell that part of the tale, I'll be
delighted to refresh your memory, Abbé." What else could
I have done?

' "Is that all?" he says, laughing. "Let me refresh your
memory. In a month from now I can give you a hundred
dollars for your account of the conversation."

' "Make it five hundred, Abbé," I says.

' "Five, then," says he.

' "That will suit me admirably," I says. "Red Jacket will
be in town again by then, and the moment he gives me leave
I'll claim the money."

'He had a hard fight to be civil but he come out smiling.

' "Monsieur," he says, "I beg your pardon as sincerely as
I envy the noble Huron your loyalty. Do me the honour to
sit down while I explain."

'There wasn't another chair, so I sat on the button-box.

'He was a clever man. He had got hold of the gossip that the President meant to make a peace treaty with England at any cost. He had found out – from Genêt, I reckon, who was with the President on the day the two chiefs met him. He'd heard that Genêt had had a huff with the President and had ridden off leaving his business at loose ends. What he wanted – what he begged and blustered to know – was just the very words which the President had said to his gentlemen *after* Genêt had left, concerning the peace treaty with England. He put it to me that in helping him to those very words I'd be helping three great countries as well as mankind. The room was as bare as the palm of your hand, but I couldn't laugh at him.

' "I'm sorry," I says, when he wiped his forehead. "As soon as Red Jacket gives permission—"

' "You don't believe me, then?" he cuts in.

' "Not one little, little word, Abbé," I says; "except that you mean to be on the winning side. Remember, I've been fiddling to all your old friends for months."

'Well, then his temper fled him and he called me names.

' "Wait a minute, *ci-devant*," I says at last. "I *am* half English and half French, but I am not the half of a man. I will tell thee something the Indian told me. Has thee seen the President?"

' "Oh yes!" he sneers. "I had letters from the Lord Lansdowne to that estimable old man."

' "Then," I says, "thee will understand. The Red Skin said that when thee has met the President thee will feel in thy heart he is a stronger man than thee."

' "Go!" he whispers. "Before I kill thee, go."

'He looked like it. So I left him.'

'Why did he want to know so badly?' said Dan.

'The way I look at it is that if he *had* known for certain that Washington meant to make the peace treaty with England at any price, he'd ha' left old Fauchet fumbling about in Philadelphia while he went straight back to

France and told old Danton – "it's no good your wasting time and hopes on the United States, because she won't fight on our side – that I've proof of!" Then Danton might have been grateful and given Talleyrand a job, because a whole mass of things hang on knowing for sure who's your friend and who's your enemy. Just think of us poor shop-keepers, for instance.'

'Did Red Jacket let you tell, when he came back?' Una asked.

'Of course not. He said, "When Cornplanter and I ask you what Big Hand said to the whites you can tell the Lame Chief. All that talk was left behind in the timber, as Big Hand ordered. Tell the Lame Chief there will be no war. He can go back to France with that word."

'Talleyrand and me hadn't met for a long time except at *émigré* parties. When I give him the message he just shook his head. He was sorting buttons in the shop.

' "I cannot return to France with nothing better than the word of an unsophisticated savage," he says.

' "Hasn't the President said anything to you?" I asked him.

' "He has said everything that one in his position ought to say, but – but if only I had what he said to his Cabinet after Genêt rode off I believe I could change Europe – the world, maybe."

' "I'm sorry," I says. "Maybe you'll do that without my help."

'He looked at me hard. "Either you have unusual observation for one so young, or you choose to be insolent," he says.

' "It was intended for a compliment," I says. "But no odds. We're off in a few days for our summer trip, and I've come to make my good-byes."

' "I go on my travels too," he says. "If ever we meet again you may be sure I will do my best to repay what I owe you."

' "Without malice, Abbé, I hope," I says.

' "None whatever," says he. "Give my respects to your adorable Dr Pangloss" (that was one of his side-names for Toby) "and the Huron." I never *could* teach him the difference betwixt Hurons and Senecas.

'Then Sister Haga came in for a paper of what we call "pilly buttons," and that was the last I saw of Talleyrand in those parts.'

'But after that you met Napoleon, didn't you?' said Una.

'Wait just a little, dearie. After that, Toby and I went to Lebanon and the Reservation, and, being older and knowing better how to manage him, I enjoyed myself well that summer with fiddling and fun. When we came back, the Brethren got after Toby because I wasn't learning any lawful trade, and he had hard work to save me from being apprenticed to Helmbold and Geyer the printers. 'Twould have ruined our music together, indeed it would. And when we escaped that, old Mattes Roush, the leather-breeches maker round the corner, took a notion I was cut out for skin-dressing. But we were rescued. Along towards Christmas there comes a big sealed letter from the Bank saying that a Monsieur Talleyrand had put five hundred dollars – a hundred pounds – to my credit there to use as I pleased. There was a little note from him inside – he didn't give any address – to thank me for past kindnesses and my believing in his future, which he said was pretty cloudy at the time of writing. I wished Toby to share the money. *I* hadn't done more than bring Talleyrand up to Hundred and Eighteen. The kindnesses were Toby's. But Toby said, "No! Liberty and Independence for ever. I have all my wants, my son." So I gave him a set of new fiddle-strings, and the Brethren didn't advise us any more. Only Pastor Meder he preached about the deceitfulness of riches, and Brother Adam Goos said if there was war the English 'ud surely shoot down the Bank. *I* knew there wasn't going to be any war, but I drew the money out and on Red Jacket's advice I put it into horse-flesh, which I sold to Bob Bicknell for the Baltimore stage-coaches. That way, I doubled my money inside the twelvemonth.'

'You gipsy! You proper gipsy!' Puck shouted.

'Why not? 'Twas fair buying and selling. Well, one thing leading to another, in a few years I had made the beginning of a worldly fortune and was in the tobacco trade.'

'Ah!' said Puck, suddenly. 'Might I inquire if you'd ever sent any news to your people in England – or in France?'

'O' course I had. I wrote regular every three months after I'd made money in the horse trade. We Lees don't like coming home empty-handed. If it's only a turnip or an egg, it's something. Oh yes, I wrote good and plenty to Uncle Aurette, and – Dad don't read very quickly – Uncle used to slip over Newhaven way and tell Dad what was going on in the tobacco trade.'

'I see—

> 'Aurettes and Lees –
> Like as two peas.

Go on, Brother Square-toes,' said Puck. Pharaoh laughed and went on.

'Talleyrand he'd gone up in the world same as me. He'd sailed to France again, and was a great man in the Government there awhile, but they had to turn him out on account of some story about bribes from American shippers. All our poor *émigrés* said he was surely finished this time, but Red Jacket and me we didn't think it likely, not unless he was quite dead. Big Hand had made his peace treaty with Great Britain, just *as* he said he would, and there was a roaring trade 'twixt England and the United States for such as 'ud take the risk of being searched by British and French men-o'-war. Those two was fighting, and just *as* his gentlemen told Big Hand 'ud happen – the United States was catching it from both. If an English man-o'-war met an American ship he'd press half the best men out of her, and swear they was British subjects. Most of 'em was! If a Frenchman met her he'd, likely, have the cargo out of her, swearing it was meant to aid and comfort the English; and if a Spaniard or a Dutchman met her – they was hanging on to England's coattails too – Lord only knows what *they* wouldn't do! It came over me that what I wanted in my tobacco trade was a fast-sailing ship and a man who could be French, English, or American at a pinch. Luckily I could lay my hands on both articles. So along towards the end of September in the year 'Ninety-nine I sailed from Philadelphia with a hundred and eleven hogshead o' good Virginia tobacco, in the brig *Berthe Aurette*, named after Mother's maiden name, hoping 'twould bring me luck, which she didn't – and yet she did.'

'Where was you bound for?' Puck asked.

'Er – any port I found handiest. I didn't tell Toby or the Brethren. They don't understand the ins and outs of the tobacco trade.'

Puck coughed a small cough as he shifted a piece of wood with his bare foot.

'It's easy for you to sit and judge,' Pharaoh cried. 'But think o' what *we* had to put up with! We spread our wings and run across the broad Atlantic like a hen through a horse-fair. Even so, we was stopped by an English frigate, three days out. He sent a boat alongside and pressed seven able seamen. I remarked it was hard on honest traders, but the officer said they was fighting all creation and hadn't time to argue. The next English frigate we escaped with no more than a shot in our quarter. Then we was chased two days and a night by a French privateer, firing between squalls, and the dirty little English ten-gun brig which made him sheer off had the impudence to press another five of our men. That's how we reached to the chops of the Channel. Twelve good men pressed out of thirty-five; an eighteen-pound shot-hole close beside our rudder; our mainsail looking like spectacles where the Frenchman had hit us – and the Channel crawling with short-handed British cruisers. Put *that* in your pipe and smoke it next time you grumble at the price of tobacco!

'Well, then, to top it off, while we was trying to get at our leaks, a French lugger come swooping at us out o' the dusk. We warned him to keep away, but he fell aboard us, and up climbed his jabbering red-caps. We couldn't endure any more – indeed we couldn't. We went at 'em with all we could lay hands on. It didn't last long. They was fifty odd to our twenty-three. Pretty soon I heard the cutlasses thrown down and some one bellowed for the *sacré* captain.

' "Here I am!" I says. "I don't suppose it makes any odds to you thieves, but this is the United States brig *Berthe Aurette*."

' "My aunt!" the man says, laughing. "Why is she named that?"

' "Who's speaking?" I said. 'Twas too dark to see, but I thought I knew the voice.

' "Enseigne de Vaisseau Estèphe L'Estrange," he sings out, and then I was sure.

' "Oh!" I says. "It's all in the family, I suppose, but you *have* done a fine day's work, Stephen."

'He whips out the binnacle-light and holds it to my face. He was young L'Estrange, my full cousin, that I hadn't seen since the night the smack sank off Telscombe Tye – six years before.

' "Whew!" he says. "That's why she was named for Aunt Berthe, is it? What's your share in her, Pharaoh?"

' "Only half owner, but the cargo's mine."

' "That's bad," he says. "I'll do what I can, but you shouldn't have fought us."

' "Steve," I says, "you aren't ever going to report our little fall-out as a fight! Why, a Revenue cutter 'ud laugh at it!"

' "So'd I if I wasn't in the Republican Navy," he says. "But two of our men are dead, d'ye see, and I'm afraid I'll have to take you to the Prize Court at Le Havre."

' "Will they condemn my 'baccy?" I asks.

' "To the last ounce. But I was thinking more of the ship. She'd make a sweet little craft for the Navy if the Prize Court 'ud let me have her," he says.

'Then I knew there was no hope. I don't blame him – a man must consider his own interests – but nigh every dollar

I had was in ship or cargo, and Steve kept on saying, "You shouldn't have fought us."

'Well, then, the lugger took us to Le Havre, and that being the one time we *did* want a British ship to rescue us, why, o' course we never saw one. My cousin spoke his best for us at the Prize Court. He owned he'd no right to rush alongside in the face o' the United States flag, but we couldn't get over those two men killed, d'ye see, and the Court condemned both ship and cargo. They was kind enough not to make us prisoners – only beggars – and young L'Estrange was given the *Berthe Aurette* to re-arm into the French Navy.

' "I'll take you round to Boulogne," he says. "Mother and the rest'll be glad to see you, and you can slip over to Newhaven with Uncle Aurette. Or you can ship with me, like most o' your men, and take a turn at King George's loose trade. There's plenty pickings," he says.

'Crazy as I was, I couldn't help laughing.

' "I've had my allowance of pickings and stealings," I says. "Where are they taking my tobacco?" 'Twas being loaded on to a barge.

' "Up the Seine to be sold in Paris," he says. "Neither you nor I will ever touch a penny of that money."

' "Get me leave to go with it," I says. "I'll see if there's justice to be gotten out of our American Ambassador."

' "There's not much justice in this world," he says, "without a Navy." But he got me leave to go with the barge and he gave me some money. That tobacco was all I had, and I followed it like a hound follows a snatched bone. Going up the river I fiddled a little to keep my spirits up, as well as to make friends with the guard. They was only doing their duty. Outside o' that they were the reasonablest o' God's creatures. They never even laughed at me. So we come to Paris, by river, along in November, which the French had christened Brumaire. They'd given new names to all the months, and after such an outrageous silly piece o' business as *that*, they wasn't likely to trouble 'emselves with my rights and wrongs. They didn't. The barge was laid up below Notre Dame church in charge of a caretaker, and he let me sleep aboard after I'd run about all day from office to office, seeking justice and fair dealing, and getting speeches concerning liberty. None heeded me. Looking back on it I can't rightly blame 'em. I'd no money, my clothes was filthy mucked; I hadn't changed my linen in weeks, and I'd no proof of my claims except the ship's papers, which, they said, I might have stolen. The thieves! The door-keeper to the American Ambassador – for I never saw even the Secretary – he swore I spoke French a sight too well for an American citizen. Worse than that – I had spent my money, d'ye see, and I – I took to fiddling in the streets for my keep; and – and, a ship's captain with a fiddle under his arm – well, I *don't* blame 'em that they didn't believe me.

'I come back to the barge one day – late in this month Brumaire it was – fair beazled out. Old Maingon, the care-taker, he'd lit a fire in a bucket and was grilling a herring.

' "Courage, mon ami," he says. "Dinner is served."

' "I can't eat," I says. "I can't do any more. It's stronger than I am."

' "Bah!" he says. "Nothing's stronger than a man. Me, for example! Less than two years ago I was blown up in the *Orient* in Aboukir Bay, but I descended again and hit the water like a fairy. Look at me now," he says. He wasn't much to look at, for he'd only one leg and one eye, but the cheerfullest soul that ever trod shoe-leather. "That's worse than a hundred and eleven hogshead of 'baccy," he goes on. "You're young, too! What wouldn't I give to be young in France at this hour! There's nothing you couldn't do," he says. "The ball's at your feet – kick it!" he says. He kicks the old fire-bucket with his peg-leg. "General Buonaparte, for example!" he goes on. "That man's a babe compared to me, and see what he's done already. He's conquered Egypt and Austria and Italy – oh! half Europe!" he says, "and now he sails back to Paris, and he sails out to St Cloud down the river here – *don't* stare at the river, you young fool! – and all in front of these pig-jobbing lawyers and citizens he makes himself Consul, which is as good as a King. He'll *be* King, too, in the next three turns of the capstan – King of France, England, and the world! Think o' that!" he shouts, "and eat your herring."

'I says something about Boney. If he hadn't been fighting England I shouldn't have lost my 'baccy – should I?

' "Young fellow," says Maingon, "you don't under-stand."

'We heard cheering. A carriage passed over the bridge with two in it.

' "That's the man himself," says Maingon. "He'll give 'em something to cheer for soon." He stands at the salute.

' "Who's t'other in black beside him?" I asks, fairly shaking all over.

' "Ah! he's the clever one. You'll hear of him before long. He's that scoundrel-bishop, Talleyrand."

' "It is!" I said, and up the steps I went with my fiddle, and run after the carriage calling, "Abbé, Abbé!"

'A soldier knocked the wind out of me with the back of his sword, but I had sense to keep on following till the carriage stopped – and there just was a crowd round the house-door! I must have been half-crazy else I wouldn't have struck up "*Si le Roi m'avait donné Paris la grande ville!*" I thought it might remind him.

' "That is a good omen!" he says to Boney sitting all hunched up; and he looks straight at me.

' "Abbé – oh, Abbé!" I says. "Don't you remember Toby and Hundred and Eighteen Second Street?"

'He said not a word. He just crooked his long white finger to the guard at the door while the carriage steps were let down, and I skipped into the house, and they slammed the door in the crowd's face.

' "You go there," says a soldier, and shoves me into an empty room, where I catched my first breath since I'd left the barge. Presently I heard plates rattling next door – there were only folding doors between – and a cork drawn. "I tell you," some one shouts with his mouth full, "it was all that sulky ass Sieyès' fault. Only my speech to the Five Hundred saved the situation."

' "Did it save your coat?" says Talleyrand. "I hear they tore it when they threw you out. Don't gasconade to me. You may be in the road of victory, but you aren't there yet."

'Then I guessed t'other man was Boney. He stamped about and swore at Talleyrand.

' "You forget yourself, Consul," says Talleyrand, "or rather you remember yourself – Corsican."

' "Pig!" says Boney, and worse.

' "Emperor!" says Talleyrand, but, the way he spoke, it sounded worst of all. Some one must have backed against the folding doors, for they flew open and showed me in the middle of the room. Boney whipped out his pistol before I could stand up. "General," says Talleyrand to him, "this gentleman has a habit of catching us canaille *en déshabillé*. Put that thing down."

'Boney laid it on the table, so I guessed which was master. Talleyrand takes my hand – "Charmed to see you again, Candide," he says. "How is the adorable Dr Pangloss and the noble Huron?"

' "They were doing very well when I left," I said. "But I'm not."

' "Do *you* sell buttons now?" he says, and fills me a glass of wine off the table.

' "Madeira," says he. "Not so good as some I have drunk."

' "You mountebank!" Boney roars. "Turn that out." (He didn't even say "man," but Talleyrand, being gentle-born, just went on.)

' "Pheasant is not so good as pork," he says. "You will find some at that table if you will do me the honour to sit down. Pass him a clean plate, General." And, as true as I'm here, Boney slid a plate along just like a sulky child. He was a lanky-haired, yellow-skinned little man, as nervous as a cat – and as dangerous. I could feel that.

'You mountebank!' Boney roars. 'Turn that out'

' "And now," said Talleyrand, crossing his game leg over his sound one, "will you tell me your story?"

'I was in a fluster, but I told him nearly everything from the time he left me the five hundred dollars in Philadelphia, up to my losing ship and cargo at Le Havre. Boney began by listening, but after a bit he dropped into his own thoughts and looked at the crowd sideways through the front-room curtains. Talleyrand called to him when I'd done.

' "Eh? What we need now," says Boney, "is peace for the next three or four years."

' "Quite so," says Talleyrand. "Meantime I want the Consul's order to the Prize Court at Le Havre to restore my friend here his ship."

' "Nonsense!" says Boney. "Give away an oak-built brig of two hundred and seven tons for sentiment? Certainly not! She must be armed into my Navy with ten – no, fourteen twelve-pounders and two long fours. Is she strong enough to bear a long twelve forward?"

'Now I could ha' sworn he'd paid no heed to my talk, but that wonderful head-piece of his seemingly skimmed off every word of it that was useful to him.

' "Ah, General!" says Talleyrand. "You are a magician – a magician without morals. But the brig is undoubtedly American, and we don't want to offend them more than we have."

' "Need anybody talk about the affair?" he says. He didn't look at me, but I knew what was in his mind – just cold murder because I worried him; and he'd order it as easy as ordering his carriage.

' "You can't stop 'em," I said. "There's twenty-two other men besides me." I felt a little more 'ud set me screaming like a wired hare.

' "Undoubtedly American," Talleyrand goes on. "You would gain something if you returned the ship – with a message of fraternal good-will – published in the *Moniteur*" (that's a French paper like the Philadelphia *Aurora*).

' "A good idea!" Boney answers. "One could say much in a message."

' "It might be useful," says Talleyrand. "Shall I have the message prepared?" He wrote something in a little pocket ledger.

' "Yes – for me to embellish this evening. The *Moniteur* will publish it tonight."

' "Certainly. Sign, please," says Talleyrand, tearing the leaf out.

' "But that's the order to return the brig," says Boney. "Is that necessary? Why should I lose a good ship? Haven't I lost enough ships already?"

'Talleyrand didn't answer any of those questions. Then Boney sidled up to the table and jabs his pen into the ink. Then he shies at the paper again: "My signature alone is useless," he says. "You must have the other two Consuls as well. Sieyès and Roger Ducos must sign. We must preserve the Laws."

' "By the time my friend presents it," says Talleyrand, still looking out of window, "only one signature will be necessary."

'Boney smiles. "It's a swindle," says he, but he signed and pushed the paper across.

' "Give that to the President of the Prize Court at Le Havre," says Talleyrand, "and he will give you back your ship. I will settle for the cargo myself. You have told me how much it cost. What profit did you expect to make on it?"

'Well, then, as man to man, I was bound to warn him that I'd set out to run it into England without troubling the Revenue, and so I couldn't rightly set bounds to my profits.'

'I guessed that all along,' said Puck.

> 'There was never a Lee to Warminghurst –
> That wasn't a smuggler last and first.'

The children laughed.

'It's comical enough now,' said Pharaoh. 'But I didn't

laugh then. Says Talleyrand after a minute, "I am a bad accountant and I have several calculations on hand at present. Shall we say twice the cost of the cargo?"

'Say? I couldn't say a word. I sat choking and nodding like a China image while he wrote an order to his secretary to pay me, I won't say how much, because you wouldn't believe it.

' "Oh! Bless you, Abbe! God bless you!" I got it out at last.

' "Yes," he says, "I am a priest in spite of myself, but they call me Bishop now. Take this for my episcopal blessing," and he hands me the paper.

' "He stole all that money from me," says Boney over my shoulder. "A Bank of France is another of the things we must make. Are you mad?" he shouts at Talleyrand.

' "Quite," says Talleyrand, getting up. "But be calm. The disease will never attack you. It is called gratitude. This gentleman found me in the street and fed me when I was hungry."

' "I see; and he has made a fine scene of it and you have paid him, I suppose. Meantime, France waits."

' "Oh! poor France!" says Talleyrand. "Good-bye, Candide," he says to me. "By the way," he says, "have you yet got Red Jacket's permission to tell me what the President said to his Cabinet after Monsieur Genêt rode away?"

'I couldn't speak, I could only shake my head, and Boney – so impatient he was to go on with his doings – he ran at me and fair pushed me out of the room. And that was all there was to it.'

Pharaoh stood up and slid his fiddle into one of his big skirt-pockets as though it were a dead hare.

'Oh! but we want to know lots and lots more,' said Dan. 'How you got home – and what old Maingon said on the barge – and wasn't your cousin surprised when he had to give back the *Berthe Aurette*, and—'

'Tell us more about Toby!' cried Una.

'Yes, and Red Jacket,' said Dan.

'Won't you tell us any more?' they both pleaded.

Puck kicked the oak branch on the fire, till it sent up a column of smoke that made them sneeze. When they had finished the Shaw was empty except for old Hobden stamping through the larches.

'They gipsies have took two,' he said. "My black pullet and my liddle gingy-speckled cockrel.'

'I thought so,' said Dan, picking up one tail-feather that the old woman had overlooked.

'Which way did they go? Which way did the runagates go?' said Hobden.

'Hobby!' said Una. 'Would you like it if we told Keeper Ridley all your goings and comings?'

'POOR HONEST MEN'

Your jar of Virginny
Will cost you a guinea,
Which you reckon too much by five shilling or ten;
But light your churchwarden
And judge it accordin'
When I've told you the troubles of poor honest men.

From the Capes of the Delaware,
As you are well aware,
We sail with tobacco for England – but then
Our own British cruisers,
They watch us come through, sirs,
And they press half a score of us poor honest men.

Or if by quick sailing
(Thick weather prevailing)
We leave them behind (as we do now and then)
We are sure of a gun from
Each frigate we run from,
Which is often destruction to poor honest men!

Broadsides the Atlantic
We tumble short-handed,
With shot-holes to plug and new canvas to bend,
And off the Azores,
Dutch, Dons and Monsieurs
Are waiting to terrify poor honest men!

Napoleon's embargo
Is laid on all cargo
Which comfort or aid to King George may intend;
And since roll, twist and leaf,
Of all comforts is chief,
They try for to steal it from poor honest men!

With no heart for fight,
We take refuge in flight,
But fire as we run, our retreat to defend,
Until our stern-chasers
Cut up her fore-braces,
And she flies off the wind from us poor honest men!

Twix' the Forties and Fifties,
South-eastward the drift is,
And so, when we think we are making Land's End,
Alas, it is Ushant
With half the King's Navy,
Blockading French ports against poor honest men!

But they may not quit station
(Which is our salvation),
So swiftly we stand to the Nor'ard again;
And finding the tail of
A homeward-bound convoy,
We slip past the Scillies like poor honest men.

'Twix' the Lizard and Dover,
We hand our stuff over,
Though I may not inform how we do it, nor when;
But a light on each quarter
Low down on the water
Is well understanded by poor honest men.

Even then we have dangers
From meddlesome strangers,
Who spy on our business and are not content
To take a smooth answer,
Except with a handspike . . .
And they say they are murdered by poor honest men!

To be drowned or be shot
Is our natural lot,
Why should we, moreover, be hanged in the end –
After all our great pains
For to dangle in chains,
As though we were smugglers, not poor honest men?

The Conversion of St Wilfrid

EDDI'S SERVICE

Eddi, priest of St Wilfrid
  In the chapel at Manhood End,
Ordered a midnight service
  For such as cared to attend.

But the Saxons were keeping Christmas,
  And the night was stormy as well.
Nobody came to service
  Though Eddi rang the bell.

'Wicked weather for walking,'
  Said Eddi of Manhood End.
'But I must go on with the service
  For such as care to attend.'

The altar candles were lighted, –
  An old marsh donkey came,
Bold as a guest invited,
  And stared at the guttering flame.

The storm beat on at the windows,
  The water splashed on the floor,
And a wet yoke-weary bullock
  Pushed in through the open door.

'How do I know what is greatest,
  How do I know what is least?
That is My Father's business,'
  Said Eddi, Wilfrid's priest.

'But, three are gathered together –
  Listen to me and attend.
I bring good news, my brethren!'
  Said Eddi, of Manhood End.

And he told the Ox of a manger
    And a stall in Bethlehem,
And he spoke to the Ass of a Rider
    That rode to Jerusalem.

They steamed and dripped in the chancel,
    They listened and never stirred,
While, just as though they were Bishops,
    Eddi preached them The Word.

Till the gale blew off on the marshes
    And the windows showed the day,
And the Ox and the Ass together
    Wheeled and clattered away.

And when the Saxons mocked him,
    Said Eddi of Manhood End,
'I dare not shut His chapel
    On such as care to attend.'

The Conversion of St Wilfrid

THEY had bought peppermints up at the village, and were coming home past little St Barnabas' Church, when they saw Jimmy Kidbrooke, the carpenter's baby, kicking at the churchyard gate, with a shaving in his mouth and the tears running down his cheeks.

Una pulled out the shaving and put in a peppermint. Jimmy said he was looking for his grand-daddy – he never seemed to take much notice of his father – so they went up between the old graves, under the leaf-dropping limes, to the porch, where Jim trotted in, looked about the empty Church, and screamed like a gate-hinge.

Young Sam Kidbrooke's voice came from the bell-tower and made them jump.

'Why, Jimmy,' he called, 'what are you doin' here? Fetch him, Father!'

Old Mr Kidbrooke stumped downstairs, jerked Jimmy on to his shoulder, stared at the children beneath his brass spectacles, and stumped back again. They laughed: it was so exactly like Mr Kidbrooke.

'It's all right,' Una called up the stairs. 'We found him, Sam. Does his mother know?'

'He's come off by himself. She'll be justabout crazy,' Sam answered.

'Then I'll run down street and tell her.' Una darted off.

'Thank you, Miss Una. Would you like to see how we're mendin' the bell-beams, Mus' Dan?'

Dan hopped up, and saw young Sam lying on his stomach in a most delightful place among beams and ropes, close to the five great bells. Old Mr Kidbrooke on the floor beneath was planing a piece of wood, and Jimmy was eating the shavings as fast as they came away. He never looked at

Jimmy; Jimmy never stopped eating; and the broad gilt-bobbed pendulum of the church clock never stopped swinging across the white-washed wall of the tower.

Dan winked through the sawdust that fell on his upturned face. 'Ring a bell,' he called.

'I mustn't do that, but I'll buzz one of 'em a bit for you,' said Sam. He pounded on the sound-bow of the biggest bell, and waked a hollow groaning boom that ran up and down the tower like creepy feelings down your back. Just when it almost began to hurt, it died away in a hurry of beautiful sorrowful cries, like a wine-glass rubbed with a wet finger. The pendulum clanked – one loud clank to each silent swing.

Dan heard Una return from Mrs Kidbrooke's, and ran down to fetch her. She was standing by the font staring at some one who kneeled at the Altar-rail.

'Is that the Lady who practises the organ?' she whispered.

'No. She's gone into the organ-place. Besides, she wears black,' Dan replied.

The figure rose and came down the nave. It was a white-haired man in a long white gown with a sort of scarf looped low on the neck, one end hanging over his shoulder. His loose long sleeves were embroidered with gold, and a deep strip of gold embroidery waved and sparkled round the hem of his gown.

'Go and meet him,' said Puck's voice behind the font. 'It's only Wilfrid.'

'Wilfrid who?' said Dan. 'You come along too.'

'Wilfrid – Saint of Sussex, and Archbishop of York. *I* shall wait till he asks me.' He waved them forward. Their feet squeaked on the old grave-slabs in the centre aisle. The Archbishop raised one hand with a pink ring on it, and said something in Latin. He was very handsome, and his thin face looked almost as silvery as his thin circle of hair.

'Are you alone?' he asked.

'Puck's here, of course,' said Una. 'Do you know him?'

'I know him better now than I used to.' He beckoned over

Dan's shoulder, and spoke again in Latin. Puck pattered forward, holding himself as straight as an arrow. The Archbishop smiled.

'Be welcome,' said he. 'Be very welcome.'

'Welcome to you also, O Prince of the church,' Puck replied. The Archbishop bowed his head and passed on, till he glimmered like a white moth in the shadow by the font.

'He does look awfully princely,' said Una. 'Isn't he coming back?'

'Oh yes. He's only looking over the church. He's very fond of churches,' said Puck. 'What's that?'

The Lady who practises the organ was speaking to the blower-boy behind the organ-screen. 'We can't very well talk here,' Puck whispered. 'Let's go to Panama Corner.'

He led them to the end of the south aisle, where there is a slab of iron which says in queer, long-tailed letters: *Orate p. annema Jhone Coline*. The children always called it Panama Corner.

The Archbishop moved slowly about the little church, peering at the old memorial tablets and the new glass windows. The Lady who practises the organ began to pull out stops and rustle hymn-books behind the screen.

'I hope she'll do all the soft lacey tunes – like treacle on porridge,' said Una.

'I like the trumpety ones best,' said Dan. 'Oh, look at Wilfrid! He's trying to shut the Altar-gates!'

'Tell him he mustn't,' said Puck, quite seriously.

'He can't, anyhow,' Dan muttered, and tiptoed out of Panama Corner while the Archbishop patted and patted at the carved gates that always sprang open again beneath his hand.

'That's no use, sir,' Dan whispered. 'Old Mr Kidbrooke says Altar-gates are just *the* one pair of gates which no man can shut. He made 'em so himself.'

The Archbishop's blue eyes twinkled. Dan saw that he knew all about it.

'I beg your pardon,' Dan stammered – very angry with Puck.

'Yes, I know! He made them so Himself.' The Archbishop smiled, and crossed to Panama Corner, where Una dragged up a certain padded arm-chair for him to sit on.

The organ played softly. 'What does that music say?' he asked.

Una dropped into the chant without thinking: ' "O all ye works of the Lord, bless ye the Lord; praise him and magnify him for ever." We call it the Noah's Ark, because it's all lists of things – beasts and birds and whales, you know.'

'Whales?' said the Archbishop quickly.

'Yes – "O ye whales, and all that move in the waters," ' Una hummed – ' "Bless ye the Lord." It sounds like a wave turning over, doesn't it?'

'Holy Father,' said Puck with a demure face, 'is a little seal also "one who moves in the water"?'

'Eh? Oh yes – yess!' he laughed. 'A seal moves wonderfully in the waters. Do the seal come to my island still?'

Puck shook his head. 'All those little islands have been swept away.'

'Very possible. The tides ran fiercely down there. Do you know the land of the Sea-calf, maiden?'

'No – but we've seen seals – at Brighton.'

'The Archbishop is thinking of a little farther down the coast. He means Seal's Eye – Selsey – down Chichester way – where he converted the South Saxons,' Puck explained.

'Yes – yess; if the South Saxons did not convert me,' said the Archbishop, smiling. 'The first time I was wrecked was on that coast. As our ship took ground and we tried to push her off, an old fat fellow of a seal, I remember, reared breast-high out of the water, and scratched his head with his flipper as if he were saying: "What *does* that excited person with the pole think he is doing?" I was very wet and miserable, but I could not help laughing, till the natives came down and attacked us.'

'What did you do?' Dan asked.

'One couldn't very well go back to France, so one tried to make them go back to the shore. All the South Saxons are born wreckers, like my own Northumbrian folk. I was bringing over a few things for my old church at York, and some of the natives laid hands on them, and – and I'm afraid I lost my temper.'

'It is said—' Puck's voice was wickedly meek – 'that there was a great fight.'

'Eh, but I must ha' been a silly lad.' Wilfrid spoke with a sudden thick burr in his voice. He coughed, and took up his silvery tones again. 'There was no fight really. My men thumped a few of them, but the tide rose half an hour before its time, with a strong wind, and we backed off. What I wanted to say, though, was, that the seas about us were full of sleek seals watching the scuffle. My good Eddi – my chaplain – insisted that they were demons. Yes – yess! That was my first acquaintance with the South Saxons and their seals.'

'But not the only time you were wrecked, was it?' said Dan.

'Alas, no! On sea and land my life seems to have been one long shipwreck.' He looked at the Jhone Coline slab as old Hobden sometimes looks into the fire. 'Ah, well!'

'But did you ever have any more adventures among the seals?' said Una, after a little.

'Oh, the seals! I beg your pardon. They are the important things. Yes – yess! I went back to the South Saxons after twelve – fifteen – years. No, I did not come by water, but overland from my own Northumbria, to see what I could do. It's little one *can* do with that class of native except make them stop killing each other and themselves—'

'Why did they kill themselves?' Una asked, her chin in her hand.

'Because they were heathen. When they grew tired of life (as if *they* were the only people!) they would jump into the sea. They called it going to Wotan. It wasn't want of food always – by any means. A man would tell you that he felt grey in the heart, or a woman would say that she saw nothing but long days in front of her; and they'd saunter away to the mud-flats and – that would be the end of them, poor souls, unless one headed them off! One had to run quick, but one can't allow people to lay hands on themselves because they happen to feel grey. Yes – yess – Extraordinary people, the South Saxons. Disheartening, sometimes. . . . What does that say now?' The organ had changed tune again.

'Only a hymn for next Sunday,' said Una. ' "The Church's One Foundation." Go on, please, about running over the mud. I should like to have seen you.'

'I dare say you would, and I really *could* run in those days. Ethelwalch the King gave me some five or six muddy parishes by the sea, and the first time my good Eddi and I rode there we saw a man slouching along the slob, among the seals at Manhood End. My good Eddi disliked seals – but he swallowed his objections and ran like a hare.'

'Why?' said Dan.

'For the same reason that I did. We thought it was one of our people going to drown himself. As a matter of fact, Eddi and I were nearly drowned in the pools before we overtook him. To cut a long story short, we found ourselves very muddy, very breathless, being quietly made fun of in good Latin by a very well-spoken person. No – he'd no idea of going to Wotan. He was fishing on his own beaches, and he showed us the beacons and turf-heaps that divided his lands from the church property. He took us to his own house, gave us a good dinner, some more than good wine, sent a guide with us into Chichester, and became one of my best and most refreshing friends. He was a Meon by descent, from the west edge of the kingdom; a scholar educated, curiously enough, at Lyons, my old school; had travelled the world over, even to Rome, and was a brilliant talker. We found we had scores of acquaintances in common. It seemed he was a small chief under King Ethelwalch, and I fancy the King was somewhat afraid of him. The South Saxons mistrust a man who talks too well. Ah! *Now*, I've left out the very point of my story. He kept a great grey-muzzled old dog-seal that he had brought up from a pup. He called it Padda – after one of my clergy. It *was* rather like fat, honest old Padda. The creature followed him everywhere, and nearly knocked down my good Eddi when we first met him. Eddi loathed it. It used to sniff at his thin legs and cough at him. I can't say I ever took much notice of it (I was not fond of animals), till one day Eddi came to me with a circumstantial account of some witchcraft that Meon worked. He would tell the seal to go down to the beach the last thing at night, and bring him word of the weather. When it came back, Meon might say to his slaves, "Padda thinks we shall have wind tomorrow. Haul up the boats!" I spoke to Meon casually about the story, and he laughed.

'He told me he could judge by the look of the creature's coat and the way it sniffed what weather was brewing. Quite possible. One need not put down everything one does not understand to the work of bad spirits – or good ones, for that matter.' He nodded towards Puck, who nodded gaily in return.

'I say so,' he went on, 'because to a certain extent I have been made a victim of that habit of mind. Some while after I was settled at Selsey, King Ethelwalch and Queen Ebba ordered their people to be baptized. I fear I'm too old to believe that a whole nation can change its heart at the King's command, and I had a shrewd suspicion that their real motive was to get a good harvest. No rain had fallen for two or three years, but as soon as we had finished baptizing, it fell heavily, and they all said it was a miracle.'

'And was it?' Dan asked.

'Everything in life is a miracle, but' – the Archbishop twisted the heavy ring on his finger – 'I should be slow – ve-ry slow should I be – to assume that a certain sort of miracle happens whenever lazy and improvident people say they are going to turn over a new leaf if they are paid for it. My friend Meon had sent his slaves to the font, but he had not come himself, so the next time I rode over – to return a manuscript – I took the liberty of asking why. He was perfectly open about it. He looked on the King's action as a heathen attempt to curry favour with the Christians' God through me the Archbishop, and he would have none of it. "My dear man," I said, "admitting that that is the case, surely you, as an educated person, don't believe in Wotan and all the other hobgoblins any more than Padda here?" The old seal was hunched up on his ox-hide behind his master's chair.

' "Even if I don't," he said, "why should I insult the memory of my fathers' Gods? I have sent you a hundred and three of my rascals to christen. Isn't that enough?"

' "By no means," I answered. "I want *you*."

' "He wants us! What do you think of that, Padda?" He pulled the seal's whiskers till it threw back its head and roared, and he pretended to interpret. "No! Padda says he won't be baptized yet awhile. He says you'll stay to dinner and come fishing with me tomorrow, because you're overworked and need a rest."

' "I wish you'd keep yon brute in its proper place," I said, and Eddi, my chaplain, agreed.

' "I do," said Meon. "I keep him just next my heart. He can't tell a lie, and he doesn't know how to love any one except me. It 'ud be the same if I were dying on a mud-bank, wouldn't it, Padda?"

' "Augh! Augh!" said Padda, and put up his head to be scratched.

'Then Meon began to tease Eddi: "Padda says, if Eddi saw his Archbishop dying on a mud-bank Eddi would tuck up his gown and run. Padda knows Eddi can run too! Padda came into Wittering Church last Sunday – all wet – to hear the music, and Eddi ran out."

'My good Eddi rubbed his hands and his shins together, and flushed. "Padda is a child of the Devil, who is the father of lies!" he cried, and begged my pardon for having spoken. I forgave him.

' "Yes. You are just about stupid enough for a musician,"
said Meon. "But here he is. Sing a hymn to him, and see if
he can stand it. You'll find my small harp beside the fire-
place."

'Eddi, who is really an excellent musician, played and
sang for quite half an hour. Padda shuffled off his ox-hide,
hunched himself on his flippers before him, and listened with
his head thrown back. Yes – yess! A rather funny sight!
Meon tried not to laugh, and asked Eddi if he were satisfied.

'It takes some time to get an idea out of my good Eddi's
head. He looked at me.

' "Do you want to sprinkle him with holy water, and see if
he flies up the chimney? Why not baptize him?" said Meon.

'Eddi was really shocked. I thought it was bad taste
myself.

' "That's not fair," said Meon. "You call him a demon
and a familiar spirit because he loves his master and likes
music, and when I offer you a chance to prove it you won't
take it. Look here! I'll make a bargain. I'll be baptized if
you'll baptize Padda too. He's more of a man than most of
my slaves."

' "One doesn't bargain – or joke – about these matters," I
said. He was going altogether too far.

' "Quite right," said Meon; "I shouldn't like any one to
joke about Padda. Padda, go down to the beach and bring
us tomorrow's weather!"

'My good Eddi must have been a little over-tired with his
day's work. "I am a servant of the church," he cried. "My
business is to save souls, not to enter into fellowships and
understandings with accursed beasts."

' "Have it your own narrow way," said Meon. "Padda,
you needn't go." The old fellow flounced back to his ox-hide
at once.

' "Man could learn obedience at least from that creature,"
said Eddi, a little ashamed of himself. Christians should not
curse.

' "Don't begin to apologise just when I am beginning to

like you," said Meon. "We'll leave Padda behind tomorrow – out of respect to your feelings. Now let's go to supper. We must be up early tomorrow for the whiting."

'The next was a beautiful crisp autumn morning – a weather-breeder, if I had taken the trouble to think; but it's refreshing to escape from kings and converts for half a day. We three went by ourselves in Meon's smallest boat, and we got on the whiting near an old wreck, a mile or so off shore. Meon knew the marks to a yard, and the fish were keen. Yes – yess! A perfect morning's fishing! If a Bishop can't be a fisherman, who can?' He twiddled his ring again. 'We stayed there a little too long, and while we were getting up our stone, down came the fog. After some discussion, we decided to row for the land. The ebb was just beginning to make round the point, and sent us all ways at once like a coracle.'

'Selsey Bill,' said Puck under his breath. 'The tides run something furious there.'

'I believe you,' said the Archbishop. 'Meon and I have spent a good many evenings arguing as to where exactly we drifted. All I know is we found ourselves in a little rocky cove that had sprung up round us out of the fog, and a swell lifted the boat on to a ledge, and she broke up beneath our feet. We had just time to shuffle through the weed before the next wave. The sea was rising.

' "It's rather a pity we didn't let Padda go down to the beach last night," said Meon. "He might have warned us this was coming."

' "Better fall into the hands of God than the hands of demons," said Eddi, and his teeth chattered as he prayed. A nor'-west breeze had just got up – distinctly cool.

' "Save what you can of the boat," said Meon; "we may need it," and we had to drench ourselves again, fishing out stray planks.'

'What for?' said Dan.

'For firewood. We did not know when we should get off. Eddi had flint and steel, and we found dry fuel in the old gulls' nests and lit a fire. It smoked abominably, and we guarded it with boat-planks up-ended between the rocks. One gets used to that sort of thing if one travels. Unluckily I'm not so strong as I was. I fear I must have been a trouble to my friends. It was blowing a full gale before midnight. Eddi wrung out his cloak, and tried to wrap me in it, but I ordered him on his obedience to keep it. However, he held me in his arms all the first night, and Meon begged his pardon for what he'd said the night before – about Eddi running away if he found me on a sandbank, you remember.

' "You are right in half your prophecy," said Eddi. "I have tucked up my gown, at any rate." (The wind had blown it over his head.) "Now let us thank God for His mercies."

' "Hum!" said Meon. "If this gale lasts, we stand a very fair chance of dying of starvation."

' "If it be God's will that we live, God will provide," said Eddi. "At least help me to sing to Him." The wind almost whipped the words out of his mouth, but he braced himself against a rock and sang psalms.

'I'm glad I never concealed my opinion – from myself – that Eddi was a better man than I. Yet I have worked hard in my time – very hard! Yes – yess! So the morning and the evening were our second day on that islet. There was rain-water in the rock-pools, and, as a churchman, I knew how to fast, but I admit we were hungry. Meon fed our fire chip by chip to eke it out, and they made me sit over it, the dear fellows, when I was too weak to object. Meon held me in his arms the second night, just like a child. My good Eddi was a little out of his senses, and imagined himself teaching a York choir to sing. Even so, he was beautifully patient with them.

'I heard Meon whisper, "If this keeps up we shall go to our Gods. I wonder what Wotan will say to me. He must know I don't believe in him. On the other hand, I can't do what Ethelwalch finds so easy – curry favour with your God at the last minute, in the hope of being saved – as you call it. How do you advise, Bishop?"

' "My dear man," I said, "if that is your honest belief, I

take it upon myself to say you had far better not curry favour with any God. But if it's only your Jutish pride that holds you back, lift me up, and I'll baptize you even now."

' "Lie still," said Meon. "I could judge better if I were in my own hall. But to desert one's fathers' Gods – even if one doesn't believe in them – in the middle of a gale, isn't quite – What would you do yourself?"

'I was lying in his arms, kept alive by the warmth of his big, steady heart. It did not seem to me the time or the place for subtle arguments, so I answered, "No, I certainly should not desert my God." I don't see even now what else I could have said.

' "Thank you. I'll remember that, if I live," said Meon, and I must have drifted back to my dreams about Northumbria and beautiful France, for it was broad daylight when I heard him calling on Wotan in that high, shaking heathen yell that I detest so.

' "Lie quiet. I'm giving Wotan his chance," he said. Our dear Eddi ambled up, still beating time to his imaginary choir.

' "Yes. Call on your Gods," he cried, "and see what gifts they will send you. They are gone on a journey, or they are hunting."

'I assure you the words were not out of his mouth when old Padda shot from the top of a cold wrinkled swell, drove himself over the weedy ledge, and landed fair in our laps with a rock-cod between his teeth. I could not help smiling at Eddi's face. "A miracle! A miracle!" he cried, and kneeled down to clean the cod.

' "You've been a long time winding us, my son," said Meon. "Now fish – fish for all our lives. We're starving, Padda."

'The old fellow flung himself quivering like a salmon backward into the boil of the currents round the rocks, and Meon said, "We're safe. I'll send him to fetch help when this wind drops. Eat and be thankful."

'I never tasted anything so good as those rock-codlings we

'A miracle! A miracle!' he cried

took from Padda's mouth and half roasted over the fire. Between his plunges Padda would hunch up and purr over Meon with the tears running down his face. I never knew before that seals could weep for joy – as I have wept.

'"Surely," said Eddi, with his mouth full, "God has made the seal the loveliest of His creatures in the water. Look how Padda breasts the current! He stands up against it like a rock; now watch the chain of bubbles where he dives; and now – there is his wise head under that rock-ledge! Oh, a blessing be on thee, my little brother Padda!"

'"You *said* he was a child of the Devil!" Meon laughed.

'"There I sinned," poor Eddi answered. "Call him here, and I will ask his pardon. God sent him out of the storm to humble me, a fool."

'"I won't ask you to enter into fellowships and understandings with any accursed brute," said Meon, rather unkindly. "Shall we say he was sent to our Bishop as the ravens were sent to your prophet Elijah?"

'"Doubtless that is so," said Eddi. "I will write it so if I live to get home."

'"No – no!" I said. "Let us three poor men kneel and thank God for His mercies."

'We kneeled, and old Padda shuffled up and thrust his head under Meon's elbows. I laid my hand upon it and blessed him. So did Eddi.

'"And now, my son," I said to Meon, "shall I baptize thee?"

'"Not yet," said he. "Wait till we are well ashore and at home. No God in any Heaven shall say that I came to him or left him because I was wet and cold. I will send Padda to my people for a boat. Is that witchcraft, Eddi?"

'"Why, no. Surely Padda will go and pull them to the beach by the skirts of their gowns as he pulled me in Wittering Church to ask me to sing. Only then I was afraid, and did not understand," said Eddi.

'"You are understanding now," said Meon, and at a wave of his arm off went Padda to the mainland, making a wake like a war-boat till we lost him in the rain. Meon's people could not bring a boat across for some hours; even so it was ticklish work among the rocks in that tideway. But they hoisted me aboard, too stiff to move, and Padda swam behind us, barking and turning somersaults all the way to Manhood End!'

'Good old Padda!' murmured Dan.

'When we were quite rested and re-clothed, and his people had been summoned – not an hour before – Meon offered himself to be baptized.'

'Was Padda baptized too?' Una asked.

'No, that was only Meon's joke. But he sat blinking on his ox-hide in the middle of the hall. When Eddi (who thought I wasn't looking) made a little cross in holy water on his wet muzzle, he kissed Eddi's hand. A week before Eddi wouldn't have touched him. *That* was a miracle, if you like! But seriously, I was more glad than I can tell you to get Meon. A rare and splendid soul that never looked back – never looked back!' The Archbishop half closed his eyes.

'But, sir,' said Puck, most respectfully, 'haven't you left out what Meon said afterwards?' Before the Bishop could speak he turned to the children and went on: 'Meon called all his fishers and ploughmen and herdsmen into the hall and he said: "Listen, men! Two days ago I asked our Bishop whether it was fair for a man to desert his fathers' Gods in a time of danger. Our Bishop said it was not fair. You needn't shout like that, because you are all Christians now. My red war-boat's crew will remember how near we all were to death when Padda fetched them over to the Bishop's islet. You can tell your mates that even in that place, at that time, hanging on the wet, weedy edge of death, our Bishop, a Christian, counselled me, a heathen, to stand by my fathers' Gods. I tell you now that a faith which takes care that every man shall keep faith, even though he may save his soul by breaking faith, is the faith for a man to believe in. So I believe in the Christian God, and in Wilfrid His Bishop, and in the Church that Wilfrid rules. You have been baptized

once by the King's orders. I shall not have you baptized
again; but if I find any more old women being sent to
Wotan, or any girls dancing on the sly before Balder, or any
men talking about Thun or Lok or the rest, I will teach you
with my own hands how to keep faith with the Christian
God. Go out quietly; you'll find a couple of beefs on the
beach." Then of course they shouted "Hurrah!" which
meant "Thor help us!" and – I think you laughed, sir?'

'I think you remember it all too well,' said the Archbishop,
smiling. 'It was a joyful day for me. I had learned a great
deal on that rock where Padda found us. Yes – yess! One
should deal kindly with all the creatures of God, and gently
with their masters. But one learns late.'

He rose, and his gold-embroidered sleeves rustled thickly.
The organ clacked and took deep breaths.

'Wait a minute,' Dan whispered. 'She's going to do the
trumpety one. It takes all the wind you can pump. It's in
Latin, sir.'

'There is no other tongue,' the Archbishop answered.

'It's not a real hymn,' Una explained. 'She does it as a
treat after her exercises. She isn't a real organist, you know.
She just comes down here sometimes, from the Albert Hall.'

'Oh, what a miracle of a voice!' said the Archbishop.

It rang out suddenly from a dark arch of lonely noises –
every word spoken to the very end:

> 'Dies Irae, dies illa,
>   Solvet saeclum in favilla,
>   Teste David cum Sibylla.'

The Archbishop caught his breath and moved forward.

The music carried on by itself a while.

'Now it's calling all the light out of the windows,' Una
whispered to Dan.

'I think it's more like a horse neighing in battle,' he
whispered back. The voice cried:

> 'Tuba mirum spargens sonum
>   Per sepulchra regionum.'

Deeper and deeper the organ dived down, but far below its deepest note they heard Puck's voice joining in the last line:

'Coget omnes ante thronum.'

As they looked in wonder, for it sounded like the dull jar of one of the very pillars shifting, the little fellow turned and went out through the south door.

'Now's the sorrowful part, but it's very beautiful.' Una found herself speaking to the empty chair in front of her.

'What are you doing that for?' Dan said behind her. 'You spoke so politely too.'

'I don't know . . . I thought . . .' said Una. 'Funny!'

' 'Tisn't. It's the part you like best,' Dan grunted.

The music had turned soft – full of little sounds that chased each other on wings across the broad gentle flood of the main tune. But the voice was ten times lovelier than the music.

'Recordare Jesu pie,
Quod sum causa Tuae viae,
Ne me perdas illâ die!'

There was no more. They moved out into the centre aisle.

' 'That you?' the Lady called as she shut the lid. 'I thought I heard you, and I played it on purpose.'

'Thank you awfully,' said Dan. 'We hoped you would, so we waited. Come on, Una, it's pretty nearly dinner-time.'

SONG OF THE RED WAR-BOAT

Shove off from the wharf-edge! Steady!
   Watch for a smooth! Give way!
If she feels the lop already
   She'll stand on her head in the bay.
It's ebb – it's dusk – it's blowing,
   The shoals are a mile of white,
But (snatch her along!) we're going
   To find our master tonight.

      For we hold that in all disaster
         Of shipwreck, storm, or sword,
      A man must stand by his master
         When once he has pledged his word!

Raging seas have we rowed in,
   But we seldom saw them thus;
Our master is angry with Odin –
   Odin is angry with us!
Heavy odds have we taken,
   But never before such odds.
The Gods know they are forsaken,
   We must risk the wrath of the Gods!

Over the crest she flies from,
   Into its hollow she drops,
Crouches and clears her eyes from
   The wind-torn breaker-tops,
Ere out on the shrieking shoulder
   Of a hill-high surge she drives.
Meet her! Meet her and hold her!
   Pull for your scoundrel lives!

The thunders bellow and clamour
   The harm that they mean to do;
There goes Thor's Own Hammer
   Cracking the dark in two!

Close! But the blow has missed her,
  Here comes the wind of the blow!
Row or the squall'll twist her
  Broadside on to it! – *Row!*

Hearken, Thor of the Thunder!
  We are not here for a jest –
For wager, warfare, or plunder,
  Or to put your power to test.
This work is none of our wishing –
  We would stay at home if we might –
But our master is wrecked out fishing,
  We go to find him tonight.

    For we hold that in all disaster –
      As the Gods Themselves have said –
    A man must stand by his master
      Till one of the two is dead.

That is our way of thinking,
  Now you can do as you will,
While we try to save her from sinking,
  And hold her head to it still.
Bale her and keep her moving,
  Or she'll break her back in the trough . . .
Who said the weather's improving,
  And the swells are taking off?

Sodden, and chafed and aching,
  Gone in the loins and knees –
No matter – the day is breaking,
  And there's far less weight to the seas!
Up mast, and finish baling –
  In oars, and out with the mead –
The rest will be two-reef sailing . . .
  That was a night indeed!

    But we hold that in all disaster
      (And faith, we have found it true!)
    If only you stand by your master,
      The Gods will stand by you!

A Doctor of Medicine

AN ASTROLOGER'S SONG

To the Heavens above us
   Oh, look and behold
The planets that love us
   All harnessed in gold!
What chariots, what horses,
   Against us shall bide
While the Stars in their courses
   Do fight on our side?

All thought, all desires,
   That are under the sun,
Are one with their fires,
   As we also are one;
All matter, all spirit,
   All fashion, all frame,
Receive and inherit
   Their strength from the same.

(Oh, man that deniest
   All power save thine own,
Their power in the highest
   Is mightily shown.
Not less in the lowest
   That power is made clear.
Oh, man, if thou knowest,
   What treasure is here!)

Earth quakes in her throes
   And we wonder for why!
But the blind planet knows
   When her ruler is nigh;
And, attuned since Creation,
   To perfect accord,
She thrills in her station
   And yearns to her Lord.

The waters have risen,
   The springs are unbound –
The floods break their prison,
   And ravin around.
No rampart withstands 'em,
   Their fury will last,
Till the Sign that commands 'em
   Sinks low or swings past.

Through abysses unproven,
   And gulfs beyond thought,
Our portion is woven,
   Our burden is brought.
Yet They that prepare it,
   Whose Nature we share,
Make us who must bear it
   Well able to bear.

Though terrors o'ertake us
   We'll not be afraid,
No Power can unmake us
   Save that which has made.
Nor yet beyond reason
   Nor hope shall we fall –
All things have their season,
   And Mercy crowns all.

Then, doubt not, ye fearful –
   The Eternal is King –
Up, heart, and be cheerful,
   And lustily sing:
What chariots, what horses,
   Against us shall bide
While the Stars in their courses
   Do fight on our side?

A Doctor of Medicine

THEY were playing hide-and-seek with bicycle lamps after tea. Dan had hung his lamp on the apple tree at the end of the hellebore bed in the walled garden, and was crouched by the gooseberry bushes ready to dash off when Una should spy him. He saw her lamp come into the garden and disappear as she hid it under her cloak. While he listened for her footsteps, somebody (they both thought it was Phillips the gardener) coughed in the corner of the herb-beds.

'All right,' Una shouted across the asparagus; 'we aren't hurting your old beds, Phippsey!'

She flashed her lantern towards the spot, and in its circle of light they saw a Guy Fawkes-looking man in a black cloak and a steeple-crowned hat, walking down the path beside Puck. They ran to meet him, and the man said something to them about *rooms* in their head. After a time they understood he was warning them not to catch colds.

'You've a bit of a cold yourself, haven't you?' said Una, for he ended all his sentences with a consequential cough. Puck laughed.

'Child,' the man answered, 'if it hath pleased Heaven to afflict me with an infirmity—'

'Nay, nay,' Puck struck in, 'the maid spoke out of kindness. *I* know that half your cough is but a catch to trick the vulgar; and that's a pity. There's honesty enough in you, Nick, without rasping and hawking.'

'Good people' – the man shrugged his lean shoulders – 'the vulgar crowd love not truth unadorned. Wherefore we philosophers must needs dress her to catch their eye or – ahem! – their ear.'

'And what d'you think of *that*?' said Puck solemnly to Dan.

'I don't know,' he answered. 'It sounds like lessons.'

'Ah – well! There have been worse men than Nick Culpeper to take lessons from. Now, where can we sit that's not indoors?'

'In the hay-mow, next to old Middenboro,' Dan suggested. '*He* doesn't mind.'

'Eh?' Mr Culpeper was stooping over the pale hellebore blooms by the light of Una's lamp. 'Does Master Middenboro need my poor services, then?'

'Save him, no!' said Puck. 'He is but a horse – next door to an ass, as you'll see presently. Come!'

Their shadows jumped and slid on the fruit-tree walls. They filed out of the garden by the snoring pig-pound and the crooning hen-house, to the shed where Middenboro the old lawn-mower pony lives. His friendly eyes showed green in the light as they set their lamps down on the chickens' drinking-trough outside, and pushed past to the hay-mow. Mr Culpeper stooped at the door.

'Mind where you lie,' said Dan. 'This hay's full of hedge-brishings.'

'In! in!' said Puck. 'You've lain in fouler places than this, Nick. Ah! Let us keep touch with the stars!' He kicked open the top of the half-door, and pointed to the clear sky. 'There be the planets you conjure with! What does your wisdom make of that wandering and variable star behind those apple boughs?'

The children smiled. A bicycle that they knew well was being walked down the steep lane.

'Where?' Mr Culpeper leaned forward quickly. 'That? Some countryman's lantern.'

'Wrong, Nick,' said Puck. ' 'Tis a singular bright star in Virgo, declining towards the house of Aquarius the water-carrier, who hath lately been afflicted by Gemini. Aren't I right, Una?'

Mr Culpeper snorted contemptuously.

'No. It's the village nurse going down to the Mill about some fresh twins that came there last week. Nurse,' Una called, as the light stopped on the flat, 'when can I see the Morris twins? And how are they?'

'Next Sunday, perhaps. Doing beautifully,' the Nurse called back, and with a *ping-ping-ping* of the bell brushed round the corner.

'Her uncle's a vetinary surgeon near Banbury,' Una explained, 'and if you ring her bell at night, it rings right beside her bed – not downstairs at all. Then she jumps up – she always keeps a pair of dry boots in the fender, you know – and goes anywhere she's wanted. We help her bicycle through gaps sometimes. Most of her babies do beautifully. She told us so herself.'

'I doubt not, then, that she reads in my books,' said Mr Culpeper quietly. 'Twins at the Mill!' he muttered half aloud. ' "And again He sayeth, Return, ye children of men." '

'Are you a doctor or a rector?' Una asked, and Puck with a shout turned head over heels in the hay. But Mr Culpeper was quite serious. He told them that he was a physician-astrologer – a doctor who knew all about the stars as well as all about herbs for medicine. He said that the sun, the moon, and five Planets, called Jupiter, Mars, Mercury, Saturn, and Venus, governed everybody and everything in the world. They all lived in Houses – he mapped out some of them against the dark with a busy forefinger – and they moved from House to House like pieces at draughts; and they went loving and hating each other all over the skies. If you knew their likes and dislikes, he said, you could make them cure your patient and hurt your enemy, and find out the secret causes of things. He talked of these five Planets as though they belonged to him, or as though he were playing long games against them. The children burrowed in the hay up to their chins, and looked out over the half-door at the solemn, star-powdered sky till they seemed to be falling upside down into it, while Mr Culpeper talked about 'trines' and 'oppositions' and 'conjunctions' and 'sympathies' and 'antipathies' in a tone that just matched things.

A rat ran between Middenboro's feet, and the old pony stamped.

'Mid hates rats,' said Dan, and passed him over a lock of hay. 'I wonder why.'

'Divine Astrology tells us,' said Mr Culpeper. 'The horse, being a martial beast that beareth man to battle, belongs naturally to the red planet Mars – the Lord of War. I would show you him, but he's too near his setting. Rats and mice, doing their businesses by night, come under the dominion of our Lady the Moon. Now between Mars and Luna, the one red, t'other white, the one hot, t'other cold and so forth, stands, as I have told you, a natural antipathy, or, as you say, hatred. Which antipathy their creatures do inherit. Whence, good people, you may both see and hear your cattle stamp in their stalls for the self-same causes as decree the passages of the stars across the unalterable face of Heaven! Ahem!'

Puck lay along chewing a leaf. They felt him shake with laughter, and Mr Culpeper sat up stiffly.

'I myself,' said he, 'have saved men's lives, and not a few neither, by observing at the proper time – there is a time, mark you, for all things under the sun – by observing, I say, so small a beast as a rat in conjunction with so great a matter as this dread arch above us.' He swept his hand across the sky. 'Yet there are those,' he went on sourly, 'who have years without knowledge.'

'Right,' said Puck. 'No fool like an old fool.'

Mr Culpeper wrapped his cloak round him and sat still while the children stared at the Great Bear on the hill-top.

'Give him time,' Puck whispered behind his hand. 'He turns like a timber-tug – all of a piece.'

'Ahem!' Mr Culpeper said suddenly. 'I'll prove it to you. When I was physician to Saye's Horse, and fought the King – or rather the man Charles Stuart – in Oxfordshire (I had *my* learning at Cambridge), the plague was very hot all around us. I saw it at close hands. He who says I am ignorant of the plague, for example, is altogether beside the bridge.'

'We grant it,' said Puck solemnly. 'But why talk of the plague this rare night?'

'To prove my argument. This Oxfordshire plague, good people, being generated among rivers and ditches, was of a werish, watery nature. Therefore it was curable by drenching the patient in cold water, and laying him in wet cloths; or at least, so I cured some of them. Mark this. It bears on what shall come after.'

'Mark also, Nick,' said Puck, 'that we are not your College of Physicians, but only a lad and a lass and a poor lubberkin. Therefore be plain, old Hyssop on the Wall!'

'To be plain and in order with you, I was shot in the chest while gathering of betony from a brookside near Thame, and was took by the King's men before their Colonel, one Blagg or Bragge, whom I warned honestly that I had spent the week past among our plague-stricken. He flung me off into a cowshed, much like this here, to die, as I supposed; but one of their priests crept in by night and dressed my wound. He was a Sussex man like myself.'

'Who was that?' said Puck suddenly. 'Zack Tutshom?'

'No, Jack Marget,' said Mr Culpeper.

'Jack Marget of New College? The little merry man that stammered so? Why a plague was stuttering Jack at Oxford then?' said Puck.

'He had come out of Sussex in hope of being made a Bishop when the King should have conquered the rebels, as he styled us Parliament men. His College had lent the King some monies too, which they never got again, no more than simple Jack got his bishopric. When we met he had had a bitter bellyful of King's promises, and wished to return to his wife and babes. This came about beyond expectation, for, so soon as I could stand of my wound, the man Blagge made excuse that I had been among the plague, and Jack had been tending me, to thrust us both out from their camp. The King had done with Jack now that Jack's College had lent the money, and Blagge's physician could not abide me because I would not sit silent and see him butcher the sick. (He was a College of Physicians man!) So Blagge, I say, thrust us both out, with many vile words, for a pair of pestilent, prating, pragmatical rascals.'

'Ha! Called *you* pragmatical, Nick?' Puck started up. 'High time Oliver came to purge the land! How did you and honest Jack fare next?'

'We were in some sort constrained to each other's company. I was for going to my house in Spitalfields, he would go to his parish in Sussex; but the plague was broke out and spreading through Wiltshire, Berkshire, and Hampshire, and he was so mad distracted to think that it might even then be among his folk at home that I bore him company. He had comforted me in my distress. I could not have done less; and I remembered that I had a cousin at Great Wigsell, near by Jack's parish. Thus we footed it from Oxford, cassock and buff coat together, resolute to leave wars on the left side henceforth; and either through our mean appearances, or the plague making men less cruel, we were not hindered. To be sure, they put us in the stocks one half-day for rogues and vagabonds at a village under St Leonard's forest, where, as I have heard, nightingales never sing; but the constable very honestly gave me back my Astrological Almanac, which I carry with me.' Mr Culpeper tapped his thin chest. 'I dressed a whitlow on his thumb. So we went forward.

'Not to trouble you with impertinences, we fetched over against Jack Marget's parish in a storm of rain about the day's end. Here our roads divided, for I would have gone on to my cousin at Great Wigsell, but while Jack was pointing me out his steeple, we saw a man lying drunk, as he conceived, athwart the road. He said it would be one Hebden, a parishioner, and till then a man of good life; and he accused himself bitterly for an unfaithful shepherd, that had left his flock to follow princes. But I saw it was the plague, and not the beginnings of it neither. They had set out the plague-stone, and the man's head lay on it.'

But I saw it was the plague

'What's a plague-stone?' Dan whispered.

'When the plague is so hot in a village that the neighbours shut the roads against 'em, people set a hollowed stone, pot, or pan, where such as would purchase victual from outside may lay money and the paper of their wants, and depart. Those that would sell come later – what will a man not do for gain? – snatch the money forth, and leave in exchange such goods as their conscience reckons fair value. I saw a silver groat in the water, and the man's list of what he would buy was rain-pulped in his wet hand.

' "My wife! Oh, my wife and babes!" says Jack of a sudden, and makes uphill – I with him.

'A woman peers out from behind a barn, crying out that the village is stricken with the plague, and that for our lives' sake we must avoid it.

' "Sweetheart!" says Jack. "Must I avoid thee?" and she leaps at him and says the babes are safe. She was his wife.

'When he had thanked God, even to tears, he tells me this was not the welcome he had intended, and presses me to flee the place while I was clean.

' "Nay! The Lord do so to me and more also if I desert thee now," I said. "These affairs are, under God's leave, in some fashion my strength."

' "Oh, sir," she says, "are you a physician? We have none."

' "Then, good people," said I, "I must e'en justify myself to you by my works."

' "Look – look ye," stammers Jack, "I took you all this time for a crazy Roundhead preacher." He laughs, and she, and then I – all three together in the rain are overtook by an unreasonable gust or clap of laughter, which none the less eased us. We call it in medicine the Hysterical Passion. So I went home with 'em.'

'Why did you not go on to your cousin at Great Wigsell, Nick?' Puck suggested. ' 'Tis barely seven mile up the road.'

'But the plague was here,' Mr Culpeper answered, and pointed up the hill. 'What else could I have done?'

'What were the parson's children called?' said Una.

'Elizabeth, Alison, Stephen, and Charles – a babe. I scarce saw them at first, for I separated to live with their father in a cart-lodge. The mother we put – forced – into the house with her babes. She had done enough.

'And now, good people, give me leave to be particular in this case. The plague was worst on the north side of the street, for lack, as I showed 'em, of sunshine; which, proceeding from the *primum mobile*, or source of life (I speak astrologically), is cleansing and purifying in the highest degree. The plague was hot too by the corn-chandler's, where they sell forage to the carters; extreme hot in both Mills, along the river, and scatteringly in other places, *except*, mark you, at the smithy. Mark here, that all forges and smith shops belong to Mars, even as corn and meat and wine shops acknowledge Venus for their mistress. There was no plague in the smithy at Munday's Lane—'

'Munday's Lane? You mean our village? I thought so when you talked about the two Mills,' cried Dan. 'Where did we put the plague-stone? I'd like to have seen it.'

'Then look at it now,' said Puck, and pointed to the chickens' drinking-trough where they had set their bicycle lamps. It was a rough, oblong stone pan, rather like a small kitchen sink, which Phillips, who never wastes anything, had found in a ditch and had used for his precious hens.

'That?' said Dan and Una, and stared, and stared, and stared.

Mr Culpeper made impatient noises in his throat and went on.

'I am at these pains to be particular, good people, because I would have you follow, so far as you may, the operations of my mind. That plague which I told you I had handled outside Wallingford in Oxfordshire was of a watery nature, conformable to the brookish riverine country it bred in, and curable, as I have said, by drenching in water. This plague

of ours here, for all that it flourished along watercourses –
every soul at both Mills died of it, – could not be so handled.
Which brought me to a stand. Ahem!'

'And your sick people in the meantime?' Puck demanded.

'We persuaded them on the north side of the street to lie
out in Hitheram's field. Where the plague had taken one,
or at most two, in a house, folk would not shift for fear of
thieves in their absence. They cast away their lives to die
among their goods.'

'Human nature,' said Puck. 'I've seen it time and again.
How did your sick do in the fields?'

'They died not near so thick as those that kept within
doors, and even then they died more out of distraction and
melancholy than plague. But I confess, good people, I could
not in any sort master the sickness, or come at a glimmer of
its nature or governance. To be brief, I was flat bewildered
at the brute malignity of the disease, and so – did what I
should have done before – dismissed all conjectures and
apprehensions that had grown up within me, chose a good
hour by my Almanac, clapped my vinegar-cloth to my face,
and entered some empty houses, resigned to wait upon the
stars for guidance.'

'At night? Were you not horribly frightened?' said Puck.

'I dared to hope that the God who hath made man so
nobly curious to search out His mysteries might not destroy
a devout seeker. In due time – there is a time, as I have said,
for everything under the sun – I spied a whitish rat, very
puffed and scabby, which sat beneath the dormer of an attic
through which shined our Lady the Moon. Whilst I looked
on him – and her – she was moving towards old cold Saturn,
her ancient ally – the rat creeped languishingly into her light,
and there, before my eyes, died. Presently his mate or companion came out, laid him down beside there, and in like
fashion died too. Later – an hour or less to midnight – a
third rat did e'en the same; always choosing the moonlight to
die in. This threw me into an amaze, since, as we know, the
moonlight is favourable, not hurtful, to the creatures of the

Moon; and Saturn, being friends with her, as you would say, was hourly strengthening her evil influence. Yet these three rats had been stricken dead in very moonlight. I leaned out of the window to see which of Heaven's host might be on our side, and there beheld I good trusty Mars, very red and heated, bustling about his setting. I straddled the roof to see better.

'Jack Marget came up street going to comfort our sick in Hitheram's field. A tile slipped under my foot.

'Says he, heavily enough, "Watchman, what of the night?"

' "Heart up, Jack," says I. "Methinks there's one fighting for us that, like a fool, I've forgot all this summer." My meaning was naturally the planet Mars.

' "Pray to Him then," says he. "I forgot Him too this summer."

'He meant God, whom he always bitterly accused himself of having forgotten up in Oxfordshire, among the King's men. I called down that he had made amends enough for his sin by his work among the sick, but he said he would not believe so till the plague was lifted from 'em. He was at his strength's end – more from melancholy than any just cause. I have seen this before among priests and over-cheerful men. I drenched him then and there with a half-cup of waters, which I do not say cure the plague, but are excellent against heaviness of the spirits.'

'What were they?' said Dan.

'White brandy rectified, camphor, cardamoms, ginger, two sorts of pepper, and aniseed.'

'Whew!' said Puck. 'Waters you call 'em!'

'Jack coughed on it valiantly, and went downhill with me. I was for the Lower Mill in the valley, to note the aspect of the Heavens. My mind had already shadowed forth the reason, if not the remedy, for our troubles, but I would not impart it to the vulgar till I was satisfied. That practice may be perfect, judgment ought to be sound, and to make judgment sound is required an exquisite knowledge. Ahem!

I left Jack and his lantern among the sick in Hitheram's field. He still maintained the prayers of the so-called Church, which were rightly forbidden by Cromwell.'

'You should have told your cousin at Wigsell,' said Puck, 'and Jack would have been fined for it, and you'd have had half the money. How did you come so to fail in your duty, Nick?'

Mr Culpeper laughed – his only laugh that evening – and the children jumped at the loud neigh of it.

'We were not fearful of *men's* judgment in those days,' he answered. 'Now mark me closely, good people, for what follows will be to you, though not to me, remarkable. When I reached the empty Mill, old Saturn, low down in the House of the Fishes, threatened the Sun's rising-place. Our Lady the Moon was moving towards the help of him (understand, I speak astrologically). I looked abroad upon the high Heavens, and I prayed the Maker of 'em for guidance. Now Mars sparkingly withdrew himself below the sky. On the instant of his departure, which I noted, a bright star or vapour leaped forth above his head (as though he had heaved up his sword), and broke all about in fire. The cocks crowed midnight through the valley, and I sat me down by the mill-wheel, chewing spearmint (though that's an herb of Venus), and calling myself all the asses' heads in the world! 'Twas plain enough *now*!'

'What was plain?' said Una.

'The true cause and cure of the plague. Mars, good fellow, had fought for us to the uttermost. Faint though he had been in the Heavens, and this had made me overlook him in my computations, he more than any of the other planets had kept the Heavens – which is to say, had been visible some part of each night wellnigh throughout the year. Therefore his fierce and cleansing influence, warring against the Moon, had stretched out to kill those three rats under my nose, and under the nose of their natural mistress, the Moon. I had known Mars lean half across Heaven to deal our Lady the Moon some shrewd blow from under his shield, but I had never before seen his strength displayed so effectual.'

'I don't understand a bit. Do you mean Mars killed the rats because he hated the Moon?' said Una.

'*That* is as plain as the pikestaff with which Blagge's men pushed me forth,' Mr Culpeper answered. 'I'll prove it. Why had the plague not broken out at the blacksmith's shop in Munday's Lane? Because, as I've shown you, forges and smithies belong naturally to Mars, and, for his honour's sake, Mars 'ud keep 'em clean from the creatures of the Moon. But was it like, think you, that he'd come down and rat-catch in general for lazy, ungrateful mankind? That were working a willing horse to death. So, then, you can see that the meaning of the blazing star above him when he set was simply this: "Destroy and burn the creatures of the Moon, for they are the root of your trouble. And thus, having shown you a taste of my power, good people, adieu." '

'Did Mars really say all that?' Una whispered.

'Yes, and twice so much as that to any one who had ears to hear. Briefly, he enlightened me that the plague was spread by the creatures of the Moon. The Moon, our Lady of Ill-aspect, was the offender. My own poor wits showed me that I, Nick Culpeper, had the people in my charge, God's good providence aiding me, and no time to lose neither.

'I posted up the hill, and broke into Hitheram's field amongst 'em all at prayers.

' "Eureka, good people!" I cried, and cast down a dead mill-rat which I'd found. "Here's your true enemy, revealed at last by the stars."

' "Nay, but I'm praying," says Jack. His face was as white as washed silver.

' "There's a time for everything under the sun," says I. "If you would stay the plague, take and kill your rats."

' "Oh, mad, stark mad!" says he, and wrings his hands.

'A fellow lay in the ditch beside him, who bellows that he'd as soon die mad hunting rats as be preached to death on a cold fallow. They laughed round him at this, but Jack

Marget falls on his knees, and very presumptuously petitions that he may be appointed to die to save the rest of his people. This was enough to thrust 'em back into their melancholy.

'"You are an unfaithful shepherd, Jack," I says. "Take a bat" (which we call a stick in Sussex) "and kill a rat if you die before sunrise. 'Twill save your people."

'"Aye, aye. Take a bat and kill a rat," he says ten times over, like a child, which moved 'em to ungovernable motions of that hysterical passion before mentioned, so that they laughed all, and at least warmed their chill bloods at that very hour — one o'clock or a little after — when the fires of life burn lowest. Truly there is a time for everything; and the physician must work with it — ahem! — or miss his cure. To be brief with you, I persuaded 'em, sick or sound, to have at the whole generation of rats throughout the village. And there's a reason for all things too, though the wise physician need not blab 'em all. *Imprimis*, or firstly, the mere sport of it, which lasted ten days, drew 'em most markedly out of their melancholy. I'd defy sorrowful Job himself to lament or scratch while he's routing rats from a rick. *Secundo*, or secondly, the vehement act and operation of this chase or war opened their skins to generous transpiration — more vulgarly, sweated 'em handsomely; and this further drew off their black bile — the mother of sickness. Thirdly, when we came to burn the bodies of the rats, I sprinkled sulphur on the faggots, whereby the onlookers were as handsomely suffumigated. This I could not have compassed if I had made it a mere physician's business; they'd have thought it some conjuration. Yet more, we cleansed, limed, and burned out a hundred foul poke-holes, sinks, slews, and corners of unvisited filth in and about the houses in the village, and by good fortune (mark here that Mars was in opposition to Venus) burned the corn-handler's shop to the ground. Mars loves not Venus. Will Noakes the saddler dropped his lantern on a truss of straw while he was rat-hunting there.'

'Had ye given Will any of that gentle cordial of yours, Nick, by any chance?' said Puck.

'A glass – or two glasses – not more. But as I would say, in fine, when we had killed the rats, I took ash, slag, and charcoal from the smithy, and burnt earth from the brick-yard (I reason that a brickyard belongs to Mars), and rammed it with iron crowbars into the rat-runs and buries, and beneath all the house floors. The Creatures of the Moon hate all that Mars hath used for his own clean ends. For example – rats bite not iron.'

'And how did poor stuttering Jack endure it?' said Puck.

'He sweated out his melancholy through his skin, and catched a loose cough, which I cured with electuaries, according to art. It is noteworthy, were I speaking among my equals, that the venom of the plague translated, or turned itself into, and evaporated, or went away as, a very heavy hoarseness and thickness of the head, throat, and chest. (Observe from my books which planets govern these portions of man's body, and your darkness, good people, shall be illuminated – ahem!) None the less, the plague, *qua* plague, ceased and took off (for we only lost three more, and two of 'em had it already on 'em) from the morning of the day that Mars enlightened me by the Lower Mill.' He coughed – almost trumpeted – triumphantly.

'It is proved,' he jerked out. 'I say I have proved my contention, which is, that by Divine Astrology and humble search into the veritable causes of things – at the proper time – the sons of wisdom may combat even the plague.'

'H'm!' Puck replied. 'For my own part I hold that a simple soul—'

'Mine? – simple, forsooth?' said Mr Culpeper.

'A very simple soul, a high courage tempered with sound and stubborn conceit, is stronger than all the stars in their courses. So I confess truly that you saved the village, Nick.'

'I stubborn? I stiff-necked? I ascribed all my poor success, under God's good providence, to Divine Astrology. Not to me the glory! You talk as that dear weeping ass Jack

Marget preached before I went back to my work in Red
Lion House, Spitalfields.'

'Oh! Stammering Jack preached, did he? They say he
loses his stammer in the pulpit.'

'And his wits with it. He delivered a most idolatrous dis-
course when the plague was stayed. He took for his text:
"The wise man that delivered the city." I could have given
him a better, such as: "There is a time for—" '

'But what made you go to church to hear him?' Puck
interrupted. 'Wail Attersole was your lawfully appointed
preacher, and a dull dog he was!'

Mr Culpeper wriggled uneasily.

'The vulgar,' said he, 'the old crones and – ahem! – the
children, Alison and the others, they dragged me to the
House of Rimmon by the hand. I was in two minds to
inform on Jack for maintaining the mummeries of the falsely-
called Church, which, I'll prove to you, are founded merely
on ancient fables—'

'Stick to your herbs and planets,' said Puck, laughing.
'You should have told the magistrates, Nick, and had Jack
fined. Again, why did you neglect your plain duty?'

'Because – because I was kneeling, and praying, and
weeping with the rest of 'em at the Altar-rails. In medicine
this is called the Hysterical Passion. It may be – it may
be.'

'That's as may be,' said Puck. They heard him turn the
hay. 'Why, your hay is half hedge-brishings,' he said. 'You
don't expect a horse to thrive on oak and ash and thorn
leaves, do you?'

Ping-ping-ping went the bicycle bell round the corner. Nurse
was coming back from the Mill.

'Is it all right?' Una called.

'All quite right,' Nurse called back. 'They're to be
christened next Sunday.'

'What? What?' They both leaned forward across the
half-door. It could not have been properly fastened, for it

opened, and tilted them out with hay and leaves sticking all over them.

'Come on! We must get those two twins' names,' said Una, and they charged uphill shouting over the hedge, till Nurse slowed up and told them.

When they returned, old Middenboro had got out of his stall, and they spent a lively ten minutes chasing him in again by starlight.

'OUR FATHERS OF OLD'

EXCELLENT herbs had our fathers of old –
  Excellent herbs to ease their pain –
Alexanders and Marigold,
  Eyebright, Orris, and Elecampane,
Basil, Rocket, Valerian, Rue,
  (Almost singing themselves they run)
Vervain, Dittany, Call-me-to-you –
  Cowslip, Melilot, Rose of the Sun.
    Anything green that grew out of the mould
    Was an excellent herb to our fathers of old.

Wonderful tales had our fathers of old –
  Wonderful tales of the herbs and the stars –
The Sun was Lord of the Marigold,
  Basil and Rocket belonged to Mars.
Pat as a sum in division it goes –
  (Every plant had a star bespoke) –
Who but Venus should govern the Rose?
  Who but Jupiter own the Oak?
    Simply and gravely the facts are told
    In the wonderful books of our fathers of old.

Wonderful little, when all is said,
  Wonderful little our fathers knew.
Half their remedies cured you dead –
  Most of their teaching was quite untrue -
'Look at the stars when a patient is ill,
  (Dirt has nothing to do with disease,)
Bleed and blister as much as you will,
  Blister and bleed him as oft as you please.'
    Whence enormous and manifold
    Errors were made by our fathers of old.

Yet when the sickness was sore in the land,
    And neither planet nor herb assuaged,
They took their lives in their lancet-hand
    And, oh, what a wonderful war they waged!
Yes, when the crosses were chalked on the door –
    Yes, when the terrible dead-cart rolled,
Excellent courage our fathers bore –
    Excellent heart had our fathers of old.
        Not too learned, but nobly bold,
        Into the fight went our fathers of old.

If it be certain, as Galen says,
    And sage Hippocrates holds as much –
'That those afflicted by doubts and dismays
    Are mightily helped by a dead man's touch,'
Then, be good to us, stars above!
    Then, be good to us, herbs below!
We are afflicted by what we can prove;
    We are distracted by what we know –
            So – ah, so!
        Down from your Heaven or up from your mould,
        Send us the hearts of our fathers of old!

Simple Simon

THE THOUSANDTH MAN

ONE man in a thousand, Solomon says,
   Will stick more close than a brother.
And it's worth while seeking him half your days
   If you find him before the other.
Nine hundred and ninety-nine depend
   On what the world sees in you,
But the Thousandth Man will stand your friend
   With the whole round world agin you.

'Tis neither promise nor prayer nor show
   Will settle the finding for 'ee.
Nine hundred and ninety-nine of 'em go
   By your looks or your acts or your glory.
But if he finds you and you find him,
   The rest of the world don't matter;
For the Thousandth Man will sink or swim
   With you in any water.

You can use his purse with no more shame
   Than he uses yours for his spendings;
And laugh and mention it just the same
   As though there had been no lendings.
Nine hundred and ninety-nine of 'em call
   For silver and gold in their dealings;
But the Thousandth Man he's worth 'em all,
   Because you can show him your feelings!

His wrong's your wrong, and his right's your right,
   In season or out of season.
Stand up and back it in all men's sight —
   With *that* for your only reason!
Nine hundred and ninety-nine can't bide
   The shame or mocking or laughter,
But the Thousandth Man will stand by your side
   To the gallows-foot — and after!

Simple Simon

CATTIWOW came down the steep lane with his five-horse timber-tug. He stopped by the wood-lump at the back gate to take off the brakes. His real name was Brabon, but the first time the children met him, years and years ago, he told them he was 'carting wood,' and it sounded so exactly like 'cattiwow' that they never called him anything else.

'Hi!' Una shouted from the top of the wood-lump, where they had been watching the lane. 'What are you doing? Why weren't we told?'

'They've just sent for me,' Cattiwow answered. 'There's a middlin' big log sticked in the dirt at Rabbit Shaw, and' – he flicked his whip back along the line – 'so they've sent for us all.'

Dan and Una threw themselves off the wood-lump almost under black Sailor's nose. Cattiwow never let them ride the big beam that makes the body of the timber-tug, but they hung on behind while their teeth thuttered.

The Wood road beyond the brook climbs at once into the woods, and you see all the horses' backs rising, one above another, like moving stairs. Cattiwow strode ahead in his sackcloth woodman's petticoat, belted at the waist with a leather strap; and when he turned and grinned, his red lips showed under his sackcloth-coloured beard. His cap was sackcloth too, with a flap behind, to keep twigs and bark out of his neck. He navigated the tug among pools of heather-water that splashed in their faces, and through clumps of young birches that slashed at their legs, and when they hit an old toadstooled stump, they never knew whether it would give way in showers of rotten wood, or jar them back again.

At the top of Rabbit Shaw half-a-dozen men and a team of horses stood round a forty-foot oak log in a muddy hollow. The ground about was poached and stoached with sliding hoof-marks, and a wave of dirt was driven up in front of the butt.

'What did you want to bury her for this way?' said Cattiwow. He took his broad-axe and went up the log tapping it.

'She's sticked fast,' said 'Bunny' Lewknor, who managed the other team.

Cattiwow unfastened the five wise horses from the tug. They cocked their ears forward, looked, and shook themselves.

'I believe Sailor knows,' Dan whispered to Una.

'He do,' said a man behind them. He was dressed in flour sacks like the others, and he leaned on his broad-axe, but the children, who knew all the wood-gangs, knew he was a stranger. In his size and oily hairiness he might have been Bunny Lewknor's brother, except that his brown eyes were as soft as a spaniel's, and his rounded black beard, beginning close up under them, reminded Una of the walrus in 'The Walrus and the Carpenter.'

'Don't he justabout know?' he said shyly, and shifted from one foot to the other.

'Yes. "What Cattiwow can't get out of the woods must have roots growing to her"' – Dan had heard old Hobden say this a few days before.

At that minute Puck pranced up, picking his way through the pools of black water in the ling.

'Look *out*!' cried Una, jumping forward. 'He'll see you, Puck!'

'Me and Mus' Robin are pretty middlin' well acquainted,' the man answered with a smile that made them forget all about walruses.

'This is Simon Cheyneys,' Puck began, and cleared his throat. 'Shipbuilder of Rye Port; burgess of the said town, and the only—'

'Oh, look! Look ye! That's a knowing one,' said the man. Cattiwow had fastened his team to the thin end of the log, and was moving them about with his whip till they stood at right angles to it, heading downhill. Then he grunted. The horses took the strain, beginning with Sailor next the log, like a tug-of-war team, and dropped almost to their knees. The log shifted a nail's breadth in the clinging dirt, with the noise of a giant's kiss.

'You're getting her!' Simon Cheyneys slapped his knee. 'Hing on! Hing on, lads, or she'll master ye! Ah!'

Sailor's left hind hoof had slipped on a heather-tuft. One of the men whipped off his sack apron and spread it down. They saw Sailor feel for it, and recover. Still the log hung, and the team grunted in despair.

'Hai!' shouted Cattiwow, and brought his dreadful whip twice across Sailor's loins with the crack of a shot-gun. The horse almost screamed as he pulled that extra last ounce which he did not know was in him. The thin end of the log left the dirt and rasped on dry gravel. The butt ground round like a buffalo in his wallow. Quick as an axe-cut, Lewknor snapped on his five horses, and sliding, trampling, jingling, and snorting, they had the whole thing out on the heather.

'Dat's the very first time I've knowed you lay into Sailor – to hurt him,' said Lewknor.

'It is,' said Cattiwow, and passed his hand over the two wheals. 'But I'd ha' laid my own brother open at that pinch. Now we'll twitch her down the hill a piece – she lies just about right – and get her home by the low road. My team'll do it, Bunny; you bring the tug along. Mind out!'

He spoke to the horses, who tightened the chains. The great log half rolled over, and slowly drew itself out of sight downhill, followed by the wood-gang and the timber-tug. In half a minute there was nothing to see but the deserted hollow of the torn-up dirt, the birch undergrowth still shaking, and the water draining back into the hoof-prints.

'Ye heard him?' Simon Cheyneys asked. 'He cherished his horse, but he'd ha' laid him open in that pinch.'

'Not for his own advantage,' said Puck quickly. ' 'Twas only to shift the log.'

'I reckon every man born of woman has his log to shift in the world – if so be you're hintin' at any o' Frankie's doings. *He* never hit beyond reason or without reason,' said Simon.

'*I* never said a word against Frankie,' Puck retorted, with a wink at the children. 'An' if I did, do it lie in your mouth to contest my say-so, seeing how you—'

'Why don't it lie in my mouth, seeing I was the first which knowed Frankie for all he was?' The burly sack-clad man puffed down at cool little Puck.

'Yes, and the first which set out to poison him – Frankie – on the high seas—'

Simon's angry face changed to a sheepish grin. He waggled his immense hands, but Puck stood off and laughed mercilessly.

'But let me tell you, Mus' Robin,' he pleaded.

'I've heard the tale. Tell the children here. Look, Dan! Look, Una!' – Puck's straight brown finger levelled like an arrow. 'There's the only man that ever tried to poison Sir Francis Drake!'

'Oh, Mus' Robin! 'Tidn't fair. You've the 'vantage of us all in your upbringin's by hundreds o' years. Stands to nature you know all the tales against every one.'

He turned his soft eyes so helplessly on Una that she cried, 'Stop ragging him, Puck! You know he didn't really.'

'I do. But why are you so sure, little maid?'

'Because – because he doesn't look like it,' said Una stoutly.

'I thank you,' said Simon to Una. 'I – I was always trustable-like with children if you let me alone, you double handful o' mischief!' He pretended to heave up his axe on Puck; and then his shyness overtook him afresh.

'Where did you know Sir Francis Drake?' said Dan, not liking being called a child.

'At Rye Port, to be sure,' said Simon, and seeing Dan's bewilderment, repeated it.

'Yes, but look here,' said Dan. ' "Drake he was a Devon man." The song says so.'

' "*And* ruled the Devon seas," ' Una went on. 'That's what I was thinking – if you don't mind.'

Simon Cheyneys seemed to mind very much indeed, for he swelled in silence while Puck laughed.

'Hutt!' he burst out at last, 'I've heard that talk too. If you listen to them West Country folk, you'll listen to a pack o' lies. I believe Frankie was born somewhere out west among the Shires, but his father had to run for it when Frankie was a baby, because the neighbours was wishful to kill him, d'ye see? He run to Chatham, old Parson Drake did, an' Frankie was brought up in a old hulks of a ship moored in the Medway river, same as it might ha' been the Rother. Brought up *at* sea, you might say, before he could walk *on* land – nigh Chatham in Kent. And ain't Kent back-door to Sussex? And don't that make Frankie Sussex? O' course it do. Devon man! Bah! Those West Country boats they're always fishin' in other folks' water.'

'I beg your pardon,' said Dan. 'I'm sorry.'

'No call to be sorry. You've been misled. I met Frankie at Rye Port when my Uncle, that was the shipbuilder there, pushed me off his wharf-edge on to Frankie's ship. Frankie had put in from Chatham with his rudder splutted, and a man's arm – Moon's that 'ud be – broken at the tiller. "Take this boy aboard an' drown him," says my Uncle, "and I'll mend your rudder-piece for love." '

'What did your Uncle want you drowned for?' said Una.

'That was only his fashion of say-so, same as Mus' Robin. I'd a foolishness in my head that ships could be builded out of iron. Yes – iron ships! I'd made me a liddle toy one of iron plates beat out thin – and she floated a wonder! But my Uncle, bein' a burgess of Rye, and a shipbuilder, he 'prenticed me to Frankie in the fetchin' trade, to cure this foolishness.'

'What was the fetchin' trade?' Dan interrupted.

'Fetchin' poor Flemishers and Dutchmen out o' the Low

Countries into England. The King o' Spain, d'ye see, he was burnin' 'em in those parts, for to make 'em Papishers, so Frankie he fetched 'em away to *our* parts, and a risky trade it was. His master wouldn't never touch it while he lived, but he left his ship to Frankie when he died, and Frankie turned her into this fetchin' trade. Outrageous cruel hard work – on besom-black nights bulting back and forth off they Dutch roads with shoals on all sides, and having to hark out for the *frish-frish-frish*-like of a Spanish galliwopses' oars creepin' up on ye. Frankie 'ud have the tiller and Moon he'd peer forth at the bows, our lantern under his skirts, till the boat we was lookin' for 'ud blurt up out o' the dark, and we'd lay hold and haul aboard whoever 'twas – man, woman, or babe – an' round we'd go again, the wind bewling like a kite in our riggin's, and they'd drop into the hold and praise God for happy deliverance till they was all sick.

'I had nigh a year at it, an' we must have fetched off – oh, a hundred pore folk, I reckon. Outrageous bold, too, Frankie growed to be. Outrageous cunnin' he was. Once we was as near as nothin' nipped by a tall ship off Tergoes Sands in a snowstorm. She had the wind of us, and spooned straight before it, shootin' all bow guns. Frankie fled inshore smack for the beach, till he was atop of the first breakers. Then he hove his anchor out, which nigh tore our bows off, but it twitched us round end-for-end into the wind, d'ye see, an' we clawed off them sands like a drunk man rubbin' along a tavern bench. When we could see, the Spanisher was laid flat along in the breakers with the snows whitening on his wet belly. He thought he could go where Frankie went.'

'What happened to the crew?' said Una.

'We didn't stop,' Simon answered. 'There was a very liddle new baby in our hold, and the mother she wanted to get to some dry bed middlin' quick. We runned into Dover, and said nothing.'

'Was Sir Francis Drake very much pleased?'

'Heart alive, maid, he'd no head to his name in those days.

He was just a outrageous, valiant, crop-haired, tutt-mouthed boy, roarin' up an' down the narrer seas, with his beard not yet quilled out. He made a laughing-stock of everything all day, and he'd hold our lives in the bight of his arm all the besom-black night among they Dutch sands; and we'd ha' jumped overside to behove him any one time, all of us.'

'Then why did you try to poison him?' Una asked wickedly, and Simon hung his head like a shy child.

'Oh, that was when he set me to make a pudden, for because our cook was hurted. *I* done my uttermost, but she all fetched adrift like in the bag, an' the more I biled the bits of her, the less she favoured any fashion o' pudden. Moon he chawed and chammed his piece, and Frankie chawed and chammed his'n, and – no words to it – he took me by the ear an' walked me out over the bow-end, an' him an' Moon hove the pudden at me on the bowsprit gub by gub, something cruel hard!' Simon rubbed his hairy cheek.

' "Nex' time you bring me anything," says Frankie, "you bring me cannon-shot an' I'll know what I'm getting." But as for poisonin'—' He stopped, the children laughed so.

'Of course you didn't,' said Una. 'Oh, Simon, we *do* like you!'

'I was always likeable with children.' His smile crinkled up through the hair round his eyes. 'Simple Simon they used to call me through our yard gates.'

'Did Sir Francis mock you?' Dan asked.

'Ah, no. He was gentle-born. Laugh he did – he was always laughing – but not so as to hurt a feather. An' I loved 'en. I loved 'en before England knew 'en, or Queen Bess she broke his heart.'

'But he hadn't really done anything when you knew him, had he?' Una insisted. 'Armadas and those things, I mean.'

Simon pointed to the scars and scrapes left by Cattiwow's great log. 'You tell me that that good ship's timber never done nothing against winds and weathers since her up-springing, and I'll confess ye that young Frankie never done nothing neither. Nothing? He adventured and suffered and made shift on they Dutch sands *as* much in any one month as ever he had occasion for to do in a half-year on the high seas afterwards. An' what was his tools? A coaster boat – a liddle box o' walty plankin' an' some few fathom feeble rope held together an' made able by *him* sole. He drawed our spirits up in our bodies same as a chimney-towel draws a fire. 'Twas *in* him, and it comed out all times and shapes.'

'I wonder did he ever 'magine what he was going to be? Tell himself stories about it?' said Dan with a flush.

'I expect so. We mostly do – even when we're grown. But bein' Frankie, he took good care to find out beforehand what his fortune might be. Had I rightly ought to tell 'em this piece?' Simon turned to Puck, who nodded.

'My Mother, she was just a fair woman, but my Aunt, her sister, she had gifts by inheritance laid up in her,' Simon began.

'Oh, that'll never do,' cried Puck, for the children stared blankly. 'Do you remember what Robin promised to the Widow Whitgift so long as her blood and get lasted?'[1]

'Yes. There was always to be one of them that could see farther through a millstone than most,' Dan answered promptly.

'Well, Simon's Aunt's mother,' said Puck slowly, 'married the Widow's blind son on the Marsh, and Simon's Aunt was the one chosen to see farthest through millstones. Do you understand?'

'That was what I was gettin' at,' said Simon, 'but you're so desperate quick. My Aunt she knew what was comin' to people. My Uncle being a burgess of Rye, he counted all such things odious, and my Aunt she couldn't be got to practise her gifts hardly at all, because it hurted her head for a week afterwards; but when Frankie heard she had 'em, he was all for nothin' till she foretold on him – till she looked in his hand to tell his fortune, d'ye see? One time we was at Rye she come aboard with my other shirt and some apples, and he fair beazled the life out of her about it.

[1] See 'Dymchurch Flit' in *Puck of Pook's Hill*.

' "Oh, you'll be twice wed, and die childless," she says, and pushes his hand away.

' "That's the woman's part," he says. "What'll come to me – to me?" an' he thrusts it back under her nose.

' "Gold – gold, past belief or counting," she says. "Let go o' me, lad."

' "Sink the gold!" he says. "What'll I *do*, mother?" He coaxed her like no woman could well withstand. I've seen him with 'em – even when they were sea-sick.

' "If you *will* have it," she says at last, "you shall have it. You'll do a many things, and eating and drinking with a dead man beyond the world's end will be the least of them. For you'll open a road from the East unto the West, and back again, and you'll bury your heart with your best friend by that road-side, and the road you open none shall shut so long as you're let lie quiet in your grave."[1]

' "And if I'm not?" he says.

' "Why, then," she says, "Sim's iron ships will be sailing on dry land. Now ha' done with this foolishness. Where's Sim's shirt?"

'He couldn't fetch no more out of her, and when we come up from the cabin, he stood mazed-like by the tiller, playing with a apple.

' "My Sorrow!" says my Aunt; "d'ye see that? The great world lying in his hand, liddle and round like a apple."

' "Why, 'tis one you gived him," I says.

' "To be sure," she says. " 'Tis just a apple," and she went ashore with her hand to her head. It always hurted her to show her gifts.

'Him and me puzzled over that talk plenty. It sticked in his mind quite extravagant. The very next time we slipped out for some fetchin' trade, we met Mus' Stenning's boat

[1] The old lady's prophecy is in a fair way to come true, for now the Panama Canal is finished, one end of it opens into the very bay where Sir Francis Drake was buried. So ships are taken through the Canal, and the road round Cape Horn which Sir Francis opened is very little used.

over by Calais sands; and he warned us that the Spanishers had shut down all their Dutch ports against us English, and their galliwopses was out picking up our boats like flies off hogs' backs. Mus' Stenning he runs for Shoreham, but Frankie held on a piece, knowin' that Mus' Stenning was jealous of our good trade. Over by Dunkirk a great gor-bellied Spanisher, with the Cross on his sails, came rampin' at us. We left him. We left him all they bare seas to conquest in.

'"Looks like this road was going to be shut pretty soon," says Frankie, humourin' her at the tiller. "I'll have to open that other one your Aunt foretold of."

'"The Spanisher's crowdin' down on us middlin' quick," I says.

'"No odds," says Frankie, "he'll have the inshore tide against him. Did your Aunt say I was to lie quiet in my grave for ever?"

'"Till my iron ships sailed dry land," I says.

'"That's foolishness," he says. "Who cares where Frankie Drake makes a hole in the water now or twenty years from now?"

'The Spanisher kept muckin' on more and more canvas. I told him so.

'"He's feelin' the tide," was all he says. "If he was among Tergoes Sands with this wind, we'd be picking his bones proper. I'd give my heart to have all their tall ships there some night before a north gale, and me to windward. There'd be gold in my hands then. Did your Aunt say she saw the world settin' in my hand, Sim?"

'"Yes, but 'twas a apple," says I, and he laughed like he always did at me. "Do you ever feel minded to jump over-side and be done with everything?" he asks after a while.

'"No. What water comes aboard is too wet as 'tis," I says. "The Spanisher's going about."

'"I told you," says he, never looking back. "He'll give us the Pope's Blessing as he swings. Come down off that rail. There's no knowin' where stray shots may hit." So I came down off the rail, and leaned against it, and the Spanisher he ruffled round in the wind, and his port-lids opened all red inside.

' "Now what'll happen to my road if they don't let me lie quiet in my grave?" he says. "Does your Aunt mean there's two roads to be found and kept open – or what does she mean? I don't like that talk about t'other road. D'you believe in your iron ships, Sim?"

'He knowed I did, so I only nodded, and he nodded back again.

' "Anybody but me 'ud call you a fool, Sim," he says. "Lie down. Here comes the Pope's Blessing!"

'The Spanisher gave us his broadside as he went about. They all fell short except one that smack-smooth hit the rail behind my back, an' I felt most won'erful cold.

' "Be you hit anywhere to signify?" he says. "Come over to me."

' "O Lord, Mus' Drake," I says, "my legs won't move," and that was the last I spoke for months.'

'Why? What had happened?' cried Dan and Una together.

'The rail had jarred me in here like.' Simon reached behind him clumsily. 'From my shoulders down I didn't act no shape. Frankie carried me piggy-back to my Aunt's house, and I lay bed-rid and tongue-tied while she rubbed me day and night, month in and month out. She had faith in rubbing with the hands. P'raps she put some of her gifts into it, too. Last of all, something loosed itself in my pore back, and lo! I was whole restored again, but kitten-feeble.

' "Where's Frankie?" I says, thinking I'd been a longish while abed.

' "Down-wind amongst the Dons – months ago," says my Aunt.

' "When can I go after 'en?" I says.

' "Your duty's to your town and trade now," says she. "Your Uncle he died last Michaelmas and he've left you and me the yard. So no more iron ships, mind ye."

Frankie carried me piggy-back to my Aunt's house

' "What?" I says. "And you the only one that beleft in 'em!"

' "Maybe I do still," she says, "but I'm a woman before I'm a Whitgift, and wooden ships is what England needs us to build. I lay on ye to do so."

'That's why I've never teched iron since that day – not to build a toy ship of. I've never even drawed a draft of one for my pleasure of evenings.' Simon smiled down on them all.

'Whitgift blood is terrible resolute – on the she-side,' said Puck.

'Didn't you ever see Sir Francis Drake again?' Dan asked.

'With one thing and another, and my being made a burgess of Rye, I never clapped eyes on him for the next twenty years. Oh, I had the news of his mighty doings the world over. They was the very same bold, cunning shifts and passes he'd worked with beforetimes off they Dutch sands, but, naturally, folk took more note of them. When Queen Bess made him knight, he sent my Aunt a dried orange stuffed with spiceries to smell to. She cried outrageous on it. She blamed herself for her foretellings, having set him on his won'erful road; but I reckon he'd ha' gone that way all withstanding. Curious how close she foretelled it! The world in his hand like an apple, an' he burying his best friend, Mus' Doughty—'

'Never mind for Mus' Doughty,' Puck interrupted. 'Tell us where you met Sir Francis next.'

'Oh, ha! That was the year I was made a burgess of Rye – the same year which King Philip sent his ships to take England without Frankie's leave.'

'The Armada!' said Dan contentedly. 'I was hoping that would come.'

'*I* knowed Frankie would never let 'em smell London smoke, but plenty good men in Rye was two-three minded about the upshot. 'Twas the noise of the gun-fire tarrified us. The wind favoured it our way from off behind the Isle of Wight. It made a mutter like, which growed and growed, and by the end of a week women was shruckin' in the streets.

Then *they* come slidderin' past Fairlight in a great smoky
pat vambrished with red gun-fire, and our ships flyin' forth
and duckin' in again. The smoke-pat sliddered over to the
French shore, so I knowed Frankie was edgin' the Spanishers
toward they Dutch sands where he was master. I says to my
Aunt, "The smoke's thinnin' out. I lay Frankie's just about
scrapin' his hold for a few last rounds shot. 'Tis time for me
to go."

' "Never in them clothes," she says. "Do on the doublet I
bought you to be made burgess in, and don't you shame this
day."

'So I mucked it on, and my chain, and my stiffed Dutch
breeches and all.

' "I be comin', too," she says from her chamber, and
forth she come pavisandin' like a peacock – stuff, ruff,
stomacher and all. She was a notable woman.'

'But how did you go? You haven't told us,' said Una.

'In my own ship – but half-share was my Aunt's. In the
Antony of Rye, to be sure; and not empty-handed. I'd been
loadin' her for three days with the pick of our yard. We was
ballasted on cannon-shot of all three sizes; and iron rods
and straps for his carpenters; and a nice passel of clean
three-inch oak planking and hide breech-ropes for his
cannon, and gubs of good oakum, and bolts o' canvas, and
all the sound rope in the yard. What else could I ha' done?
I knowed what he'd need most after a week's such work. I'm
a shipbuilder, little maid.

'We'd a fair slant o' wind off Dungeness, and we crept on
till it fell light airs and puffed out. The Spanishers was all in
a huddle over by Calais, and our ships was strawed about
mending 'emselves like dogs lickin' bites. Now and then a
Spanisher would fire from a low port, and the ball 'ud troll
across the flat swells, but both sides was finished fightin' for
that tide.

'The first ship we foreslowed on, her breastworks was
crushed in, an' men was shorin' 'em up. She said nothing.
The next was a black pinnace, his pumps clackin' middling

quick, and he said nothing. But the third, mending shot-holes, he spoke out plenty. I asked him where Mus' Drake might be, and a shiny-suited man on the poop looked down into us, and saw what we carried.

' "Lay alongside you!" he says. "We'll take that all."

' " 'Tis for Mus' Drake," I says, keeping away lest his size should lee the wind out of my sails.

' "Hi! Ho! Hither! We're Lord High Admiral of England! Come alongside, or we'll hang ye," he says.

' 'Twas none of my affairs who he was if he wasn't Frankie, and while he talked so hot I slipped behind a green-painted ship with her top-sides splintered. We was all in the middest of 'em then.

' "Hi! Hoi!" the green ship says. "Come alongside, honest man, and I'll buy your load. I'm Fenner that fought the seven Portugals – clean out of shot or bullets. Frankie knows me."

' "Ay, but I don't," I says, and I slacked nothing.

'He was a masterpiece. Seein' I was for goin' on, he hails a Bridport hoy beyond us and shouts, "George! Oh, George! Wing that duck. He's fat!" An' true as we're all here, that squatty Bridport boat rounds to acrost our bows, intendin' to stop us by means o' shooting.

'My Aunt looks over our rail. "George," she says, "you finish with your enemies afore you begin on your friends."

'Him that was laying the liddle swivel-gun at us sweeps off his hat an' calls her Queen Bess, and asks if she was selling liquor to pore dry sailors. My Aunt answered him quite a piece. She was a notable woman.

'Then *he* come up – his long pennant trailing overside – his waistcloths and netting tore all to pieces where the Spanishers had grappled, and his sides black-smeared with their gun-blasts like candle-smoke in a bottle. We hooked on to a lower port and hung.

' "Oh, Mus' Drake! Mus' Drake!" I calls up.

'He stood on the great anchor cathead, his shirt open to the middle, and his face shining like the sun.

' "Why, Sim!" he says. Just like that – after twenty year! "Sim," he says, "what brings you?"

' "Pudden," I says, not knowing whether to laugh or cry. "You told me to bring cannon-shot next time, an' I've brought 'em."

'He saw we had. He ripped out a fathom and a half o' brimstone Spanish, and he swung down on our rail, and he kissed me before all his fine young captains. His men was swarming out of the lower ports ready to unload us. When he saw how I'd considered all his likely wants, he kissed me again.

' "Here's a friend that sticketh closer than a brother!" he says. "Mistress," he says to my Aunt, "all you foretold on me was true. I've opened that road from the East to the West, and I've buried my heart beside it."

' "I know," she says. "That's why I be come."

' "But ye never foretold this"; he points to both they great fleets.

' "This don't seem to me to make much odds compared to what happens *to* a man," she says. "Do it?"

' "Certain sure a man forgets to remember when he's proper mucked up with work. Sim," he says to me, "we must shift every living Spanisher round Dunkirk corner on to our Dutch sands before morning. The wind'll come out of the North after this calm – same as it used – and then they're our meat."

' "Amen," says I. "I've brought you what I could scutchel up of odds and ends. Be you hit anywhere to signify?"

' "Oh, our folk'll attend to all that when we've time," he says. He turns to talk to my Aunt, while his men flew the stuff out of our hold. I think I saw old Moon amongst 'em, but we was too busy to more than nod like. Yet the Spanishers was going to prayers with their bells and candles before we'd cleaned out the *Antony*. Twenty-two ton o' useful stuff I'd fetched him.

' "Now, Sim," says my Aunt, "no more devouring of

Mus' Drake's time. He's sending us home in the Bridport
hoy. I want to speak to them young springalds again."

' "But here's our ship all ready and swept," I says.

' "Swep' an' garnished," says Frankie. "I'm going to fill
her with devils in the likeness o' pitch and sulphur. We must
shift the Dons round Dunkirk corner, and if shot can't do it,
we'll send down fireships."

' "I've given him my share of the *Antony*," says my Aunt.
"What do you reckon to do about yours?"

' "She offered it," said Frankie, laughing.

' "She wouldn't have if I'd overheerd her," I says;
"because I'd have offered my share first." Then I told him
how the *Antony's* sails was best trimmed to drive before the
wind, and seeing he was full of occupations we went acrost
to that Bridport hoy, and left him.

'But Frankie was gentle-born, d'ye see, and that sort they
never overlook any folks' dues.

'When the hoy passed under his stern, he stood bare-
headed on the poop same as if my Aunt had been his Queen,
and his musicianers played "Mary Ambree" on their silver
trumpets quite a long while. Heart alive, little maid! I never
meaned to make you look sorrowful—'

Bunny Lewknor in his sackcloth petticoats burst through the
birch scrub wiping his forehead.

'We've got the stick to rights now! She've been a whole
hatful o' trouble. You come an' ride her home, Mus' Dan
and Miss Una!'

They found the proud wood-gang at the foot of the slope,
with the log double-chained on the tug.

'Cattiwow, what are you going to do with it?' said Dan,
as they straddled the thin part.

'She's going down to Rye to make a keel for a Lowestoft
fishin'-boat, I've heard. Hold tight!'

Cattiwow cracked his whip, and the great log dipped and
tilted, and leaned and dipped again, exactly like a stately
ship upon the high seas.

FRANKIE'S TRADE

Old Horn to All Atlantic said:
    (*A-hay O! To me O!*)
'Now where did Frankie learn his trade?
For he ran me down with a three-reef mains'le.'
    (*All round the Horn!*)

Atlantic answered: 'Not from me!
You'd better ask the cold North Sea,
For he ran me down under all plain canvas.'
    (*All round the Horn!*)

The North Sea answered: 'He's my man,
For he came to me when he began –
Frankie Drake in an open coaster.
    (*All round the Sands!*)

'I caught him young and I used him sore,
So you never shall startle Frankie more,
Without capsizing Earth and her waters.
    (*All round the Sands!*)

'I did not favour him at all,
I made him pull and I made him haul –
And stand his trick with the common sailors.
    (*All round the Sands!*)

'I froze him stiff and I fogged him blind,
And kicked him home with his road to find
By what he could see of a three-day snow-storm.
    (*All round the Sands!*)

'I learned him his trade o' winter nights,
'Twixt Mardyk Fort and Dunkirk lights
On a five-knot tide with the forts a-firing.
    (*All round the Sands!*)

'Before his beard began to shoot,
I showed him the length of the Spaniard's foot –
And I reckon he clapped the boot on it later.
    (*All round the Sands!*)

'If there's a risk which you can make
That's worse than he was used to take
Nigh every week in the way of his business;
    (*All round the Sands!*)

'If there's a trick that you can try
Which he hasn't met in time gone by,
Not once or twice, but ten times over;
    (*All round the Sands!*)

'If you can teach him aught that's new,
    (*A-hay O! To me O!*)
I'll give you Bruges and Niewport too,
And the ten tall churches that stand between 'em.'
    Storm along, my gallant Captains!
    (*All round the Horn!*)

The Tree of Justice

THE BALLAD OF MINEPIT SHAW

ABOUT the time that taverns shut
   And men can buy no beer,
Two lads went up by the keepers' hut
   To steal Lord Pelham's deer.

Night and the liquor was in their heads –
   They laughed and talked no bounds,
Till they waked the keepers on their beds,
   And the keepers loosed the hounds.

They had killed a hart, they had killed a hind,
   Ready to carry away,
When they heard a whimper down the wind
   And they heard a bloodhound bay.

They took and ran across the fern,
   Their crossbows in their hand,
Till they met a man with a green lantern
   That called and bade 'em stand.

'What are you doing, O Flesh and Blood,
   And what's your foolish will,
That you must break into Minepit Wood
   And wake the Folk of the Hill?'

'Oh, we've broke into Lord Pelham's park,
   And killed Lord Pelham's deer,
And if ever you heard a little dog bark
   You'll know why we come here!'

'We ask you let us go our way,
   As fast as we can flee,
For if ever you heard a bloodhound bay,
   You'll know how pressed we be.'

'Oh, lay your crossbows on the bank
      And drop the knife from your hand,
And though the hounds are at your flank
      I'll save you where you stand!'

They laid their crossbows on the bank,
      They threw their knives in the wood,
And the ground before them opened and sank
      And saved 'em where they stood.

'Oh, what's the roaring in our ears
      That strikes us well-nigh dumb?'
'Oh, that is just how things appears
      According as they come.'

'What are the stars before our eyes
      That strike us well-nigh blind?'
'Oh, that is just how things arise
      According as you find.'

'And why's our bed so hard to the bones
      Excepting where it's cold?'
'Oh, that's because it is precious stones
      Excepting where 'tis gold.

'Think it over as you stand,
      For I tell you without fail,
If you haven't got into Fairyland
      You're not in Lewes Gaol.'

All night long they thought of it,
      And, come the dawn, they saw
They'd tumbled into a great old pit,
      At the bottom of Minepit Shaw.

And the keepers' hound had followed 'em close
      And broke her neck in the fall;
So they picked up their knives and their cross-bows
      And buried the dog. That's all.

But whether the man was a poacher too
      Or a Pharisee so bold —
I reckon there's more things told than are true,
      And more things true than are told.

The Tree of Justice

It was a warm, dark winter day with the Sou'-West wind singing through Dallington Forest, and the woods below the Beacon. The children set out after dinner to find old Hobden, who had a three months' job in the Rough at the back of Pound's Wood. He had promised to get them a dormouse in its nest. The bright leaf still clung to the beech coppice; the long chestnut leaves lay orange on the ground, and the rides were speckled with scarlet-lipped sprouting acorns. They worked their way by their own short cuts to the edge of Pound's Wood, and heard a horse's feet just as they came to the beech where Ridley the keeper hangs up the vermin. The poor little fluffy bodies dangled from the branches – some perfectly good, but most of them dried to twisted strips.

'Three more owls,' said Dan, counting. 'Two stoats, four jays, and a kestrel. That's ten since last week. Ridley's a beast.'

'In my time this sort of tree bore heavier fruit.' Sir Richard Dalyngridge[1] reined up his grey horse, Swallow, in the ride behind them. 'What play do you make?' he asked.

'Nothing, sir. We're looking for old Hobden,' Dan replied. 'He promised to get us a sleeper.'

'Sleeper? A *dormeuse*, do you say?'

'Yes, a dormouse, sir.'

'I understand. I passed a woodman on the low grounds. Come!'

He wheeled up the ride again, and pointed through an opening to the patch of beech-stubs, chestnut, hazel, and

[1] This is the Norman knight they met the year before in *Puck of Pook's Hill*. See 'Young Men at the Manor,' 'The Knights of the Joyous Venture,' and 'Old Men at Pevensey,' in that book.

birch that old Hobden would turn into firewood, hop-poles, pea-boughs, and house-faggots before spring. The old man was as busy as a beaver.

Something laughed beneath a thorn, and Puck stole out, his finger on his lip.

'Look!' he whispered. 'Along between the spindle-trees. Ridley has been there this half-hour.'

The children followed his point, and saw Ridley the keeper in an old dry ditch, watching Hobden as a cat watches a mouse.

'Huhh!' cried Una. 'Hobden always 'tends to his wires before breakfast. He puts his rabbits into the faggots he's allowed to take home. He'll tell us about 'em tomorrow.'

'We had the same breed in my day,' Sir Richard replied, and moved off quietly, Puck at his bridle, the children on either side between the close-trimmed beech stuff.

'What did you do to them?' said Dan, as they repassed Ridley's terrible tree.

'That!' Sir Richard jerked his head toward the dangling owls.

'Not he!' said Puck. 'There was never enough brute Norman in you to hang a man for taking a buck.'

'I – I cannot abide to hear their widows screech. But why am I on horseback while you are afoot?' He dismounted lightly, tapped Swallow on the chest, so that the wise thing backed instead of turning in the narrow ride, and put himself at the head of the little procession. He walked as though all the woods belonged to him. 'I have often told my friends,' he went on, 'that Red William the King was not the only Norman found dead in a forest while he hunted.'

'D'you mean William Rufus?' said Dan.

'Yes,' said Puck, kicking a clump of red toad-stools off a dead log.

'For example, there was a knight new from Normandy,' Sir Richard went on, 'to whom Henry our King granted a manor in Kent near by. He chose to hang his forester's son the day before a deer-hunt that he gave to pleasure the King.'

'Now when would that be?' said Puck, and scratched an ear thoughtfully.

'The summer of the year King Henry broke his brother Robert of Normandy at Tenchebrai fight. Our ships were even then at Pevensey loading for the war.'

'What happened to the knight?' Dan asked.

'They found him pinned to an ash, three arrows through his leather coat. *I* should have worn mail that day.'

'And did you see him all bloody?' Dan continued.

'Nay, I was with De Aquila at Pevensey, counting horse-shoes, and arrow-sheaves, and ale-barrels into the holds of the ships. The army only waited for our King to lead them against Robert in Normandy, but he sent word to De Aquila that he would hunt with him here before he set out for France.'

'Why did the King want to hunt so particularly?' Una demanded.

'If he had gone straight to France after the Kentish knight was killed, men would have said he feared being slain like the knight. It was his duty to show himself debonair to his English people as it was De Aquila's duty to see that he took no harm while he did it. But it was a great burden! De Aquila, Hugh, and I ceased work on the ships, and scoured all the Honour of the Eagle – all De Aquila's lands – to make a fit, and, above all, a safe sport for our King. Look!'

The ride twisted, and came out on the top of Pound's Hill Wood. Sir Richard pointed to the swells of beautiful, dappled Dallington, that showed like a woodcock's breast up the valley. 'Ye know the forest?' said he.

'You ought to see the bluebells there in Spring!' said Una.

'I have seen,' said Sir Richard, gazing, and stretched out his hand. 'Hugh's work and mine was first to move the deer gently from all parts into Dallington yonder, and there to hold them till the King came. Next, we must choose some three hundred beaters to drive the deer to the stands within bowshot of the King. Here was our trouble! In the mellay of a deer-drive a Saxon peasant and a Norman King may come over-close to each other. The conquered do not love their conquerors all at once. So we needed sure men, for whom their village or kindred would answer in life, cattle, and land if any harm come to the King. Ye see?'

'If one of the beaters shot the King,' said Puck, 'Sir Richard wanted to be able to punish that man's village. Then the village would take care to send a good man.'

'So! So it was. But, lest our work should be too easy, the King had done such a dread justice over at Salehurst, for the killing of the Kentish knight (twenty-six men he hanged, as I heard), that our folk were half mad with fear before we began. It is easier to dig out a badger gone to earth than a Saxon gone dumb-sullen. And atop of their misery the old rumour waked that Harold the Saxon was alive and would bring them deliverance from us Normans. This has happened every autumn since Santlache fight.'

'But King Harold was killed at Hastings,' said Una.

'So it was said, and so it was believed by us Normans, but our Saxons always believed he would come again. *That* rumour did not make our work any more easy.'

Sir Richard strode on down the far slope of the wood, where the trees thin out. It was fascinating to watch how he managed his long spurs among the lumps of blackened ling.

'But we did it!' he said. 'After all, a woman is as good as a man to beat the woods, and the mere word that deer are afoot makes cripples and crones young again. De Aquila laughed when Hugh told him over the list of beaters. Half were women; and many of the rest were clerks – Saxon and Norman priests.

'Hugh and I had not time to laugh for eight days, till De Aquila, as Lord of Pevensey, met our King and led him to the first shooting-stand – by the Mill on the edge of the forest. Hugh and I – it was no work for hot heads or heavy hands – lay with our beaters on the skirts of Dallington to watch both them and the deer. When De Aquila's great horn blew we went forward, a line half a league long. Oh, to see the fat clerks, their gowns tucked up, puffing and roaring, and the sober millers dusting the undergrowth with their staves; and, like as not, between them a Saxon wench, hand in hand with her man, shrilling like a kite as she ran, and leaping high through the fern, all for joy of the sport.'

'*Ah! How! Ah! How! How-ah! Sa-how-ah!*' Puck bellowed without warning, and Swallow bounded forward, ears cocked, and nostrils cracking.

'*Hal-lal-lal-lal-la-hai-ie!*' Sir Richard answered in a high clear shout.

The two voices joined in swooping circles of sound, and a heron rose out of a red osier-bed below them, circling as though he kept time to the outcry. Swallow quivered and swished his glorious tail. They stopped together on the same note.

A hoarse shout answered them across the bare woods.

'That's old Hobden,' said Una.

'Small blame to him. It is in his blood,' said Puck. 'Did your beaters cry so, Sir Richard?'

'My faith, they forgot all else. (Steady, Swallow, steady!) They forgot where the King and his people waited to shoot. They followed the deer to the very edge of the open till the first flight of wild arrows from the stands flew fair over them.

'I cried, " 'Ware shot! 'Ware shot!" and a knot of young knights new from Normandy, that had strayed away from the Grand Stand, turned about, and in mere sport loosed off at our line shouting: " 'Ware Santlache arrows! 'Ware Santlache arrows!" A jest, I grant you, but too sharp. One of our beaters answered in Saxon: " 'Ware New Forest arrows! 'Ware Red William's arrow!" so I judged it time to end the jests, and when the boys saw my old mail gown (for, to shoot with strangers *I* count the same as war), they ceased shooting. So *that* was smoothed over, and we gave our beaters ale to wash down their anger. They were excusable! We – they had sweated to show our guests good sport, and our reward was a flight of hunting-arrows which no man loves, and worse, a churl's jibe over hard-fought, fair-lost Hastings fight. So, before the next beat, Hugh and I assembled and called the beaters over by name, to steady them. The greater part we knew, but among the Netherfield men I saw an old, old man, in the dress of a pilgrim.

'The Clerk of Netherfield said he was well known by repute for twenty years as a witless man that journeyed without rest to all the shrines of England. The old man sits, Saxon fashion, head between fists. We Normans rest the chin on the left palm.

' "Who answers for him?" said I. "If he fails in his duty, who will pay his fine?"

' "Who will pay my fine?" the pilgrim said. "I have asked that of all the Saints in England these forty years, less three months and nine days! They have not answered!" When he lifted his thin face I saw he was one-eyed, and frail as a rush.

' "Nay, but, Father," I said, "to whom hast thou commended thyself?" He shook his head, so I spoke in Saxon: "Whose man art thou?"

' "I think I have a writing from Rahere, the King's Jester," said he after a while. "I am, as I suppose, Rahere's man."

'He pulled a writing from his scrip, and Hugh, coming up, read it.

'It set out that the pilgrim was Rahere's man, and that Rahere was the King's Jester. There was Latin writ at the back.

' "What a plague conjuration's here?" said Hugh, turning it over. "*Pum-quum-sum oc-occ.* Magic?"

' "Black Magic," said the Clerk of Netherfield (he had been a monk at Battle). "They say Rahere is more of a priest than a fool and more of a wizard than either. Here's Rahere's name writ, and there's Rahere's red cockscomb mark drawn below for such as cannot read." He looked slyly at me.

' "Then read it," said I, "and show thy learning." He was a vain little man, and he gave it us after much mouthing.

' "The charm, which I think is from Virgilius the Sorcerer, says: 'When thou art once dead, and Minos' (which is a heathen judge) 'has doomed thee, neither cunning, nor speechcraft, nor good works will restore thee!' A terrible thing! It denies any mercy to a man's soul!"

' "Does it serve?" said the pilgrim, plucking at Hugh's cloak. "Oh, man of the King's blood, does it cover me?"

'Hugh was of Earl Godwin's blood, and all Sussex knew it, though no Saxon dared call him kingly in a Norman's hearing. There can be but one King.

' "It serves," said Hugh. "But the day will be long and hot. Better rest here. We go forward now."

' "No, I will keep with thee, my kinsman," he answered like a child. He was indeed childish through great age.

'The line had not moved a bowshot when De Aquila's great horn blew for a halt, and soon young Fulke – our false Fulke's son – yes, the imp that lit the straw in Pevensey Castle[1] – came thundering up a woodway.

' "Uncle," said he (though he was a man grown, he called me Uncle), "those young Norman fools who shot at you this morn are saying that your beaters cried treason against the King. It has come to Harry's long ears, and he bids you give account of it. There are heavy fines in his eye, but I am with you to the hilt, Uncle!"

'When the boy had fled back, Hugh said to me: "It was Rahere's witless man that cried, ' 'Ware Red William's arrow!' I heard him, and so did the Clerk of Netherfield."

' "Then Rahere must answer to the King for his man," said I. "Keep him by you till I send," and I hastened down.

'The King was with De Aquila in the Grand Stand above Welansford down in the valley yonder. His Court – knights and dames – lay glittering on the edge of the glade. I made my homage, and Henry took it coldly.

[1] See 'Old Men at Pevensey' in *Puck of Pook's Hill*.

' "How came your beaters to shout threats against me?" said he.

' "The tale has grown," I answered. "One old witless man cried out, ' 'Ware Red William's arrow,' when the young knights shot at our line. We had two beaters hit."

' "I will do justice on that man," he answered. "Who is his master?"

' "He is Rahere's man," said I.

' "Rahere's?" said Henry. "Has my fool a fool?"

'I heard the bells jingle at the back of the stand, and a red leg waved over it; then a black one. So, very slowly, Rahere the King's Jester straddled the edge of the planks, and looked down on us, rubbing his chin. Loose-knit, with cropped hair, and a sad priest's face, under his cockscomb cap, that he could twist like a strip of wet leather. His eyes were hollow-set.

' "Nay, nay, Brother," said he. "If I suffer you to keep your fool, you must e'en suffer me to keep mine."

'This he delivered slowly into the King's angry face! My faith, a King's Jester must be bolder than lions!

' "Now we will judge the matter," said Rahere. "Let these two brave knights go hang my fool because he warned King Henry against running after Saxon deer through woods full of Saxons. 'Faith, Brother, if *thy* Brother, Red William, now among the Saints as we hope, had been timely warned against a certain arrow in New Forest, one fool of us four would not be crowned fool of England this morning. Therefore, hang the fool's fool, knights!"

'Mark the fool's cunning! Rahere had himself given us order to hang the man. No King dare confirm a fool's command to such a great baron as De Aquila; and the helpless King knew it.

' "What? No hanging?" said Rahere, after a silence. "A' God's Gracious Name, kill something, then! Go forward with the hunt!"

'He splits his face ear to ear in a yawn like a fish-pond. "Henry," says he, "the next time I sleep, do not pester me with thy fooleries." Then he throws himself out of sight behind the back of the stand.

'I have seen courage with mirth in De Aquila and Hugh, but stark mad courage of Rahere's sort I had never even guessed at.'

'What did the King say?' cried Dan.

'He had opened his mouth to speak, when young Fulke, who had come into the stand with us, laughed, and, boy-like, once begun, could not check himself. He kneeled on the instant for pardon, but fell sideways, crying: "His legs! Oh, his long, waving red legs as he went backward!"'

'Like a storm breaking, our grave King laughed, – stamped and reeled with laughter till the stand shook. So, like a storm, this strange thing passed!

'He wiped his eyes, and signed to De Aquila to let the drive come on.

'When the deer broke, we were pleased that the King shot from the shelter of the stand, and did not ride out after the hurt beasts as Red William would have done. Most vilely his knights and barons shot!

'De Aquila kept me beside him, and I saw no more of Hugh till evening. We two had a little hut of boughs by the camp, where I went to wash me before the great supper, and in the dusk I heard Hugh on the couch.

' "Wearied, Hugh?" said I.

' "A little," he says. "I have driven Saxon deer all day for a Norman King, and there is enough of Earl Godwin's blood left in me to sicken at the work. Wait awhile with the torch."

'I waited then, and I thought I heard him sob.'

'Poor Hugh! Was he so tired?' said Una. 'Hobden says beating is hard work sometimes.'

'I think this tale is getting like the woods,' said Dan, 'darker and twistier every minute.'

Sir Richard had walked as he talked, and though the children thought they knew the woods well enough, they felt a little lost.

'A dark tale enough,' says Sir Richard, 'but the end was not all black. When we had washed, we went to wait on the King at meat in the great pavilion. Just before the trumpets blew for the Entry – all the guests upstanding – long Rahere comes posturing up to Hugh, and strikes him with his bauble-bladder.

' "Here's a heavy heart for a joyous meal!" he says. "But each man must have his black hour or where would be the merit of laughing? Take a fool's advice, and sit it out with my man. I'll make a jest to excuse you to the King if he remember to ask for you. That's more than I would do for Archbishop Anselm."

'Hugh looked at him heavy-eyed. "Rahere?" said he. "The King's Jester? Oh, Saints, what punishment for my King!" and smites his hands together.

' "Go – go fight it out in the dark," says Rahere, "and thy Saxon Saints reward thee for thy pity to my fool." He pushed him from the pavilion, and Hugh lurched away like one drunk.'

'But why?' said Una. 'I don't understand.'

'Ah, why indeed? Live you long enough, maiden, and you shall know the meaning of many whys.' Sir Richard smiled. 'I wondered too, but it was my duty to wait on the King at the High Table in all that glitter and stir.

'He spoke me his thanks for the sport I had helped show him, and he had learned from De Aquila enough of my folk and my castle in Normandy to graciously feign that he knew and had loved my brother there. (This, also, is part of a king's work.) Many great men sat at the High Table – chosen by the King for their wits, not for their birth. I have forgotten their names, and their faces I only saw that one night. But' – Sir Richard turned in his stride – 'but Rahere, flaming in black and scarlet among our guests, the hollow of his dark cheek flushed with wine – long, laughing Rahere, and the stricken sadness of his face when he was not twisting it about – Rahere I shall never forget.

'At the King's outgoing De Aquila bade me follow him,

with his great bishops and two great barons, to the little pavilion. We had devised jugglers and dances for the Court's sport; but Henry loved to talk gravely to grave men, and De Aquila had told him of my travels to the world's end. We had a fire of apple-wood, sweet as incense, – and the curtains at the door being looped up, we could hear the music and see the lights shining on mail and dresses.

'Rahere lay behind the King's chair. The questions he darted forth at me were as shrewd as the flames. I was telling of our fight with the apes, as ye called them, at the world's end.[1]

' "But where is the Saxon knight that went with you?" said Henry. "He must confirm these miracles."

' "He is busy," said Rahere, "confirming a new miracle."

' "Enough miracles for today," said the King. "Rahere, you have saved your long neck. Fetch the Saxon knight."

' "Pest on it," said Rahere. "Who would be a King's Jester? I'll bring him, Brother, if you'll see that none of your home-brewed bishops taste my wine while I am away." So he jingled forth between the men-at-arms at the door.

'Henry had made many bishops in England without the Pope's leave. I know not the rights of the matter, but only Rahere dared jest about it. We waited on the King's next word.

' "I think Rahere is jealous of you," said he, smiling, to Nigel of Ely. He was one bishop; and William of Exeter, the other – Wal-wist the Saxons called him – laughed long. "Rahere is a priest at heart. Shall I make him a bishop, De Aquila?" says the King.

' "There might be worse," said our Lord of Pevensey. "Rahere would never do what Anselm has done."

'This Anselm, Archbishop of Canterbury, had gone off raging to the Pope at Rome, because Henry would make bishops without *his* leave either. I knew not the rights of it, but De Aquila did, and the King laughed.

' "Anselm means no harm. He should have been a monk,

[1] See 'The Knights of the Joyous Venture' in *Puck of Pook's Hill*.

not a bishop," said the King. "I'll never quarrel with
Anselm or his Pope till they quarrel with my England. If we
can keep the King's peace till my son comes to rule, no man
will lightly quarrel with our England."

"'Amen," said De Aquila. "But the King's peace ends
when the King dies."

'That is true. The King's peace dies with the King. The
custom then is that all laws are outlaw, and men do what
they will till the new King is chosen.

' "I will amend that," said the King hotly. "I will have it
so that though King, son, and grandson were all slain in one
day, *still* the King's peace should hold over all England!
What is a man that his mere death must upheave a people?
We must have the Law."

' "Truth," said William of Exeter; but that he would
have said to any word of the King.

'The two great barons behind said nothing. This teaching
was clean against their stomachs, for when the King's peace
ends, the great barons go to war and increase their lands.
At that instant we heard Rahere's voice returning, in a
scurril Saxon rhyme against William of Exeter:

> "Well wist Wal-wist where lay his fortune
>   When that he fawned on the King for his crozier,"

and amid our laughter he burst in, with one arm round
Hugh, and one round the old pilgrim of Netherfield.

' "Here is your knight, Brother," said he, "and for the
better disport of the company, here is my fool. Hold up,
Saxon Samson, the gates of Gaza are clean carried away!"

'Hugh broke loose, white and sick, and staggered to my
side; the old man blinked upon the company.

'We looked at the King, but he smiled.

' "Rahere promised he would show me some sport after
supper to cover his morning's offence," said he to De
Aquila. "So this is thy man, Rahere?"

' "Even so," said Rahere. "My man he has been, and my

'Here is your knight, Brother,' said he

protection he has taken, ever since I found him under the gallows at Stamford Bridge telling the kites atop of it that he was – Harold of England!"

'There was a great silence upon these last strange words, and Hugh hid his face on my shoulder, woman-fashion.

' "It is most cruel true," he whispered to me. "The old man proved it to me at the beat after you left, and again in our hut even now. It is Harold, my King!"

'De Aquila crept forward. He walked about the man and swallowed.

' "Bones of the Saints!" said he, staring.

' "Many a stray shot goes too well home," said Rahere.

'The old man flinched as at an arrow. "Why do you hurt me still?" he said in Saxon. "It was on some bones of some Saints that I promised I would give my England to the Great Duke." He turns on us all crying, shrilly: "Thanes, he had caught me at Rouen – a lifetime ago. If I had not promised, I should have lain there all my life. What else could I have done? I have lain in a strait prison all my life none the less. There is no need to throw stones at me." He guarded his face with his arms, and shivered.

' "Now his madness will strike him down," said Rahere. "Cast out the evil spirit, one of you new bishops."

'Said William of Exeter: "Harold was slain at Santlache fight. All the world knows it."

' "I think this man must have forgotten," said Rahere. "Be comforted, Father. Thou wast well slain at Hastings forty years gone, less three months and nine days. Tell the King."

'The man uncovered his face. "I thought they would stone me," he said. "I did not know I spoke before a King." He came to his full towering height – no mean man, but frail beyond belief.

'The King turned to the tables, and held him out his own cup of wine. The old man drank, and beckoned behind him, and, before all the Normans, my Hugh bore away the empty cup, Saxon-fashion, upon the knee.

' "It is Harold!" said De Aquila. "His own stiff-necked blood kneels to serve him."

' "Be it so," said Henry. "Sit, then, thou that hast been Harold of England."

'The madman sat, and hard, dark Henry looked at him between half-shut eyes. We others stared like oxen, all but De Aquila, who watched Rahere as I have seen him watch a far sail on the sea.

'The wine and the warmth cast the old man into a dream. His white head bowed; his hands hung. His eye indeed was opened, but the mind was shut. When he stretched his feet, they were scurfed and road-cut like a slave's.

' "Ah, Rahere," cried Hugh, "why hast thou shown him thus? Better have let him die than shame him – and me!"

' "Shame thee?" said the King. "Would any baron of mine kneel to me if I were witless, discrowned, and alone, and Harold had my throne?"

' "No," said Rahere. "I am the sole fool that might do it, Brother, unless" – he pointed at De Aquila, whom he had only met that day – "yonder tough Norman crab kept me company. But, Sir Hugh, I did not mean to shame him. He hath been somewhat punished through, maybe, little fault of his own."

' "Yet he lied to my Father, the Conqueror," said the King, and the old man flinched in his sleep.

' "Maybe," said Rahere, "but thy Brother Robert, whose throat we purpose soon to slit with our own hands—'

' "Hutt!" said the King, laughing. "I'll keep Robert at my table for a life's guest when I catch him. Robert means no harm. It is all his cursed barons."

' "None the less," said Rahere, "Robert may say that thou hast not always spoken the stark truth to him about England. I should not hang too many men on *that* bough, Brother."

' "And it is certain," said Hugh, "that" – he pointed to the old man – "Harold was forced to make his promise to the Great Duke."

‘ "Very strongly forced," said De Aquila. He had never any pride in the Duke William's dealings with Harold before Hastings. Yet, as he said, one cannot build a house all of straight sticks.

‘ "No matter how he was forced," said Henry, "England was promised to my Father William by Edward the Confessor. Is it not so?" William of Exeter nodded. "Harold confirmed that promise to my Father on the bones of the Saints. Afterwards he broke his oath and would have taken England by the strong hand."

‘ "Oh! Là! Là!" Rahere rolled up his eyes like a girl. "That ever England should be taken by the strong hand!"

‘Seeing that Red William and Henry after him had each in just that fashion snatched England from Robert of Normandy, we others knew not where to look. But De Aquila saved us quickly.

‘ "Promise kept or promise broken," he said, "Harold came near enough to breaking us Normans at Santlache."

‘ "Was it so close a fight, then?" said Henry.

‘ "A hair would have turned it either way," De Aquila answered. "His house-carles stood like rocks against rain. Where wast thou, Hugh, in it?"

‘ "Among Godwin's folk beneath the Golden Dragon till your front gave back, and we broke our ranks to follow," said Hugh.

‘ "But I bade you stand! I bade you stand! I knew it was all a deceit!" Harold had waked, and leaned forward as one crying from the grave.

‘ "Ah, now we see how the traitor himself was betrayed!" said William of Exeter, and looked for a smile from the King.

‘ "I made thee Bishop to preach at *my* bidding," said Henry; and turning to Harold, "Tell us here how thy people fought us?" said he. "Their sons serve me now against my Brother Robert!"

‘The old man shook his head cunningly. "Na – Na – Na!" he cried. "I know better. Every time I tell my tale men stone me. But, Thanes, I will tell you a greater thing. Listen!" He told us how many paces it was from some Saxon Saint's shrine to another shrine, and how many more back to the Abbey of the Battle.

' "Ay," said he. "I have trodden it too often to be out even ten paces. I move very swiftly. Harold of Norway knows that, and so does Tostig my brother. They lie at ease at Stamford Bridge, and from Stamford Bridge to the Battle Abbey it is—" he muttered over many numbers and forgot us.

' "Ay," said De Aquila, all in a muse. "That man broke Harold of Norway at Stamford Bridge, and came near to breaking us at Santlache – all within one month."

' "But how did he come alive from Santlache fight?" asked the King. "Ask him! Hast thou heard it, Rahere?"

' "Never. He says he has been stoned too often for telling the tale. But he can count you off Saxon and Norman shrines till daylight," said Rahere and the old man nodded proudly.

' "My faith!" said Henry after a while. "I think even my Father the Great Duke would pity if he could see him."

' "How if he *does* see?" said Rahere.

'Hugh covered his face with his sound hand. "Ah, why hast thou shamed him?" he cried again to Rahere.

' "No – no," says the old man, reaching to pluck at Rahere's cape. "I am Rahere's man. None stone me now," and he played with the bells on the scollops of it.

' "How if he had been brought to me when you found him?" said the King to Rahere.

' "You would have held him prisoner again – as the Great Duke did," Rahere answered.

' "True," said our King. "He is nothing except his name. Yet that name might have been used by stronger men to trouble my England. Yes. I must have made him my life's guest – as I shall make Robert."

' "I knew it," said Rahere. "But while this man wandered mad by the wayside, none cared what he called himself."

' "I learned to cease talking before the stones flew," says the old man, and Hugh groaned.

' "Ye have heard!" said Rahere. "Witless, landless, nameless, and, but for my protection, masterless, he can still make shift to bide his doom under the open sky."

' "Then wherefore didst thou bring him here for a mock and a shame?" cried Hugh, beside himself with woe.

' "A right mock and a just shame!" said William of Exeter.

' "Not to me," said Nigel of Ely. "I see and I tremble, but I neither mock nor judge."

' "Well spoken, Ely." Rahere falls into the pure fool again. "I'll pray for thee when I turn monk. Thou hast given thy blessing on a war between two most Christian brothers." He meant the war forward 'twixt Henry and Robert of Normandy. "I charge you, Brother," he says, wheeling on the King, "dost thou mock my fool?"

'The King shook his head, and so then did smooth William of Exeter.

' "De Aquila, dost thou mock him?" Rahere jingled from one to another, and the old man smiled.

' "By the Bones of the Saints, not I," said our Lord of Pevensey. "I know how dooms near he broke us at Sant-lache."

' "Sir Hugh, you are excused the question. But you, valiant, loyal, honourable, and devout barons, Lords of Man's Justice in your own bounds, do *you* mock my fool?"

'He shook his bauble in the very faces of those two barons whose names I have forgotten. "Na – Na!" they said, and waved him back foolishly enough.

'He hies him across to staring, nodding Harold, and speaks from behind his chair.

' "No man mocks thee. Who here judges this man? Henry of England – Nigel – De Aquila! On your souls, swift with the answer!" he cried.

'None answered. We were all – the King not least – over-borne by that terrible scarlet-and-black wizard-jester.

' "Well for your souls," he said, wiping his brow. Next, shrill like a woman: "Oh, come to me!" and Hugh ran forward to hold Harold, that had slidden down in the chair.

' "Hearken," said Rahere, his arm round Harold's neck. "The King – his bishops – the knights – all the world's crazy chessboard neither mock nor judge thee. Take that comfort with thee, Harold of England!"

'Hugh heaved the old man up and he smiled.

' "Good comfort," said Harold. "Tell me again! I have been somewhat punished—'

'Rahere hallooed it once more into his ear as the head rolled. We heard him sigh, and Nigel of Ely stood forth, praying aloud.

' "Out! I will have no Norman!" Harold said as clearly as I speak now, and he refuged himself on Hugh's sound shoulder, and stretched out, and lay all still.'

'Dead?' said Una, turning up a white face in the dusk.

'That was his good fortune. To die in the King's presence, and on the breast of the most gentlest, truest knight of his own house. Some of us envied him,' said Sir Richard, and fell back to take Swallow's bridle.

'Turn left here,' Puck called ahead of them from under an oak. They ducked down a narrow path through close ash plantation.

The children hurried forward, but cutting a corner charged full-abreast into the thorn-faggot that old Hobden was carrying home on his back.

'My! My!' said he. 'Have you scratted your face, Miss Una?'

'Sorry! It's all right,' said Una, rubbing her nose. 'How many rabbits did you get today?'

'That's tellin's,' the old man grinned as he re-hoisted his faggot. 'I reckon Mus' Ridley he've got rheumatism along o' lyin' in the dik to see I didn't snap up any. Think o' that now!'

They laughed a good deal while he told them the tale.

'An' just as he crawled away I heard some one hollerin'

to the hounds in our woods,' said he. 'Didn't you hear? You must ha' been asleep sure-ly.'

'Oh, what about the sleeper you promised to show us?' Dan cried.

' 'Ere he be – house an' all!' Hobden dived into the prickly heart of the faggot and took out a dormouse's wonderfully woven nest of grass and leaves. His blunt fingers parted it as if it had been precious lace, and tilting it toward the last of the light he showed the little, red, furry chap curled up inside, his tail between his eyes that were shut for their winter sleep.

'Let's take him home. Don't breathe on him,' said Una. 'It'll make him warm and he'll wake up and die straight off. Won't he, Hobby?'

'Dat's a heap better by my reckonin' than wakin' up and findin' himself in a cage for life. No! We'll lay him into the bottom o' this hedge. Dat's jus' right! No more trouble for him till come Spring. An' now we'll go home.'

A CAROL

Our Lord Who did the Ox command
  To kneel to Judah's King,
He binds His frost upon the land
  To ripen it for Spring —
To ripen it for Spring, good sirs,
  According to His word;
Which well must be as ye can see —
  And who shall judge the Lord?

When we poor fenmen skate the ice
  Or shiver on the wold,
We hear the cry of a single tree
  That breaks her heart in the cold —
That breaks her heart in the cold, good sirs,
  And rendeth by the board;
Which well must be as ye can see —
  And who shall judge the Lord?

Her wood is crazed and little worth
  Excepting as to burn,
That we may warm and make our mirth
  Until the Spring return —
Until the Spring return, good sirs,
  When people walk abroad;
Which well must be as ye can see —
  And who shall judge the Lord?

God bless the master of this house,
  And all that sleep therein!
And guard the fens from pirate folk,
  And keep us all from sin,
To walk in honesty, good sirs,
  Of thought and deed and word!
Which shall befriend our latter end —
  And who shall judge the Lord?

The Jungle Book 50p

illustrated

First published in 1894, *The Jungle Book* has delighted
countless people with its tales of Mowgli, Toomai, Rikki-
Tikki-Tavi, and Kaa. Fables that illustrate profound truths,
they are also thrilling and exciting stories.

The Second Jungle Book 50p

illustrated

Published one year after *The Jungle Book*, in 1895,
the *Second Jungle Book* is made up of fables which
have penetrated a wide audience with their universal appeal.

Just So Stories   50p

illustrated

These delightful stories tell you fascinating things like How the Leopard got his Spots, How the Camel got his Hump, and How the Alphabet was made.

First published in 1902 and illustrated by the author himself, this enchanting book is one of Rudyard Kipling's most famous.